HIS HIDDEN LOVE

A REVERSE HAREM ROMANCE (THEIR SECRET DESIRE 1)

MICHELLE LOVE

MEGAN LEE

HOT AND STEAMY ROMANCE

CONTENTS

Blurb	1
1. Chapter One - Wicked Game...	5
2. Chapter Two - I'll Be Seeing You	11
3. Chapter Three - Let's Get Lost	22
4. Chapter Four - Faded	29
5. Chapter Five - Pretty	33
6. Chapter Six - Here with Me	35
7. Chapter Seven - Rid of Me	42
8. Chapter Eight - Million Dollar Man	50
9. Chapter Nine - Every Breath You Take	57
10. Chapter Ten - Perfectly Lonely	65
11. Chapter Eleven - Angel	75
12. Chapter Twelve - Love is a Losing Game	80
13. Chapter Thirteen - Broken-hearted Girl	90
14. Chapter Fourteen - Hunger	96
15. Chapter Fifteen - Waiting Game	103
16. Chapter Sixteen - Scared to be Lonely	111
17. Chapter Seventeen - Dusk Till Dawn	123
18. Chapter Eighteen - Hardly Wait	132
19. Chapter Nineteen - Pillow Talk	140
20. Chapter Twenty - All the Stars	149
21. Chapter Twenty-One - Hurts	155
22. Chapter Twenty-Two – 8 Letters	166
23. Chapter Twenty-Three - Fresh Blood	171
24. Chapter Twenty-Four - Never Let Me Go	178
25. Chapter Twenty-Five - Him & I	185
26. Chapter Twenty-Six - Fake Love	196
27. Chapter Twenty-Seven - You and Me	210
28. Chapter Twenty-Eight - The Limit to Your Love	219
29. Chapter Twenty-Nine - Strangers	225

30.	Chapter Thirty – Runaways	235
31.	Chapter Thirty-One – One Last Time	248
32.	Chapter Thirty-Two – Set Fire To The Rain	253
33.	Chapter Thirty-Three – Closer to God	260
34.	Chapter Thirty-Four – Goner	269
35.	Chapter Thirty-Five – Breathe	277
36.	Chapter Thirty-Six – Secret Love Song	284
	Sneak Peek - Chapter 1 Praying	291

Made in "The United States" by:

Michelle Love & Megan Lee

© Copyright 2020

ISBN: 9781087860053

ALL RIGHTS RESERVED. No part of this publication may be reproduced or transmitted in any form whatsoever, electronic, or mechanical, including photocopying, recording, or by any informational storage or retrieval system without express written, dated and signed permission from the author

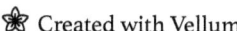 Created with Vellum

BLURB

India Blue is one of the world's most successful and beloved singers. The beautiful Seattle native fiercely guards her privacy and for good reason—when she was a teenager, a horrific attack changed her forever. Since that day, she has avoided intimacy, excepting only Sun, the gorgeous Korean pop star, India's friend and sometime lover, who would change his life for her—even going so far as leaving his true love, bandmate Tae.

When India meets superstar actor Massimo Verdi, she is thrown into a world of passion, desire, and uninhibited sensuality. India knows she is falling for the charming, sexy Italian. When he seemingly betrays that trust, India wonders if either of her lovers is the man for her or is she merely a consolation prize?

Still violently obsessed with India, her attacker will soon be released from prison. To be safe, India must disappear into

obscurity, but she cannot bring herself to part from either Massimo or Sun.
But are Sun or Massimo the men she believes them to be? Or will her heart lead her to a darker, more treacherous place than she could have imagined?

Secret Love Song is the first part in a series of connected stories with an international cast of beautiful people, stunning locations, dark storylines, and hot, hot sensual romance with no cheating and a guaranteed happy ever after!

When singer India Blue meets superstar actor Massimo Verdi, their sexual attraction is immediate and almost overwhelming. But India is plagued by a dark secret, and when her life is threatened, the two would-be-lovers find their love inundated with jeopardy and distance.

Complicating matters is India's close relationship with her friend, K-pop star Sun, who is in turmoil as well. After photographs of Massimo kissing his ex-girlfriend flood the internet, India flees to Seoul where she and the distressed Sun rekindle their sexual relationship.
With two men in her heart and another determined to kill her, India becomes mired in uncertainty and depression.

When she and Massimo reconnect, she begins to see a way of out of her gloom and falls in love with him...
...except her vengeful psychopath is never far behind. With more secrets getting revealed, India needs to decide who to love—and who to trust.

Massimo Verdi, international playboy and one of the world's sexiest actors, is still single after ending a decade-long romance when he meets American singer India Blue and is instantly bowled over by her.

Frustrated by India's apparent flightiness, Massimo tries to forget her and gets caught up in a scandal involving his manipulative ex-girlfriend, Valentina.
After photos of them kissing are published, Massimo thinks he has lost India forever but when she reaches out to him, their friendship blossoms and soon becomes romantic in nature.
As much as he is falling for her, Massimo can see that India's life is convoluted, and he fears that could lose the woman he loves to a deranged stalker.
Can he risk his heart? What about India's secret past and her love for another man in another country? Can Massimo trust her to love him alone or will he need to put his ego aside to

capture the heart of the most incredible woman he has ever met?

1
CHAPTER ONE - WICKED GAME...

Venice, Italy

INDIA BLUE INHALED as much oxygen as she could through her nose, then let it out slowly through her mouth. The breath juddered from her in a shaky, almost gasp-like hiss. It was always this way: the nerves before the concert started, the heinous half-hour of self-doubt. Her stage fright was well documented and that gave her a measure of comfort. The people who paid to hear her sing knew she got panicky; if they were a decent crowd, they'd give her that bit extra to get her adrenaline flowing.

At least that's what she hoped—that they'd be kind. Even after all this time, she had trouble believing in the screams and the joy she received when she waved to the thousands of fans that filled her concerts. She had felt like an awkward, bashful teenager when all of this started—when she was able to function once more after the incident.

God. Why are you thinking of this now?

India tasted bile and was about to dissolve into a full-blown panic attack. Not a good situation when she was due on stage in five minutes. She pulled her long dark hair back into a messy ponytail—no stylists or makeup for her—she preferred the intimacy of making herself up, of getting her hair just the way she wanted. She never was a fashionista despite the high-end designers scrambling to sign the beautiful, young Indian-American girl. India checked her reflection: huge dark-brown eyes, pink mouth, golden skin. People considered her beautiful but the haunted look in her eyes never went away, and that was *all* she could see in her reflection.

India grabbed her phone to check the time. Four minutes to curtain up. Being allowed to play at La Fenice, Venice's premier opera house, was a testament to her talent. So far, she was one of a handful of non-classical artists to do so. Her signature mix of pop, country, and jazz was unique, certainly, but she never liked being confined by genres.

"Hey, Bubba."

As soon as India heard her brother's voice, all her tension drained. Technically, Lazlo Schuler was not a blood relative but he was the one she trusted the most—and there weren't many.

"Hey bro. Just about to go on."

Lazlo gave a deep chuckle. "I wish I could be there to see

you, Bubba. This is a special night."

India sighed. "It's okay, Laz, I understand what you have to deal with over there."

"How come you're my only client who I never have trouble with?" Lazlo laughed. He was her manager, her publicist, her everything, but he also had other clients on his roster—clients who demanded his attention day and night. At forty-nine, Lazlo was resolutely single, married to his job and the best in the business. "You heard from Gabe, Bubba?" Lazlo's brother worked in Los Angeles.

"A text message. He and Selena are really splitting up, huh?"

Lazlo sighed. "At this point, it's probably the best for both. Flogging a dead horse and all that. Listen, I hate to be a nag but by my watch, you should have been on stage a minute ago."

India glanced at the clock. "Shit. Look, thanks, Laz, I'll call you later."

"Love you, Bubba. Hey, say hello to Diana and Grey."

India grinned. "Will do. Love you, bro."

As she walked to the stage, less anxious now that she had spoken to Lazlo, she thought about her plans after the show. She was having a late dinner and drinks with her best friends, Diana Harper and Grey Lynch, a married couple, two English actors she had been close friends with for years now. Back in the day, India scored a film of Diana's, when she herself was a music star, and they'd been friends ever since.

Diana was flirty, feisty, and fun; twenty-two years senior to India's twenty-eight, and India considered her a sister. Diana had counseled her through some hard times, and her husband Grey, a laidback sweetheart, had become a close friend as well.

Later this evening, she would meet with them and their friend, Massimo. India's heart began to beat a little faster. Massimo Verdi was Italy's biggest movie star: attractive, dark-brown curls, intense green eyes, a body to die for, and a rich, masculine voice that sent chills through her. She'd never met him; Diana was close friends with him and he asked to meet her, much to India's surprise. Her first instinct was to say no; the crushing weight of her tragic history stifling her. Diana had seen her discomfort and firmly sat her down.

"Sweetheart...it's *just* dinner. Massimo's a sweetie...once you get past the machismo and that marvelous face of his. He's a fan and wants to meet you. And for whatever it's worth...I think you'll like him."

So, she agreed, much to Diana's delight. A few evenings ago, she was in Rome, and Diana made them watch one of Massimo's movies. Diana was right, he is *divine*. The role he played was a tortured artist, manipulated by the woman he loved. He was hypnotic in the role, and she could not stop thinking about him ever since.

"Hey, India, you ready? They're foaming at the mouth for you."

India smiled at the stagehand, pushed her thoughts of Massimo Verdi to the back of her mind, and stepped out on the stage.

. . .

MASSIMO HUGGED Diana and Grey hello, and they walked directly to their private box to watch the show. The lights were already down as they took their seats, and the first swirling notes of music commenced. Massimo smiled at Diana.

"I've been looking forward to this day."

Diana grinned back. "Good! You know, right about now, India will be at the side of the stage trying not to vomit."

Massimo laughed. "I understand that emotion."

Diana rolled her eyes. "*Sure* you do."

Massimo smirked and shrugged. His face, his body, his voice had power. His confidence was well-earned, and he often concealed how shy he really was.

The music got louder and the screams and applause of the fans went into overdrive as India Blue stepped into the spotlight. The roar of the audience along with the sight of her in the flesh for the first time, lit dramatically by concert lights, sent adrenaline shooting through his veins and he leaned eagerly forward.

The first note she sung made him shiver. So pure and clear, then as the song continued, her legendary rasp came in —so much emotion, so much honesty. Massimo was enraptured. She was petite but leggy with breakneck curves and a small waist, and the way her dark hair was escaping from the bun on the back of her neck made him crazy. He could feel his groin tighten as he watched her move. She was not a singer with highly stylized shows, backup dancers, or intricate, well-practiced dance moves. Instead, she swayed with the rhythm when she was at the mic or sitting at her piano, her whole body seeming to merge with the instrument. It was not sexual, nor her writhing meant to titillate. India Blue was an individual so connected with her music that everything she had went into the performance.

To Massimo, it was the singularly most erotic thing he'd seen and he knew, without doubt, that he wanted India Blue in his bed and in his life.

INDIA HIGH-FIVED every member of her band making sure they got equal applause. It was one of the reasons session musicians clamored to work with her: she paid well overstandard rates; she was inclusive; collaborative; and best of all, she loved. She treated them as family and never put herself above them, even though it was her name on the marquee bringing the audiences—and the money —rolling in.

As she began the encore, she glanced up to the box where she knew Diana, Grey, and Massimo Verdi were sitting. She smiled and waved at them who smiled back, and then she looked at *Massimo*. He was staring at her, his eyes intense, and she could not tear her own eyes away from him. At the first line of the song—a slow, sensual cover of Chris Isaak's "Wicked Game"—suddenly only the two of them were in the room.

The world was on fire and all that could save me was you...
India never sung a more honest line.

CHAPTER TWO - I'LL BE SEEING YOU

India showered quickly, her heart thumping. In a few moments, she would be meeting the man who she sang a freaking *love song* to in front of thousands of people.

What were you thinking? She berated herself as she dried her hair, leaving it down so she could hide behind it. She slipped into a loose-fitting lilac swing dress that showed off her long legs and the cinnamon tone of her skin. A delicate long chain cuddled between her breasts, the lightest of makeup on her face. India glanced in the mirror. The haunted look was there. With it, something else. Something new. *Excitement.*

Before she decided to cancel, she grabbed her purse and went out to meet her friends—and the man who put that excitement in her.

. . .

DISAPPOINTMENT SHOT through her when Diana and Grey were alone. *You scared him off.* She swallowed the sting and happily greeted her friends. Diana beamed at her. "You were fantastic, darling, and utterly spellbinding." She lowered her voice to a stage-whisper. "You had quite the effect on our Italian friend."

India colored, and Grey shot his wife a warning glance tempered with a smile. "Leave the poor girl alone. Sorry, sweetheart," Grey kissed India's cheek, "I married a pimp. Massi had to use the bathroom."

"And he's returned!" Diana crowed suddenly, and India's stomach twisted into knots when he spoke behind her.

"*Buona sera.*" His voice was even deeper in person, like dark chocolate. India turned to look at him, hoping the blatant lust she was feeling wasn't too obvious. He was tall, at least six-two, dwarfing her five-five. His eyes searched her face in a way that made her feel she was already naked and about to be fucked into next Tuesday by him. He *oozed* sex. There was a precarious intensity to him that made him look angry, menacing...and then he smiled.

Oh, dear God...that smile. His expression altered from manly to boyish in a split second—from dangerous to sweet. *Damn.* India was gaping at him and hoped she wasn't *actually* drooling. She tentatively smiled back at him. "Hey there. Great to meet you at last."

Massimo Verdi leaned in and kissed her cheek, only lingering for a second longer. His scent was woodsy and clean, a tiny hint of expensive tobacco underneath. His mouth was perfectly shaped and soft against her cheek.

India took a breath to compose herself, glancing over to Diana and Grey who were talking amongst themselves. There was a gleam in Diana's eyes when her friend returned her attention. "Shall we go and dine, loves? I'm starving."

DIANA WAS AN EXPERT AT 'INNOCENT' manipulation, Massimo thought to himself with a smirk, as his friend deftly arranged them at table so he sat next to India. Not that he minded – India Blue was everything he'd imagined and so much more. The soft beauty of her features—those dark eyes and those lips—he was already having fantasies about that pink mouth of hers.

He noticed Diana slip India a phone under the table, and India, without looking, typed in something and handed it back. Massimo half-grinned when he caught India's eye. She subtly put a finger over her lips; it was obviously some kind of prank. He winked at her and gave the tiniest nod—*I got your back.*

As she sat next to him, he couldn't help but notice the bare skin of her thigh—such a glorious golden color. He wanted to run his hand along her smooth skin...

"Massi?"

Massimo tore his attention away from India's thigh. Diana was smiling at him. "Massi, we watched *Sole Scuro* the other night, and I have to tell you—sorry to rat you out, Indy—but by the end, Indy was screaming bloody murder at the television."

India and Grey laughed, and Massimo smiled, turning to the woman at his side. "You were?"

She nodded. "That guy was setting you up the entire time! I was livid!" Massimo was amused at her indignation.

"She kept yelling, '*No! Don't let him do that!*' Although the language was quite a bit coarser." Grey shook his head in mock-disappointment.

India leaned closer to Massimo. "I actually had to be reminded that it wasn't *real*."

Massimo laughed. "Well, I hope not! I died at the end of that movie."

Diana cackled, and India burst out laughing. "You heartless *wench*."

The men joined the laughter as Diana waved her hands. "No, I'm not happy about that, just at the memory of *somebody* getting a little teary." She looked pointedly at India who flushed scarlet and shot back.

"Yes. It was *Grey*."

"Fibber." Diana rolled her eyes and smirked at Massimo.

Grey decided to help India out. "I have to say, it *was* sad."

"Yeah, see?" India looked so incensed that Massimo couldn't resist brushing the back of his hand against her cheek for the briefest second.

"I'm touched that you enjoyed it."

India gratefully smiled at him. "You were amazing, Massimo, in all seriousness. Spellbinding!"

Their eyes met and, for just that brief moment, their gaze locked. They were interrupted by the arrival of their food, but the ice had been broken. Massimo was indebted to Diana; the woman knew how to make any situation seem natural and so much fun. He smiled at her appreciatively; she looked back with a question in her eyes. *You like her?* He nodded; the slight movement to acknowledge that, yes, he did like this young woman sitting next to him.

All four chatted and laughed for the rest of the feast and then lingered over drinks. For Massimo, it was nice to relax with friends and not get harassed by the press. He easily engaged India in conversation, talking about how much he enjoyed her concert.

"Your voice is like liquid silk," he said thoughtfully, "but then there's the kick of deep claret in there, too. Like a hot chili in chocolate. Sensual, dark, affecting."

India was blushing and he loved the rose pink against her golden skin. "Thank you, that's a divine thing to say."

"I was telling Massimo about your music video project," Diana interjected, all innocence but her eyes twinkling. "Indy, wouldn't Massi be the *perfect* leading man for it?"

India's face went red, but she beamed and looked at Massimo. "You *would* be," her voice shook endearingly, "but I couldn't suppose..."

"I'd love to," he said, pushing away the thought his agent would kill him for agreeing to something without consulting her. But the hell with it—anything to spend more time with this lovely woman. "We should arrange a time to discuss it while you're in the country. How long will you be here for?"

She hesitated. "A while. I'm not certain on exact dates but at least a month."

Massimo relaxed. "Then we have all the time in the

world." Again, their eyes locked and held, and if Diana and Grey hadn't been there, he would have leaned over and pressed his lips to hers...

Suddenly, tinny music erupted, and as Grey's phone belted out "I'm Too Sexy" loudly, he exclaimed "You little minx!" to India, who dissolved into giggles. "How the heck did you manage to change my ring tone...again? *Every* time!" He shook his head trying not to smile, and Massimo realized what Diana and India had been doing earlier. "She does this to me *every* time and I never catch her," Grey explained to Massimo, who started to laugh. Diana looked innocent, but India gleefully blew a kiss at Grey.

"I have my ways, Lynch. Magic sticky fingers."

"Magic *something*." Grey grumbled, then grinned at his young friend. "I suppose "I'm Too Sexy" is better than what you set it to last time." He adjusted his phone settings. "She changed it to "Ain't Nothin' like Gangbang," " he told Massimo who choked on his drink. "And my agent called me...in front of my *mother*."

India whooped and high-fived Diana and then gave Grey a cheesy sneer when he scowled at her in mock-disapproval. Massimo smiled. These were good people to be around: fun, no fake airs and graces. Their table attracted a lot of attention merely for who was sitting there but thankfully, they were left in peace to take pleasure in their evening.

"So, tell me," he asked India, who was still adorably flushed with victory from her prank, "This project....is it a music video?"

India nodded. "Actually, it's more of a short film, a story of a relationship in four songs. The theme is built around suspicion, heartbreak, separation, and tragedy. Not the most original, but I'm hoping the visuals and the music will provide the originality. I'd really like to film it here in Venice and use some masquerade visuals in it."

"Did you perform any of the songs tonight?"

India shook her head. "No, they're not quite ready...I have some clips on my phone. Would you like to hear them?"

For a world-famous music star, India Blue was not conceited in the slightest, Massimo thought, as he put in the ear buds she offered. She was nervous at allowing him to listen to the songs, her dark eyes curious and slightly fearful of his rejection.

As she pressed *play*, his ears were filled with her sweet, husky voice, and Massimo felt his whole body react to the sound. It was as if he could hear every ounce of heartbreak and pain she ever had... He closed his eyes for a moment, immersing himself in the sound, then as he looked back at her, he imagined her with her tears flowing down her cheeks as her lover left, as her heart was ripped from her. Massimo saw her darkness and knew...it wasn't just the music. *What happened to you?* The thought of anyone—a lover, an enemy—hurting her made him want to protect her. The song ended and slowly he removed the ear buds.

"Wow. Just wow." To his astonishment, his voice shook and he giggled.

"Can you find a character for that?" She said softly and without thinking, he cupped her face in his palms.

"I could—although I could kill him for hurting you." His

thumb gently stroked across her cheek. He could feel her trembling.

Unexpectedly, they noticed Diana and Grey had left the table. India, checking her watch and seeing it was after midnight, frowned. "Where'd they go?"

Massimo hid a smile. "I think they are, how do you say, being…discreet."

His arm was along the back of her chair, his fingers stroking the inside of her arm. India looked at him, studying his face. "They are?"

Massimo nodded but remained silent. India's eyes registered desire—but also panic.

"So, this was…a plan?"

Massimo shook his head. "No, not a plan, I swear. I had no idea they would leave us alone. If you prefer, I can call you a cab. Are you uncomfortable, *Bella*?"

India shook her head. One beat of hesitation, then Massimo leaned in and lightly brushed his lips against hers. She tasted like red wine, and she responded softly to the kiss. He drew back, questioning. Her dark brown eyes were unreadable.

"*Scusami, signore? Signora?* Your companions asked me to send this over with this note." The waiter put down a bottle of champagne and handed India the note.

She opened and read it, starting to both laugh and blush furiously. Massimo was curious. "What does it say, *Bella*?"

India hesitated for a second and then handed it to him. As he read it, Massimo too began to laugh. "Well, now…"

The note read:

. . .

Dear Disgracefully Gorgeous People,

Thank you for a lovely evening. Now go! Get naked and fuck each other senseless because you've been practically doing that all evening. I say, Huzzah!

We love you both!

D & G xxx

PS

The check has been settled.

India and Massimo examined the note, then each other before bursting out laughing again. Massimo rose and offered India his hand. "How about a stroll through the city?"

India accepted his hand, feeling it close over hers, his fingers warm and dry. His thumb stroked the back of her hand as they walked. Every cell in her body was reacting to this man and without a shadow of a doubt, India knew that soon they would be in bed, fucking and clawing at each other like wild bunnies. It seemed inevitable. A frisson of electricity coursed over her skin at the thought.

So...she was amazing herself. She *never* did this: a one-night stand—to her, it just wasn't worth it. But she'd never been as turned on as she was right now. She wanted him inside her, wanted to kiss him, bite him, and suck him. She felt breathless with arousal and desire, and when a few streets later, he gently backed her against a wall and kissed her, she sank into it, her hands curling around his neck as his lips moved against hers. His fingers stroked her belly, sending thrills through her.

"God, you're beautiful," he whispered, and India sighed as his hand slipped under her skirt and began to caress her through her panties. Her hand snaked down to cup his rock-hard cock. God, he was *huge*. His eyes glittered with unreleased desire, and it took her breath away.

"My place is a couple of streets away." She gazed into his eyes. He nodded, his smile replaced by a torrid look of desire. *What a dangerous man,* she thought with a shiver. *What an exciting, irresistible man...*

Her cell phone rang, and she ignored it as Massimo kissed her again, his tongue slipping in and caressing hers. His eyelashes brushed her cheek as his arms tightened around her. Her cell phone squawked again, this time with the familiar '911' ringtone she reserved for emergencies.

She broke away from Massimo, out of breath and with an apologetic smile. "I'm so sorry, I have to get that. It's my brother's emergency ring tone."

"You and your ring tones," he grinned, "I'll step over here for a moment."

He moved away to give her some privacy and for a moment India just watched him. He took out a cigarette and lit it, shooting her a smile. God, he was delicious. India smiled back and answered her phone.

"Seriously, Laz, this better be good. You have no idea what you're interrupting."

There was a silence on the other end of the phone, and India frowned. "Laz?"

"Bubba...I'm sorry...are you alone?"

"No, I'm with Massimo, a friend...what is it, Laz? What's wrong?"

"After I tell you this, can you ask this Massimo to escort you home? I don't want you alone."

India's body began to tremble. Lazlo was not a panicky guy, nor was he prone to dramatics. "Laz, you're scaring me."

"It's Carter, Bubba. The arresting officer was charged with corruption, and all of his cases have been thrown out. They let Carter out a week ago, and so far, he's in the wind. He's out. He got out of prison."

CHAPTER THREE - LET'S GET LOST

India's entire body went numb. "It can't be, Laz... How could they let him out? The evidence was overwhelming! I testified, for the love of God!" She became aware Massimo was listening, alarmed. She looked at him apologetically. He approached and put his arms around her. For a second, she resisted; she didn't want this crap to sully their evening, and he was still technically a stranger, but...oh, the feel of his big, solid body against hers was so comforting, so safe.

"Can you get back to your apartment? I need to tell you more but not in public. I've also arranged protection for you. They'll meet you there. Nevertheless, don't go home alone. Is Massimo trustworthy?"

India smiled. "Yes," she said, meeting Massimo's gaze, "I would say Massimo Verdi is trustworthy."

"*Massimo Verdi*? That makes me feel better." Lazlo was

relieved. Massimo smiled at her, touching her cheek. India held his hand to her face for a moment, gazing at him.

"Indy, you there? Can you get home?"

India nodded and then realized that was no good to Lazlo. "Yes, I can get home." She looked at Massimo, who nodded as well. Even if he knew nothing of what was going on, he clearly would be happy to accompany her home. "I'll call you when we get back to my apartment."

She hung up. To give herself a moment, she put her phone away very slowly, taking a deep breath. She looked up to see Massimo watching her, his eyes wary.

"Are you okay, *Bella*?"

India drew in a long breath. "I don't know. Something's happened, and I..." She sighed and tried to smile. "I have to go home. My brother wants to talk to me."

Massimo held out his hand. "I'll walk you back. Listen, you don't have to tell me anything, but I'm here if you need to take a dump on me."

Despite herself, India burst out laughing. "Dude, it's 'dump on me' not 'take a dump on me'. Entirely different, very niche."

He shrugged, grinning good-naturedly.

"My English idioms need improvement."

India smiled at him and stroked her hand down his face. "It's tough to dislike a guy who knows the word 'idioms.' You're perfect." He smirked, deflecting her compliment with a shrug. *He's lovely*, India thought. *Absolutely exquisite.*

She took his hand and they walked through the quiet streets.

All the sexual tension had dissipated, and India, despite the horror at Braydon Carter's release, was disappointed. *The timing sucks, that's all,* she thought. Massimo's hand dwarfed hers, his thumb stroking the back of her hand. She moved closer, and he stopped to kiss her again, before walking on. In a few hours, they had forged a connection that wouldn't easily be forgotten.

At her door, Massimo pressed his lips against hers. "I don't think I should impose on you any more tonight, *Bella*. Just promise me, we'll reconnect soon."

India smiled. There was nothing she wanted more than to invite this gorgeous man into her apartment and make love to him—something that never happened to her—but she couldn't drag him into her mess of a life. "You have my number."

"And you have mine. I'll be disappointed if someone else plays your love interest in your music video."

She laughed. "That won't happen. I'll call you." She hoped beyond hope he didn't realize she was lying.

AFTER HE WAS GONE, and she dead bolted her door and checked that her windows were locked, India curled up on the couch and called Lazlo back.

"You okay, bub?" he said.

"Not really. I can't believe they let Carter out, Laz. After everything... *everything*." Her voice broke but she was determined not to cry.

"He won't get near you, Indy, I promise." Lazlo sighed.

"The one good thing is that the tour is over, and you can go anywhere. He won't be able to find you."

"Exiled again." India closed her eyes. She knew this all too well: a life of disguise and solitude forced upon her by a man obsessed with her. She had other stalkers—it was an occupational hazard for people in the entertainment business—but no one as relentless, as destructive as Braydon Carter.

No one as *terrifying*.

"How was Massimo Verdi?"

India's heart thumped sadly. "A sweetheart. Surprisingly, a real sweetheart. Damn it."

"I'm sorry, Indy. I wish you would find someone who... well, you know."

India chuckled softly. "I don't need a white knight, Laz. I have you." She sighed. "So, what do you suggest?"

"Leave Venice, obviously. Pick a country and get on a plane. When you're there, call me, and we'll step up security and find you a place to live. You have your credit cards?"

"Yes."

"Good. Listen, Jess knows about this, too, and she's going to challenge the release."

Jess Olden was India's best friend and her lawyer, a stunningly beautiful woman who was a pit bull in the courtroom. India smiled fondly. "I bet she is. Tell her I love her and thank you."

"I will. Jesus, Indy, I'm so sorry about this. I thought we had finally gotten past this cloak and dagger stuff."

India stared out of the window at the Venetian night and tried not to cry. "Me, too, Laz. Me, too."

MASSIMO VERDI SPENT the next few days on a press junket for his new movie but every moment he thought about India Blue: her soft, dark hair that fell below her shoulders, those large brown eyes, and perfect rose lips. He could still smell her delicate scent and his body felt charged and on edge. He needed to see her again; that was now an imperative.

After his last interview, he fended off the meeting requests from his agent and his publicist and retreated to his hotel room, decompressing from talking all day. Massimo enjoyed the junkets to a certain extent, but he also valued his privacy. He changed out of the Saville Row suit he wore and got into a sweater and jeans, flicking on the TV and ordering room service. Before the food arrived, he called Diana, and she grilled him about what happened. "Your note was the opposite of subtle, Diana."

Diana was unrepentant. "So? Did you fuck each other silly?"

Massimo laughed. "No, we didn't. We were interrupted and India had something else to deal with."

"Well, don't let her run away from you, Mass. She has a habit of pulling away even when everyone else can see what she wants. And she wants *you*, believe me. I have never seen her so…befuddled."

"*Befuddled*?" Massimo was curious.

"Okay then, aroused. She was *horny* for you. Can I make it

any clearer?" Massimo heard Grey muttering in the background, and Diana clicked her tongue at him. "I'm *not* interfering."

"Do you think it would be inappropriate for me to show up at her door?"

"Go for it. She'll get scared and try to push you away. Don't let her get away, Massi."

AFTER THE CALL, he slowly ate his steak and salad, processing what Diana said. He sensed India might be a flight risk. There was something so vulnerable about her. Why did she look so devastated when her brother called? He grabbed his laptop and did a search on her. *Strange.* For someone so high profile, there was very little information about her on the internet—plenty of gossip and speculation, but actual facts...

Weird.

Massimo closed the laptop and sat back. No, he wouldn't learn a thing from the web about this woman. To get to know her means being with her. He got up and grabbed his coat, stepping out into the cool Venice night. After all, he knew where she lived. He strode through the streets, ignoring the people who stared at him, recognizing their number one movie star.

The doorman at India's apartment building recognized him and let him in with a smile. "How can I help you tonight, Mr. Verdi? Always a pleasure to see you."

Massimo smiled back. "I'm here to see *Signora* Blue, thank you."

"Oh."

Massimo stopped. The doorman looked uncomfortable. "What is it?"

"I'm afraid *Signora* Blue has left, Mr. Verdi."

"Left? You mean she's out for the evening?" Even as he said the words, he knew what the man meant. India had left the building, the apartment, the city.

She was gone.

4
CHAPTER FOUR - FADED

Helsinki, Finland

INDIA CRANKED up the heat in the small apartment Lazlo rented for her in the Finnish capital and curled up on the couch to watch the falling snow outside. Everything was covered white in this beautiful city, and it gave India some comfort. Surely, nothing bad could happen in a place like this, right?

Lazlo had this apartment rented for her before she even boarded the plane in Venice; she admired his tenacious, efficient manner. They grew up together, overlooking their fourteen-year age difference, both living with their single mothers in a commune in Canada, living in Maupin's world in San Francisco, and finally settling in a New York apartment with no hot water and only a mattress on the floor. But they were happy. Lazlo's fiery mom, Hanna, was a radical feminist. She and India's mother, the flighty, dreamer Priya, were polar opposites but the best of friends. Even when Lazlo's father had another son, Gabriel, with another woman, and the child was dumped on Hanna to raise, they were a joyous, thoughtful, creative group of nomads, working odd jobs and helping their communities as they had very little themselves.

When Lazlo, Gabe, and India had grown and started earning an income, Hanna refused their help. "I'm happy, my darlings," she would tell them. After India's mom died, Hanna treated India as her own, raising her to be a strong, capable woman, never reliant on a man.

Any man. India sighed. Massimo Verdi wasn't just any man, and yet she ran from him the second she had reason to. Ever since that night, she dreamt of making love to him, that thick cock of his thrusting deep inside her, his full mouth kissing her, thoughts of tangling her fingers in his dark curls.

Those dreamy, green eyes...

Thinking about him wasn't a good idea now that her whole life was on hold again. *God damn you, Braydon Carter! Haven't you done enough?*

The fear of being murdered numbed her; she almost got used to the feeling that her life was limited. Staring out at the snowflakes, she rubbed her abdomen. The scars would always be there; the physical ones faded, but the psychological ones?

Fuck this. India got up from the couch and went to the

other room, where a piano stood. She would write songs. That was what she was born to do.

She ran through the tracks she played to Massimo first and began to write a treatment for the video he agreed to costar in. She tore up the first three—all of them way too raunchy for a video—but it improved her mood to daydream about filming sex scenes with Massimo.

Hurting...

As the girl sings the opening bars, she escapes a masquerade ball and runs from her lover after seeing him flirt with another woman. As the pace of the song picks up, a chase through Venice begins as the lover pursues her, desperate to win her back.

As the song reaches the bridge, they face each other across one of the beautiful piazzas. His dark-green eyes are intense, almost dangerous-looking, and she tries to resist but remembers their lovemaking—passionate, uninhibited, a meeting of true soulmates—lovers predestined. As he approaches and takes her in his arms, they dance, almost mirroring their lovemaking. Then masked enemies approach and try to tear the lovers apart. They succeed and the two are buried under a miasma of malevolence. As the song closes, the crowds disperse revealing the man holding his dead lover in his arms as the camera pans out, knowing it was his awful behavior that led to this...

. . .

INDIA PUT HER PEN DOWN. "Wow, you went dark," she noted. "*Way* dark. *Miasma of malevolence?*" She chuckled and rolled her eyes but there was something about the idea she really treasured. Something...cathartic. She wondered what Massimo would think of it.

For a moment, she chewed on her lip and then grabbed her laptop, doing what she shouldn't do at any cost.

Type the name *Massimo Verdi* into a search engine.

CHAPTER FIVE - PRETTY

January 15th

MY DARLING, my beautiful India,

EVERY DAY I wake up and your sweet face is the first I see. I say hello to you before doing anything else and picture you lying next to me. Believing it to be true, I leaned over and pressed my lips against yours.

They taste so sweet, my darling.

As the morning sunshine makes your honey skin glow, we make love, my sexual prowess making you moan and sigh as I fuck you, my cock deep inside your delicious cunt.

In case you're wondering... Yes, I'm pleasuring myself as I write this, pretending it's your hand stroking my prick, playing me the way you play your piano.

All those fans that come to see you, who stand and applaud you, do any of them know what it's like to be inside you? To love you? To taste your blood on their lips?

No. That's my privilege, my sweet darling. Only mine. No one else knows how rich and dark your blood is, how it pumps from you, luscious and hot. I'm the reason you never pose in your underwear like so many other whores in your business. Pity. I'd like to see the scars on your soft belly again, the marks that bind you to me.

And I will, someday, India. I'll see them again, up close and personally.

Soon, my darling, soon.

I love you.

Your Braydon.
  Prisoner 873927555
  Texas **State Penitentiary at Huntsville**

6
CHAPTER SIX - HERE WITH ME

New York City

"Jesus Christ." Lazlo read the letter again as Jess Olden watched his reaction. They were sitting in Lazlo's corporate office on Madison Avenue as Lazlo's eyes grew wide with terror. He put the letter down and rubbed his face. "And this one isn't the worst of them?"

"No. The police are keeping some of the more explicit letters to themselves." Jess sighed. His friend looked tired and stressed. Jess Olden was a beautiful woman, thirty-five years old, her caramel skin from her Chinese mother, her green eyes from her American father. Today there is a pronounced crease between her eyes and dark shadows below. Lazlo studied her. "Jess... did they tell you what was in them?"

Jess hesitated. She was holding back.

"Jess... please. I can't fight this unless I know everything."

"Laz... what they told me was *sickening*. Braydon's obsession with Indy is bizarre. If he finds her, he'll make sure she suffers the torments of the damned before he kills her."

"Fuck." Lazlo buried his head in his hands. "How the hell do they think letting him go will end up? The man is a maniac."

"Yeah, boo. We have to make sure he can't get to her."

"More exile. Indy deserves more. She deserves a *life*."

Jess nodded. "Look, we'll figure it out. The best thing is to try and keep a check on where he is and, God, I don't know, always keep Indy in a different country."

"What kind of life is that?"

"It's *a* life, which is more than Indy gets if Braydon catches up with her."

Lazlo stared out of the window. "She met someone, an actor, the other night. From her voice, I think she liked him. Massimo Verdi."

Jess's eyebrows shot up. "Massimo Verdi? Damn, he's a good-looking man. He's a player."

"That's what I found out." He grinned guiltily at Jess. "I looked him up."

"Big brother."

"Always. But he appears to be a good guy. You say he's a player but that's only in the last few months. He was in a long-term relationship for over a decade. That gives me hope."

Jess laughed. "You got them married off already?"

He chuckled. "Nah, but I heard something in Indy's voice, something I haven't heard in a long time."

"What?"

Lazlo smiled. "Hope."

~

Los Angeles, California

MASSIMO VERDI SHOOK the hand of the journalist, concluding his last interview of the day. The press junkets for his new film, *Momentum*, were finished, and he could go home now to decompress and relax. Jake, his publicist, smiled at him. "You look relieved."

"You know this is my least favorite part."

They walked out of the hotel suite together. "Your return flight to Rome is in two hours. Danni packed your suitcase already, and the car will pick you up in an hour."

"Thanks, Jake. And thanks for dealing with all this stuff for me." Massimo hesitated. "Any messages?"

Jake ran through the list of calls he fielded for Massimo, but Massimo was disappointed not to hear India's name. *Mio Dio, Verdi, stop thinking about her. She's obviously not interested.*

Except... arrogance aside, he doubted that was true. He felt her quivering when he kissed her, felt her hand cupping his cock. India Blue was an intriguing, enigmatic woman, and he needed more—like a junkie needs another fix.

His attention slid back to Jake when he said, "And

Valentina called. She hopes to have lunch when you get back to Rome. She says she did an interview for *Italian Vogue*, and she might have—her words—mentioned a possible reunion."

Jake pulled a face as Massimo groaned. "I'm sorry. All the celebrity rags are running with it."

"Fuck... not your fault, Jake. *Mio Dio,* what's she thinking? The last time we talked..." Massimo blew out his cheeks, forcing himself to calm down. "Never mind, Jake. I'll deal with it. What else?"

"Oh, yeah, I forgot," Jake sorted through some notes. "Here we go. India Blue's people—you know who she is, right? The singer?"

Massimo hid his smile. "Yes, I know who she is." *She occupies my thoughts, day and night.* Jake nodded, not reading the meaning behind Massimo's words.

"Her people got in touch, wanting to know if you'd make an appearance in her next music video."

"Tell them yes," Massimo said without hesitation, and Jake was surprised by his quick reply. Massimo was notorious for keeping people waiting for his commitment to projects. "Tell them yes, whenever, wherever they want me. Whenever *she* wants me."

Understanding crept into Jake's eyes. "Ah," he said with a smile, and chuckled. "Yes, India Blue is..."

Beautiful, sexy, funny. "A great talent."

Jake snorted. "That's the word. *Talented.* And drop-dead gorgeous, which doesn't hurt."

Massimo grinned widely. "Does it ever?"

"You got a crush on her, Mass?"

Massimo laughed. "A little." A *lot*. "Anyway, tell India yes."

"Got it. Oh, and you might want to give the Bellamy's party a miss tonight. Fernanda's going."

Massimo rolled his eyes. "Thanks for that. With her and Valentina..."

Fernanda Rossi was an actress who, like Massimo, was beginning to make strides in the American film scene. She was also a clingy mess, and Massimo counted their one-night stand a few months ago as one of the biggest mistakes in his life. Fernanda was obsessive and jealous; she punched a woman for looking at Massimo at a party. Massimo didn't want drama like that; he didn't want anything to do with Fernanda *ever* again.

Massimo was a rare species in film. Uninterested in the copious amounts of drugs available to stars like him, his biggest vice was sex, especially since the end of his relationship Valentina Acri, a legend in Italian cinema. Valentina, older than Massimo by almost ten years, had guided his career from a young actor into the superstar he was today. He loved her with all his heart, but the children they planned together never came, and by the end of their relationship, they became more like siblings than lovers.

As talented as she was, Valentina, in her late forties, was finding that the roles she craved weren't being offered to her. Her latest interview—the one where she hinted at reconciliation with Massimo—was a ploy to appear younger, vital, still of interest to younger men, cinema's critical target age group between twenty-five and forty-nine. Being with Massimo would achieve that.

Massimo chewed over this and sighed. He owed Valentina his career. How could he not reach out to her? He finished up with Jake and went to his room to get ready to go home. Valentina still kept tabs on where he was at any time, and before now, it didn't bother him much.

Now, for some reason, it irritated him. Valentina knew where *he* was and yet he had no idea where India Blue was. At least her people reached out about the music video; it meant she hadn't written him off completely. Wherever she disappeared to, it must be for a good reason. He wanted to talk to her, though.

In the cab to the airport, he flicked through his phone and typed her name, clicking on the 'News' section. Nothing. Still a ghost. He clicked the *Images* tab and smiled. Jake had seriously underestimated her beauty with the 'drop-dead gorgeous' remark. Her large, deep brown eyes were warm, and her emotions were plain to see within them, even if she herself was guarded. Massimo slotted his ear buds into his ears and found her last album. That *voice*...

He got so lost in her voice that the driver had to call his name twice when they arrived at the airport. Massimo wasn't thinking as he stepped out of the car—and into a melee of press photographers. Los Angeles... He sighed.

"Hey, Massi, you and Valentina gonna get back together?"

Massimo smiled and said nothing as he pushed through to Check In. His bodyguard, a huge man called Deke, helped him work his way through as flashes went off in his face.

When he was finally installed in his business-class seat,

Massimo didn't blame India for her disappearing act; he couldn't imagine she enjoyed this part of fame either.

He idly listened to the pre-flight instructions, snagging his phone to turn it off. It was only then he noticed the text message from an unknown number. He frowned, but a second later, his brow cleared as he read the message, and his heart soared.

Thank you for saying yes. See you soon! Indy x.

CHAPTER SEVEN - RID OF ME

H*elsinki, Finland*

INDIA PLAYED the piano until her fingers ached yet no lyrics would come. She'd been trying to write for days but now, she gave up. No matter, she had enough songs for three new albums. She always pushed herself too hard. She needed to take a break sometimes, but the thought of not writing or playing was anathema to her.

Still, she ran through some cover versions of her favorite songs, throwing a slower version of FKA twigs' "Two Weeks" in there. It made her think of Massimo, with its sensual beat and explicit lyrics. India closed her eyes as she sang, imagining Massimo's hands on her body, his fingertips drifting across her skin, his mouth on hers. Dominating her in bed, his cock plunging inside her over and over, India tangling her fingers in that wild mess of curls on his head, stroking his thick brows, running her fingertips across the long, dark eyelashes... She bit her lip, her body reacting urgently to the thought of him. She grabbed her cell phone. *Fuck this, I want to see him.*

She called Lazlo. When he answered sounding sleepy, she realized it was still early morning in New York. "Laz, I'm sorry to wake you."

"No matter, Bubba, what's up?"

India took a deep breath. "I'm sick of hiding, Laz. Please, could you call Massimo's people and ask them how soon he could film the video?"

Nashville

AFTER HIS RELEASE FROM HUNTSVILLE, Braydon had been staying at a very nice hotel in downtown Nashville for a month. His benefactor, whose name he still didn't know, arranged a car to pick him up and take him to Nashville. He guessed that flying would leave a paper trail whereas this seemed all very... arranged. He would probably be required to do something for this and he wondered what it would be.

His questions were answered when his benefactor came to see him on the one-month anniversary of his release. He flicked off the television as the man entered the room, flanked by a bodyguard, and Braydon frowned. This dude? Really?

"Hello, Mr. Carter."

Braydon shook his hand, and the other man gestured to a chair. "May I?"

"Go ahead. You're paying for all of this."

The other man sat and gave him a chilly smile. "Yes, I am."

Braydon was struggling to recollect this man's name, but he'd seen him on the news before. By the cut of his suit, he was rich—as if the luxury hotel Braydon was staying in hadn't clued him in. The man's white hair was slicked back neatly, and he wore a signet ring on his left hand with some kind of crest on it. His shoes, Braydon knew, were *Bruno Magli*. He only knew that because he'd just been watching a documentary on O.J. Simpson.

"Well, Mr...?"

The other man smiled. "Just call me... Stanley."

"Well, Stanley, not that I'm not grateful for all of this, but I've been wondering. Why? Why me?"

Stanley nodded. "Fair question and that's why I'm here. You'll be leaving here today, Mr. Carter and travelling to New York City to an apartment that has been purchased for you. There, you will make plans to carry out and complete your mission."

"My mission?" This sounded like a bad movie plot.

Stanley smiled—and Braydon noticed how it didn't travel to the man's eyes. Cold. Ruthless. "Yes, Braydon. I can call you Braydon?"

Braydon nodded. "Sure."

"No need to be concerned, Braydon. From the letters found in your prison cell, apparently you were already planning exactly what I need you to do."

Braydon's eyes widened in shock. "What? You mean...?"

"Yes, Mr. Carter. I want you to kill India Blue."

Rome, Italy

Valentina called him the morning after he returned to Rome, and Massimo arranged to have a lunch with her the following day. His intensely luxurious apartment was situated in the center of the city, and he liked to walk. He was often stopped by fans asking for autographs or selfies and he didn't mind. The day was warm with a light breeze, and he breathed in the fresh air. His decision to appear in India's video was exciting, especially since she had been in contact. He didn't know where she was, but tonight, they were going to see each other face-to-face, albeit over the internet. India was going to video call him to discuss dates and the story for the music video, and he couldn't wait to see her.

Massimo was still smiling when he saw Valentina sitting outside the café, and she raised a hand in greeting. At almost fifty, Valentina was still a spectacular woman: long, wavy, tawny hair, dark blue eyes, and wide smile. She refused to get plastic surgery, so small lines around her eyes and mouth were visible. She chain-smoked, too, and as Massimo kissed her cheek, the scent of cigarettes and perfume was intense. Such a familiar smell; that fragrance meant home to him for many years. Now though, compared to India's scent of fresh linen and clean air, he knew which he preferred.

Valentina turned her head as he went to kiss her other cheek and planted a full kiss on his lips. Massimo pulled back quickly, half-smiling to ease the slight. "Val, you look beautiful."

"Likewise, Mass." She held him at arm's length and studied him as if she were appraising a work of art. "A little more grey, but it suits you."

Massimo smiled. Val was in a flattering mood, which meant she wanted something. They sat and ordered drinks, Massimo looking at the food menu while Val lit another cigarette. "Want one?"

He shrugged and took one, lighting Valentina's for her. "Are you eating today?"

She shrugged and ordered a salad. Massimo, never one to turn down food, ordered *sugo all'arrabbiata* over penne. Val had always looked after her figure, remaining slender and toned. Again, Massimo found himself comparing her sharp edges to India's curves. *Stop it, you're getting obsessed.*

"So, Val... the Vogue interview?"

She had the grace to look sheepish. "I'm sorry, Mass, I did say what they printed. You know why."

"Actually, I don't. You ended our relationship months ago, Val, and you made the right decision. We don't fit anymore." He smiled kindly. "I'll never regret our ten years together.

Never. You are my family, Val, but we've moved on. Didn't I see a story about you and Dante Tolani?"

Valentina smiled. "A passing fancy. Dante is sexy, but he's not you, Mass."

Massimo sighed. "Val... listen... There's someone else. Someone I'm... intrigued with."

Valentina gave a brittle laugh. "*Intrigued*? Is that code for fucking?"

"Actually, no. We haven't slept together." *Yet.* But soon, he hoped. An image of India naked and moaning beneath him flashed through his mind, his mouth on hers, then closing around her nipple... His cock was hard against his pants, and he hoped Valentina wouldn't see it and think she was the reason for it.

"Mass, regardless of your newest flame, you're wrong about that. We do fit. I was foolish to throw away our love." She sighed. "No one is better than you, Mass."

That was a change from what she said at the end of their relationship. Massimo would never forget that night; it was seared in his brain.

Immature, irresponsible, and slovenly. Her words to describe him. Those words that caused him the most self-examination. Was he immature? Probably. His days were spent pretending to be another person for money, for Chrissakes. Irresponsible? He still didn't know what that had been about. And slovenly? *Him?* No, he'd take a lot but he wasn't *slovenly*.

Valentine was studying him, reading his mind. "I said a lot of mean things that night, Mass. Too many things. I'm really sorry."

Massimo chewed his lip. "Val... look. We'll always be friends. As for us being together again? No. Too much has passed for that to happen."

For a moment, tears glistened in her eyes, but she rallied. "Can't blame a girl for trying. So, who is she? This new intriguing woman?"

He briefly toyed with the idea of telling her; he was longing to talk to someone about India, but Val wasn't the right person. His potential relationship with India shouldn't be sullied by a bitter ex. And if Val had one failing, it was that she didn't play nice with other women. He couldn't imagine her having the same relationship India had with Diana for instance. He remembered their teasing each other at the dinner table, and he smiled. He wanted more of that fun-loving atmosphere, less of this tension he experienced around Valentina.

They finished lunch and, ever the gentleman, Massimo walked with her to her apartment. She kissed his cheek and met his gaze. "Want to come up?"

Massimo shook his head, smiling again to smooth over the rejection. "No, thanks, Val."

She gave a small, almost incredulous laugh. "You have it bad for this girl. Who is she?"

"Someone I never thought—" he tailed off, not knowing what to say. "Just call it curiosity for now."

Val's expression softened and she touched his cheek. "You used to look like that about me, Massimo. Lucky girl," she whispered and leaned in to kiss him on the mouth.

. . .

Neither saw the paparazzo taking pictures of them from across the street. The photographer got a number of shots, then disappeared as Valentina went inside and Massimo Verdi walked away. Two minutes later, he got the call. "Did you get them?"

"I did. My editor's going to love them."

"Good."

Inside her apartment, Valentina smiled to herself and ended the call, dropping her phone onto the table. *Enjoy those pictures, my darling. Your new love won't be happy, and before long you'll come crawling back to me.*

You're mine, Massimo Verdi. Don't ever forget it.

CHAPTER EIGHT - MILLION DOLLAR MAN

H*elsinki, Finland*

IF INDIA WAS EXCITED to see Massimo again, she tried to rein in the feeling. She'd seen the photographs of him kissing his supposed-ex in the newspapers and on the internet, and she couldn't help the sharp pang of jealousy in her heart.

"Nope. Won't be that girl," she declared and sighed. The universe was telling her, as always, not to get involved; it would only lead to hurt.

India rubbed her head, closing her browser to go take a shower. It was only a few weeks before Christmas and as much as she loved Helsinki, she told Lazlo she wanted to be with him for the holidays, whether it was safe or not.

Lazlo knew she wouldn't be argued with. "Fine. We'll

make arrangements to fly you in privately. No arguments about a private plane this time, Indy."

India agreed, but even so, it would be at least another month before she could leave Helsinki. Lazlo agreed on a date in January with Massimo's people to produce the music video, and because of the photos, she was looking forward to it much less.

India dried her long dark hair, then wound it into a bun, dressing in a warm sweater and jeans. Another day at her piano was planned—she had a new album to create, after all —but she felt restless. When her cell phone bleeped with a message from one of her dearest friends, Sun, her spirits lifted immediately.

Sun, his full name Sung-Jae, was a member of one of the hottest K-pop groups on the planet. He and India met at an award show a couple of years ago and clicked immediately. He was five years younger, androgynous, and the most beautiful man India had ever seen. His face had delicate, feminine features, his eyes large and full of expression. His hair was short and neat and frequently dyed to match the project he was working on. His body, however, was as far from feminine as could be possible, with washboard abs, hard pecs and a dancer's body.

THEY HAD GONE to her hotel room and stayed up all night talking. There was a heat between them they tried to deny, but it had proved impossible, and one night, after another show, they slept together.

Neither wanted a relationship, but their bond was set for life. They never had sex again but often when their paths crossed, they spent the night together, holding each other, talking, and joking around, Sun often teasing Indy about her attempts to learn Korean. He was in love with another member of his group, a quiet, reserved boy called Tae, who was more introverted than the exuberant Sun.

Where are you, Indy? I want to see you!

Her heart ached with warmth. It was easy to adore Sun; he wasn't just beautiful on the outside, but also deep within, too.

I'm away, writing, at the moment. I want to see you, too! Where are you?

Back home in Seoul. I can come where you are.

Ha, right! Not without a huge press pack! Have to lay low at the moment. I could go to Seoul.

Come soon. I have a lot to tell you.

Me, too. I'll make the arrangements and get back to you.

Sun sent a smiling emoji along with a heart, and Indy smiled. God, yes, a few days with Sun, and the world would seem a brighter place again. She could tell him about Massimo and ask for his thoughts. He knew about longing for someone.

She could tell Lazlo wasn't happy about her plans. "Indy… those boys get very little privacy. One photo of you and Sun, and Carter might see it."

"Not unless he reads Korean newspapers."

"Don't be naive, India. You know how big that group is. Any whiff of a romance between you and Sun, and it's international news."

India was getting annoyed. "So, now I can't even see my friends? I'm tired of living like this, Laz."

"We're talking about your life, Indy."

"What kind of life is it when I'm trapped, alone, and..." She choked. "What kind of life, Lazlo?" Her voice was a whisper as she fought to stop the tears. "I want to see Sun."

There was a long silence on the end of the phone, and when he spoke again, Lazlo's voice was calmer. "Does this have anything to do with those photographs of Verdi and his ex?"

Fuck, Lazlo knew her so well. "No." *Lie.* "Well, not much. I really do want to see Sun."

"Careful with that boy's heart, Indy." Indy smiled. Lazlo was giving in.

"He's in love with Tae," she said. "I can't break a heart that isn't mine."

Lazlo sighed. "I wouldn't be so sure. There's not much difference in the way he looks at Tae and the way he looks at you. He's just a young man, Indy. Don't confuse him even more."

"I want to see my friend," she insisted, and Lazlo took a deep breath.

"Fine. But we follow the new protocol. Private planes, incognito limos, security at the hotel."

"The environment will hate me with all that jet fuel," she

said with regret, but she wanted to be selfish. "Okay, if it means I can see Sun."

"I'll make the arrangements."

INDY THANKED her brother and ended the call. Her heart felt lighter, knowing she would see her friend, but still, in the back of her mind, was Massimo. The man was drop-dead gorgeous, lathered in sex appeal and machismo. She could even blame Valentina for not wanting to let him go.

"Listen to yourself, woman," she told herself, "you don't even know this guy or that world."

She sat at the piano and began to play random new melodies, and her mind drifted back and forth between Massimo and Sun, both so different, and yet they were both so desirable in their own ways. She thought about Massimo's kiss, the way his lips commanded hers, the scratch of his stubble. Sun's kiss was soft, his skin was smooth like velvet, his smile sweet and dazzling.

Indy began to smile as a new idea came to mind. Angel and Devil. Sun and Massimo. A concept for her new album. It was just an idea, but it was something to distract herself with. She grabbed her notebook and sat down on the sofa, creating new songs for the rest of the day.

New York

. . .

Braydon got the call late at night. "She's in Helsinki."

"How do you know?"

His handler laughed. "Carter, we have spies everywhere. The girl is in Helsinki. In the morning, a car will pick you up and take you to the airport. All the details are there. Mr Carter?"

"Yes?"

"Sidney asked me to tell you to make it painful."

Braydon laughed. "I can guarantee that. India will know hell before she dies, I promise."

"Good. I expect to see news of her brutal murder in the newspapers soon."

Braydon dropped his phone and lay back on the bed. At last. Not that it wasn't fun being put up in these luxurious surroundings. The apartment had every mod con and Braydon made the most of it. He cleaned himself up, too, with the expensive clothes in the closet, the ridiculous facial cleansers and moisturizers. A barber came to shave him every day, which Braydon found amusing and slightly irritating.

But he looked a million miles from the scumbag who left prison. He looked almost... respectable. He got up and went to the bathroom, flicking on the light and gazing in the mirror. Would India recognize him now? His face had slimmed down a lot, his hair was greying... but his eyes, that darkness in them burning black, were still the same. He closed them, remembering the day he took her... India was still a kid but breathtakingly beautiful. It entertained him to think that while they were together, it was heavenly for him and hellish for her.

The terror in her eyes, the way she tried so valiantly to fight him off... the shock of the blade sinking into her skin. He was getting an erection from the memory, and he took care of it, grunting and groaning as he jerked off, ejaculating generously.

Shivering and panting hard, he returned to bed, glancing at the clock. It was after midnight. *So it's after 7 a.m. in Helsinki. Is she awake already?* He wished he could telepathically instill fear into her, then snickered at his foolishness. *What is the point if he can't see her terror firsthand?*

Tomorrow would be soon enough. With a forged passport, he can now leave the country. He could hardly wait.

CHAPTER NINE - EVERY BREATH YOU TAKE

Rome, Italy

Massimo was pissed but Valentina was unrepentant. "It's not my fault the paparazzi drew their own conclusions," she stated when he inquired about the photos. "They want us to reunite. What can I do?"

Massimo kept his temper. "Next time, don't kiss me. Let's not risk misunderstandings, shall we?"

Valentina chuckled, a high, tinkly, sarcastic sound. "Well, you could always simply refuse to see me, darling." Her voice dropped to a seductive purr. "But we both know you don't want that."

He ended the call, knowing she had taken the victory. "Fuck!" he yelled into the emptiness of his dwelling. This pissed him off much more this time than ever before... India. They were close to forming a friendship at least, sharing laughs and messages, talking on Skype... Yet, since the photos came out... nada. Zilch!

It felt like a terrible loss to Massimo. He'd be damned if Valentina's machinations wreck whatever he and India had before it even started.

It wasn't as if he could go see Indy or send her flowers. Where in the world is she? She did not offer information when they spoke last. The only clue he gleaned from their talks was it was somewhere cold because of the sweaters she wore. That could mean anywhere in the Northern Hemisphere—hardly narrowing it down.

Did he dare text her? Would she reply? Fuck it, he has to know.

Hey Bella, *hope everything is okay. Looking forward to seeing you in the New Year—although that seems way too long to wait. M.*

He made himself put his phone down so he wouldn't check it like some lovesick school kid and left his apartment.

He met his friends for lunch and then strolled around the busy streets of Rome. He was stopped often by fans and admirers, and he gladly signed autographs and took selfies with them. They were the reason he was so popular, after all.

When he got back, he changed clothes before checking his phone, then finally looked at it.

His heart sank. No message.

Fuck. He had seriously blown it?

He called Jake. "Hey, could you call India's people to double-check we're still on for the music video in January?"

"Sure. Any reason?"

"Just haven't heard from her in a while."

Jake caught on. "Ah. The photos."

"Yeah."

Jake sighed. "I'm on it, boss."

Massimo grabbed a pack of cigarettes—he'd been cutting down lately but couldn't quite kick the habit—and went out onto the balcony. The view of the city was spectacular at any time of the day, but at twilight, it took on a sensual, sultry tone that Massimo thought was unequalled.

He remained outside, staring over the city until it grew dark and he tired. He walked into the apartment and saw a message on his phone.

Hey, of course. Looking forward to working with you. India.

Even if it lacked the warmth they had built up, this was something. But he had definitely lost ground. If he wanted to pursue India the way he hoped, he needed to avoid debacles with Valentina or any other woman.

He was in too deep now; he had to follow through. India Blue was too special of a woman to let go of that easily; he felt it in his bones.

He read her message a few more times, then, almost satisfied, went to bed.

HELSINKI, **Finland**

. . .

INDIA WAS HALF-PLEASED, half-annoyed by the message from Massimo. *I see you, Verdi. I know guilt.* But she couldn't deny it pleased her.

Early morning, she'll be flying to Seoul. She could hardly wait. She needed her buddy, her confidante, and damn it, she needed his arms around her. Nothing brought her peace like being in Sun's sweet presence.

She wanted to find a gift for him, something Finnish and fun. She pulled on her heavy sweater and coat, then donned a wool hat snugged down over her hair, stuffing her long, thick strands under it. She completed the look with no makeup and thick, black-framed spectacles. No one could recognize her like this.

She walked into the city center, through crowds of early Christmas shoppers and lost herself in the shops. She forgot what it was like to be free to do this—but then again, she wasn't exactly alone. The security team that followed her here kept a respectful distance, but she knew they were there. Out of the corner of her eye, she would suddenly spot one of them and want to play games with them—losing herself in a throng of shoppers so they'd panic, only to appear behind them, touching them on the shoulder as she passed to let them know she was kidding.

On lock-down, you found your games where you could. India located a small gift shop that sold knickknacks and oddities she knew Sun would love. His quirky personality, plus his youth, meant his bedroom was stuffed with things like this, models of superheroes and anime characters. Sometimes India felt more like his big sister than his sometime-lover, and she wondered if they had already settled into those roles. It had been a couple of years since they last saw each other, after all.

Afterward, she wanted to have some hot chocolate in a cafe. Someone moved beside her. "Ms. Blue... perhaps we've been out too long?"

It was one of her security guards, Nate. She smiled. "Let me have some hot chocolate and we can go."

He nodded. "Top floor. There's an elevator."

Only two other people were in the elevator: a middle-aged woman and a man with bright bleach-blonde hair and too-blue eyes behind thick-rimmed glasses. India nodded politely, then looked away. Nate silently rode with her but kept his distance as they arrived at the café.

India ordered a cup of hot chocolate and sat at a table near the window, looking down over the streets. The evening was settling in and later, as she walked back to her residence, she realized she'd miss this place. She planned on staying in Seoul until she goes home for Christmas, but she enjoyed her time in this country and this city.

She knew Nate and the other bodyguard were close, but suddenly she stopped, her skin prickling as her sixth sense kicked in.

Someone is watching me.

She scanned the streets but it was a crapshoot.

Recognize *him*.

She turned, shot a look at Nate, who sensed that something was wrong. He made his way closer as someone from behind bumped into her.

"Sorry," the person muttered, walking past, then turning to look at her.

It was the guy from the elevator. Extremely blue eyes. *Contact lenses*, she realized. Fear was clutching at her chest but then Nate was beside her, taking her by the arm and gently steering her.

He didn't leave her side until she was in the apartment. He sat her down. "What was it?"

India blew out her cheeks. "You'll think I'm insane, but I got the craziest feeling that someone was watching me. Not you or Tom. Someone bumped into me... he was the guy from the elevator."

"The blonde guy?"

She nodded.

"Did he touch you?"

India shook her head. "Only bumped my shoulder. It's probably nothing, coincidence."

Nate didn't look happy. "Damn it."

"Nate, it's probably a mishap and just me being paranoid." She felt foolish and careless. She shouldn't put Nate and Tom in such situations. Sure, it was their job but...

"I'm sorry, Nate. I shouldn't have gone out."

Nate shook his head. "You can't completely hide away, Indy, and it was low-risk. Don't worry about it. I'll check in with Tom. You're okay?"

"Of course. Thank you, Nate."

"Anytime."

. . .

Indy took her coat off, only now noticing there was a tear in the back of it. She frowned. How did that happen? She shrugged. Did it matter?

She walked into her bedroom, peeling off the sweater that was getting hot and itchy. Tugging it over her head, she threw it on the bed and went to the bathroom, cranking on the shower and stripping the rest of her clothes off.

She sighed with relief as the hot water streamed down her body, and she took her time, shaving and buffing, then stepped out and massaged body lotion into every inch of her skin. India never felt sexier than when she was freshly showered, and she felt a thrill of excitement go through her when she thought of seeing Sun tomorrow. She toyed with a brief fantasy of being made love to by him and Massimo Verdi at the same time, both men such polar opposites, but what a turn on...

She was still smirking when she returned to her bedroom and put on the cotton nightshirt. She picked up the sweater to put it in her half-packed suitcase—and froze. An envelope lay on the bed. Her name was handwritten across it in a scrawl she recognized.

Instantly she knew.

"Nate!"

She didn't mean to scream in such a panic, but Nate came rushing in, followed by Tom.

India pointed to the envelope. "Did either of you put this here?"

They shook their heads. Indy's knees gave way, and Tom caught her as Nate grabbed the envelope and ripped it open. Her bodyguard's face paled.

"Is it from him?" She asked, her voice barely a whisper.

Nate, his expression one of shock, nodded. "Yes. It's from Carter."

He found her.

CHAPTER TEN - PERFECTLY LONELY

My darling, India,

Surprise! Did you really think you could hide from me? Didn't my letters suggest what your future would be?

I'll always be with you, beautiful girl, until the moment you take your last breath.

It won't be long now.

Yours, always,

Braydon.

. . .

India sat on the plane, her ruined coat over the nightshirt, jeans hastily pulled on. Nate barely gave her time to throw the rest of her belongings into a case before he and Tom spirited her away. They took a long and complicated route to the airport, making sure they weren't being followed. Only when Nate was satisfied, they made their way to the runway and the small private jet that idled there.

Now India was alone in the cabin, wondering how the hell Carter found her, of all places, in Helsinki. She was so careful when speaking to her friends, her colleagues—only Lazlo knew she was in Helsinki.

Lazlo... and Gabe. Her other pseudo-brother, Lazlo's half-brother, but she couldn't imagine Gabe would tell her would-be murderer where she was. No freaking way, she told herself again, ignoring the nagging doubt.

Gabe would never hurt her... but he was also a drunk with a big mouth, having always lived in Lazlo's imposing shadow. Gabe was the playboy of the family, never being faithful to a single girlfriend, not even the last one, Serena, whom Lazlo and India adored. Indy recalled the day Gabe admitted to cheating on her. Indy yelled, he yelled back, and their relationship had never been the same since. Serena thanked India for taking her side and promised to stay in touch but she drifted away. It was because she didn't want to get between Indy and Gabe's friendship.

Indy was still ticked about it, and Gabe distanced himself, but she couldn't imagine he would sell her out to the man who wants to kill her.

... the moment you take your last breath...

Jesus. She insisted on reading the letter, and when she called Lazlo, she told him point-blank. "Show me the letters! I want to see them," she requested when Lazlo admitted he had them.

"No. No way."

"Laz... there's protecting me and then there's treating me like a child. Do you think I will be shocked? After what he did to me? I want to see them."

She must have hit a nerve with Lazlo because a few minutes after she hung up, Jess called her. Lazlo always got Jess to call her on professional matters when she was in trouble.

Jess and Indy went back years, their friendship cemented in college. There was a point when Indy thought she might be in love with Jess, who was bisexual, but the crush faded into sisterhood. Unlike Lazlo, Jess was the person who could stand up to Indy when she was on a tear. The first word out of Jess's mouth was "No! No way, dude. You're not seeing these pieces of filth."

"Dude," which was how they referred to each other. "Come on. Are they really worse than getting stabbed and left for dead?"

"India... they will haunt you forever if you read them. They are not about *me,* and they give me sleepless nights! The thought of you reading them, knowing what he wants to do to you... *No!*"

That made India feel bad. "You're not sleeping?"

"Take the worst thing that could happen to someone you

love and multiply it by a thousand. Would *you* be able to sleep?"

"Oh, Jess."

Jess was clearly upset, and India heard her ragged breathing. "Okay... all right, Jess. I... if I knew what to expect..."

"What he did to you before... compared to what he's planning? That's nothing. He's not talking murder, Indy, he's talking slaughter."

India was speechless. She closed her eyes and took a deep breath. For a moment, neither said a word. Then Jess cleared her throat. "You're going to visit Sun?"

"Yes. I can't wait to see him, actually."

"He's an angel. If anyone can take your mind off this, it's him." Jess adored Sun; she treated him like her little brother, and the feeling was mutual. Sun found Jess's no-bullshit approach to everything entertaining. "And I heard about some Italian movie star. What's happening there?"

"Complications." India sighed. "But I keep thinking about him."

"Did you fuck yet?"

India chuckled. "No, Laz ran a good cockblock on that with news about Carter. But I would have."

She giggled, her friend making her feel less tense. "Do you *want* to fuck him?"

"Yes." Indy answered before she could lie about it. "I would fuck that man for hours. I might regret it, but I would."

Jess laughed. "That's my girl."

"If you promise not to tell anyone... I have a fantasy about having both Sun and Massimo at the same time."

Jess whooped. "Now that really *is* my girl!"

India laughed, although her face was burning. "It's not something I've ever done."

"Really? Well, welcome to the jungle, dude."

"You have?"

"Two men at the same time? Many times." Jess gave a throaty, dirty snicker. "Girl, if the opportunity presents itself, go for it."

India sighed. "Only we could go from discussing bloody murder to threesomes and orgies."

"Oh, sweets. Well, that's what we do. Your safety comes first! If it helps to joke about it, I'm all for that. Love you, dude."

"Love you too, Slutty Dude."

"You know it."

India's tense shoulders had eased as she chatted with Jess, and when the call ended, she went to the bedroom at the rear of the plane. The jet was Lazlo's baby, and even though India nagged him about his carbon footprint, she was glad that he had it now. Her destination can be kept more private by going to three different airports before heading to South Korea.

She took an Ambien, and it wasn't until after they landed and taken off again from Charles de Gaulle in Paris that she woke. She took a shower and went to find food. Some hot food was bought for her in Paris, and she indulged gratefully, asking Nate and Tom if they'd eaten.

"We have, thanks," Nate retorted. "Listen, do you mind if I sit for a time and talk with you?"

Indy smiled at him. "No problem, as long as you don't mind watching me eat this steak like a starving puma."

"Ha, not at all."

India began to eat as Nate sat down. "What's up?"

"I'd like to go over how we're upping the security in Seoul. I know," Nate held his hands up as Indy grimaced, "but this affects Sun and his group as well, so we had to coordinate something."

"Of course," Indy felt ashamed. "No one is going to hurt Sun. I'd stand in front of a bullet for him."

"Well, let's hope the precautions we've taken means *no one* gets hurt. We still don't know how Carter found you in Finland."

Indy looked away from Nate's stare. He was probably thinking *it's Gabe*. Gabe and his drinking and bragging about his famous 'sister.' "Okay, so what's the plan?"

"Sun's apartment building is staked out by press night and day, so you can't go there. We and his security team have worked out an arrangement. There's an apartment on the outskirts of the city. It's rented in a false name, has no cameras, and is very quiet. Sun's being taken there now. You'll join him when we land."

"Christ," Indy exclaimed. "He's really being inconvenienced. What about his management, the rest of his group?"

"Your timing is great. They're taking a break for the remainder of the year. They just finished a world tour. Management wants them to rest."

"It's about time. Have you seen their schedule? It's insane."

Nate smiled at her. "Sun sent a message. We replied that we had to change your number because of the security breach. He said to tell you he can't wait to see you."

Indy felt a rush of warmth. Seeing Sun would be like a shot of pure joy. She chewed on her steak for a moment. "The new number... who has it?"

"Security, Lazlo, Jess, the usual. Not Gabe," he added. and they exchanged a look.

"Good. It's not like we're talking at the moment anyway."

"One of the avenues we're looking at is that someone got your private number and traced it. Someone with money."

"Obviously. Carter wouldn't have that kind of money, would he?"

Nate shrugged lamely. He knew something he wasn't comfortable sharing. He can keep his secrets for now. "Nate?"

"Yes?"

Indy put her fork aside. "Massimo Verdi. Does he have the new number?"

"Do you want him to have it, Indy? Do you know him well enough to trust him?"

India wanted to say yes so badly, and the thought she might not speak or text with Massimo until after the New Year hurt... but did she trust him?

No.

She couldn't get those photographs out of her mind even though she had no right to be jealous—especially as as she was about to spend time with another man.

"No," she said, finally. "Let's not drag him into this. He can do it through Lazlo."

"I agree. The fewer people have your new number, the better. Anyway, we might have to use burner phones from now on or at least until they get Carter."

India sighed. "Get him? He's out of prison, Nate. As far as they're concerned, he hasn't committed a crime, so how exactly will they *get* him?"

"The letters are enough reason to bring him back. They're death threats, Indy. When they catch him, he's going away. He won't get near you again, I promise." He smiled. "Changing the subject, someone else wants to talk to you."

"Who?"

"Your father."

India rolled her eyes. " *No*, thanks."

"Are you sure?"

"Entirely. I have nothing to say to him."

Nate studied her. "He's a powerful man; he might be able to help."

"But he won't." India's hard tone made it clear they were done talking about her estranged father. "Look, let's discuss how it'll work when we get to Seoul."

Rome

MASSIMO TRIED her number again only to receive a dead tone. Wow. She must be really pissed at him.

Fuck it. I blew it.

Or rather Valentina had. She was a master manipulator. He was so angry at her, he could scream!

Massimo tried India's number one last time, then dialed Diana's number in England.

"Hello, handsome."

"Hey, Diana... how are you?"

"You mean how is *India* after she saw the photos of you and your ex?"

Diana knew him so well, and he couldn't help but chuckle. "Valentina's work."

"I thought as much but that won't help convince India you're worth a shot. She's extremely skittish."

"What's with her? The night we met, a call from her brother spooked her pretty bad."

There was hesitation in Diana's voice. "It's really not my place to tell you. I could say look her up on the internet, but they've managed to scrub everything relating to... Look, something happened when she was younger and it left a scar. Physically and mentally."

That made him more curious. "Something happened? Someone hurt her?"

"I've said more than enough already, Massi. Look... give her some time. If you really like her, if it's meant to be—and in my heart, I know it is—it will happen. But move on with your life until then. That's the best advice for you."

He met some friends for drinks later, but he found himself preoccupied by what Diana said. Someone hurt India? More than likely it was something very serious; the fact that it was scrubbed off the internet was pretty weird. Didn't people usually exploit their pain in this industry?

Jesus. His mind was rampant with theories on what happened. Even more insidious was the sense they missed their chance, that the incredible heat of their first meeting had long since dissipated, and by the time they met again in the New Year, it would have totally vanished.

Fuck.

He was getting too hung up on a woman who was possibly lost. *Screw it.* Later, he and his friend Ricardo went to a club, and when a sensational redhead made eyes at Massimo, he pushed all thoughts of India Blue aside and took the redhead to his apartment.

The redhead—whose name he couldn't remember—was a great fuck, and she distracted Massimo for a few hours. By the time she let herself out at dawn, he was sated, exhausted, and grateful she knew the rules of the game—after all, it was just sex. He slept for a few hours but then woke to the news that Valentina was involved in a serious car crash.

He was on the way to the hospital before the anchor finished reporting the headline.

CHAPTER ELEVEN - ANGEL

Seoul, South Korea

"I SWEAR, Sun, you get more beautiful every time I see you."

He grinned at her, the highpoints in his cheekbones coloring. As celebrated as he was, Sun was shy and humble about his beauty. "I could say the same, Indy."

He wrapped his arms around her and held her tightly. India sank into his embrace. He'd grown: he stood five-ten and was much manlier. Being held by him was bliss. He tenderly kissed her forehead and smiled.

"I missed you, Sunbeam."

They were in the rented residence, India having arrived only a few moments ago. The feeling of relief and joy at seeing her friend was overwhelming, and tears were welling up in her eyes.

"Oh... don't cry, Indy! Let's sit down and catch up!"

They lay down and cuddled on the vast couch, Sun pulling a fluffy yellow blanket around them. They always did this, swaddled together while they talk. It felt safe and a million miles away from the rest of the world.

"I'm sorry you had to upend your life because of me, Sun. You'll never know how grateful I am."

He shook his head. "Don't be. It actually worked out... Tae... Tae and I needed some time apart."

"You and Tae are together?" He shook his head.

"Not as such... we can't be together like that. It would be a scandal here... but it's hard to deny the attraction, especially after Tae said he feels it, too."

"That's wonderful!"

Sun shook his head. "No. It makes it worse. The longing."

"Oh, Sun..."

He buried his face in her neck and sighed as she held him tighter. "He loves you," she whispered.

"And I love him. It's agony."

It was sad to see the tears on his sweet face. She gently wiped them away. "Don't cry, beautiful boy."

"I'm glad you're here, Indy. I need you."

"Right back at you, baby."

He kissed her then, softly on the mouth. "Why is love so complicated? How can I be in love with two people at the same time?"

India smiled at him. "What we have is... we're soulmates,

Sun, you and I. We transcend sex. You'll always be my guy, whether you're with Tae forever—I know that's your future—or perhaps...I meet someone."

Sun studied her face. "You *did* meet someone."

"Maybe. I don't know." She never lied to Sun, ever. She couldn't do something so cruel to such a pure heart. She told him about Massimo. "I just don't know, Sun. He's not what I need. He's a player and a freaking movie star. Someone who may still be hung-up on his ex."

"How long were they together?"

"Ten years, I think."

Sun grimaced. "Ouch."

"See?"

Sun propped himself on his elbow. "What was the chemistry like?"

"Insane. Like you and me when we first met."

"Wowser."

She grinned. "Wowser?" Sun's English was exemplary, but she was always surprised when he came up with idioms and slang.

Sun stroked his finger down her cheek. "You like him."

Indy nodded. "But I don't know if he's healthy for me."

"Not everything has to be long-term. Fuck him if that's what you want."

Indy snuggled to him. His skin was so soft she could hardly believe it. "For now, selfishly, I just want to be with you."

Sun pulled her closer. "Then you have me, Indy."

. . .

LATER, she and Sun made dinner, a soft tofu stew with plenty of sticky rice and vegetables, and homemade kimchi that made India's mouth water. They ate, talking and laughing over the silliest of things.

After dinner, they lounged on the couch playing computer games and watching funny videos online until Indy was tired.

Sun pulled her up off the coach, and they walked hand-in-hand to the bedroom. There never was any doubt they would share a bed; they always had.

Sun undressed her, chuckling as she could barely keep her eyes open, and he steered her onto the bed, pulling the blanket over her. Indy stirred when he slipped in naked beside her. Sun kissed her forehead. "Good night."

Indy tried to protest, but then Sun was cradling her in his arms and singing softly to her, and she, unable to resist the peace it brought her, sank into a deep slumber.

THE LIGHT in the room was blue when she woke shivering, from a horrific nightmare where blood and terror mingled with love, hurt, and heartbreak. India panted for air, her jaw stiff from clenching. She looked at Sun, his otherworldly beauty even more pronounced in the moonlight.

India lay back down and gazed at him. Sun was her safe place, she realized. He opened his eyes and smiled at her. They lay in silence for a moment, then Sun moved closer and kissed her.

It seemed natural to have him move on top of her, his

angelic face such a contrast to his well-toned body. His hands smoothed down her skin, caressing her with the lightest touch and yet every place they brushed felt like it was set aflame. India gazed at him. "Sun?"

Was he sure that his love for Tae wouldn't be sullied if they made love tonight?

"This is our bubble," Sun whispered, "And I love you."

"I love you too, Sunbeam."

It was a special kind of love; it wasn't something that could ever be tangible, but right now, it was what they needed. Sun kissed her again, this time with more urgency, and India responded, losing herself in his soft eyes and incredible body.

By the time he was inside her, India's body had taken over completely, and at first, they moved slowly together, but soon took on an intensity that she needed.

After she came, India did something she hardly ever did. She cried! Sun wrapped her in his arms and held her until she was cried out. Then he kissed her and said he loved her once more.

They fell asleep as the sun rose, and India knew she made the right decision to come here.

She just prayed that whoever was funding Brayden Carter wouldn't trace her. She needed some time. She needed time and for Sun to not be in danger. She needed time.

And she needed peace.

CHAPTER TWELVE - LOVE IS A LOSING GAME

Rome, Italy

Massimo smirked when he saw the apparent relief on the hospital staff's faces as Valentina was discharged. Three days and she had made their lives hell with her demands and histrionics. The 'serious' injuries were nothing more than whiplash and a sprained wrist but Valentina insisted on several unnecessary tests. "What if there's something wrong with my brain? What if I can't drive again?"

The kicker was she wasn't driving the vehicle that had crashed anyway. The doctor could not help rolling his eyes, stopping when he saw Massimo watching, but Massimo winked at him. He understood.

Now, Massimo sighed as he wheeled Valentina out to a hoard of paparazzi—notified by her, of course—and he wanly smiled through their barrage of questions. Valentina, bedecked in an 'Audrey Hepburn' sunglasses-and-scarf get up, waved imperiously and gave her thanks to the staff. She managed to put her hand on Massimo possessively the whole way through but this time Massimo didn't care. When a paparazzo asked him if the two were together, he looked at the man's camera directly and shook his head. "No. We're just good friends."

Valentina waited until they were in the car before she took her sunglasses off and when she did, Massimo could see her rage. "Why did you say that? Why?"

"Because it's the truth, Val. We are not a couple. You were the one to end it, and now I'm telling you it's over. You will not manipulate me again."

"Yet you were the first to come to the hospital." Valentina took out one of her cigarettes and lit it, offering him the slim silver case—always affectionate in everything she did. Massimo shook his head as she snapped the case shut in irritation. "Is this about your singer?"

Massimo stiffened. "How do you know about India?"

Valentina smiled victoriously. "I have my sources. And she's disappeared off the map. Must be frustrating for you."

"India is none of your business."

Valentina's expression went cold. "Stop pretending to be something you're not, Massimo. You're a whore and apparently that woman doesn't play games. She'll see right through you."

She already has. "Maybe I've changed." He realized it was a mistake as soon as the words came out of his mouth. Valentina laughed.

"*Sure* you have, darling. And that redhead coming out of your apartment the day I had my accident, who was she? Your French tutor?"

Massimo grit his teeth. "I'm not pretending to be a saint, Val, either in my past or now. If and when I see India again, I'll do what it takes for her to trust me."

"You're fooling yourself." Valentina waved a dismissive hand, and Massimo turned to stare out of the window.

Maybe I am *kidding myself,* he thought, *but fuck it, I want to try.* He had a plan in place already. In three days, he will go to New York and talk to India's brother, Lazlo. Using the cover of discussing the music video, he will try and make friends with the man, to prove he could be trusted. Find out what happened to make her so elusive. It was worth a shot.

She was worth a shot.

NEW YORK CITY

BRAYDON LISTENED to his yelling liaison for a good ten minutes before he got a word in. "You *had* her. She was there. You could have finished the job. India Blue should be dead, you asshole, *dead!* It should be all over the news, her fans should be holding mass vigils, memorial concerts thrown by her music colleagues. Instead she's in the wind... *again!*"

Braydon had enough. "Listen, you little weasel, I don't answer to you. Your boss knows I will kill her but she has body guards. It was by chance I got that close. I don't want it to be half-assed. She survived the last time. You have no idea what I did to her. So, fuck you, *asshole.* I told you I'd do it and I will."

By the end of his rant, he was listening to a dead tone and in a rage, he threw his cell phone at the wall where it smashed into a million fragments. *Screw it.* Stanley's money could buy him a new one.

Calming himself, he sat down and made notes. India was gone, spirited away. Leaving the note in her apartment had been a dumb move, but the temptation to scare her proved too much to resist.

So, what now? He thought about the ways he could find out where she was and really, the easiest way was to get to her brothers. He knew the younger brother, Gabriel, was a drunk; he learned that when he asked how they found her in Helsinki.

"The brother's a drunk and big mouth. He likes to talk about his famous sister. It didn't take us long to feed him enough booze and cocaine and set him up with a hooker. He gave up the information easy enough."

Indeed, Gabe Schuler was an option. Although Carter found her in Helsinki, they figured out Gabe was the weak link. He would bet the farm that Gabe didn't know where she was now.

Which left him with the older brother, and Carter didn't like the idea of taking on Lazlo Schuler. Schuler had a reputation as a nice guy—until he was crossed or until his family was threatened. Braydon followed India's career while he was in prison and knew Lazlo managed everything. He had assistants, of course, and Braydon concentrated on finding out who else ran India's career. She was famous for being extremely private and not taking publicity away from her records or concerts, so she had hired others to handle that.

The first name he came up with was a woman in Los Angeles: Coco Conrad was a publicist, a very successful one, who handled everything for India on the west coast. He would start there. He booked a ticket for the next day.

In his bathroom, he stripped off, stepping into the shower. He needed to look different from the Viking he was in Finland. There was no recognition in India's eyes after he bumped into her, neither did she noticed when he slashed her coat with a razorblade. It was a half-hearted swipe; he didn't actually want to hurt her in case she screamed and alerted those damn bodyguards.

It would all be over if they'd caught him then. He'd never get another chance. Even the scent of her perfume drove him mad. He passed her, turning to look back... In the flesh, she was more beautiful than he remembered: those huge brown eyes, her sweet face, that perfect mouth.

He had tasted those lips and knew their softness. Knew

the shape of them when she screamed bloody murder. He couldn't wait to see that again.

Concentrate. He dyed the bleached hair black, exasperated when it turned a dirty, almost green color. He tried again and this time it seemed to stick. He inserted dark brown contact lenses and applied the fake beard. *Yes. This is good.* Thankfully he wouldn't need another fake passport inside the country, but Stanley's people provided him with enough different photo IDs with disguises to travel with ease within the States.

Braydon tried to figure out his approach to Coco Conrad. He could act as a newbie film producer looking for representation. She wouldn't take him on, of course, not when she can pick and choose her clientele but he might be able to charm her. If she would accept his dinner invitation...

Finally done with his disguise and happy with it, he removed the fake beard, laying it on the bathroom counter to wear it in the morning and switched the light off. It was after midnight. He checked his email alerts; no news about India Blue.

Braydon went to bed, thinking about her lips again. *Not long now*, he told himself as he finally went to sleep.

NEW YORK CITY

LAZLO SCHULER WORKED PAST MIDNIGHT, catching up on other clients, then sat back and sighed, exhausted with work and strain. India was hidden away in South Korea with Sun, and he hoped she was finding peace. Lazlo felt constantly on edge and paranoid, but he couldn't imagine what it must be like to live under a death threat, to never be able to put down roots, to never having relationships.

He hoped India and Sun cared for one another. He respected Sun; Lazlo was a man who was comfortable in his heterosexuality, but even *he* would turn for Sun—the guy was stunning. More than that, Sun was exactly who India needed right now: kind and funny with a big heart.

Lazlo examined the message his PA brought in. Massimo Verdi. He wanted to meet in a couple of days and it probably wasn't representation he wanted to talk about.

Lazlo had doubts about the man. The photos with his ex, the rushing to her side after the accident, and his denials they were together afterward. Verdi's playboy life is shining through. Regardless of whether he and India shared an attraction, Massimo Verdi was trouble. Lazlo could see India's disappointment after the photos of Massimo and his ex were published, and he knew she would let that go.

Besides, he sighed, India didn't need much reason to run away—not that he blamed her, but he hoped she wasn't using Sun. He deserved better, and India would be horrified at the thought of that.

He tried to call her but got no answer. It was rather early in Seoul so he wasn't alarmed. He heard someone walking into the office and frowned.

"Laz?"

Shit. Gabe. At least he sounded sober. That was a rarity. "Gabe, in here."

His half-brother smiled as he came into the office. "Hey, bro." Gabe was wary, the result of being chewed out by Lazlo after the Helsinki debacle.

Lazlo nodded. "Hey. It's late."

"Look, it's been bugging me, but I want to say again how sorry I am. I'd never knowingly put Indy in danger, you know that. I hope she knows it, too."

Lazlo scrutinized his brother. "Giving up the booze and nose candy would go a long way towards that."

"I was thinking of calling her."

Lazlo shook his head. "No. Sorry, Gabe, that won't happen. We can't trust you."

Gabe sighed. "Yeah. I don't trust myself these days."

"What is it, Gabe? What's driving you lately? First the stuff with Serena and now this? Plus... how much coke do you snort? You're always so wired."

Gabe rubbed his face. "You're right, okay? But I'm stuck in this loop where if I don't snort, then I'm exhausted, like, dead to my bones."

Lazlo leaned forward. "Go to a rehab. I'll pay for that."

"I can't take more money from you, Laz."

"You can if it'll turn your life around. When you're sober, you can work for me. The city isn't good for you."

Gabe nodded, staring out of the window at the city. "Fine. But then I pay you back."

Lazlo sighed, relieved. Gabe was a problem he didn't need at the moment. "Good."

There was a long silence. "Does she hate me?" Gabe's voice quivered, but he coughed to cover his nervousness. Lazlo softened.

"Of course she doesn't, Gabe. *Of course* not. She might be angry for a while, but she loves you like you love her. She was pissed about Serena but then, so were all of us. You fucked up the best thing that ever happened to you."

"I know." Gabe sat back in his chair. "I've been trying to call her but she won't talk to me, not that I blame her. Jeez." He smiled sheepishly. "It would probably help if I stopped catting around."

Lazlo snorted. "Perhaps. Who's the latest."

"Italian actress called Fernanda Rossi. Seriously hot redhead, incredible in bed."

That name ring a bell. "Didn't she fuck Massimo Verdi a few months back?"

Gabe rolled his eyes. "Yup. She never stops talking about how he dumped her without a second glance. Fucker."

"Glass houses, Gabe."

Gabe chuckled. "Touché." He got up. "Look, I'll find a place to get help and let you know, okay? I'll find meetings, too. AA and NA. This is a wake-up call, I mean it. If anything happened to Indy because of me… I couldn't live with it." He chewed his lip. "Are you in touch with her?"

Lazlo nodded and Gabe sighed. "Tell'er I love her, would you? Tell her I'm sorry and I miss her. Tell her I'll do anything to make things good with her and hope she finds justice with this asshole. Laz, if I'd ever catch up with Carter, I'll kill that son of a bitch myself."

"On that, brother, we can agree."

After Gabe left, Lazlo drove home. His work took all of his time, and although India was always at him to carve time out for solitude, the truth was Lazlo loved his work. He had random hook-ups but nothing permanent, and he couldn't be bothered unless he really liked someone, and that hasn't happened since...

Best not think about *her*. It was too painful. Not even Indy knew about the woman he loved and lost. That drove him to work harder and to protect his sister. He knew what fanatical love could do.

Not that he thought what Carter felt for India was love. The guy was a psychopath, pure and simple.

You won't get what you want, Carter, not this time. You will not put one finger on my little sister if it takes me killing you myself.

This time, Carter, the only one who will be dead is you.

**If you want to continue reading this story,
you can get your copy here:**

**His Hidden Love
A Reverse Harem Romance Their Secret Desire Book 1**

https://www.hotandsteamyromance.com/products/his-hidden-love-a-holiday-romance-their-secret-desire-book-1

13

CHAPTER THIRTEEN - BROKEN-HEARTED GIRL

India stretched out as she woke to a bright November morning in Seoul. The bed was empty beside her, and she heard Sun in the living room. She got up and threw her nightshirt over and padded out to see him.

Sun was arguing on the phone and his beautiful face was creased with distress. India's heart sank. The two weeks together were glorious, but Sun's mind was also on his other love: Tae.

It was obvious he was talking to him, so Indy gave him privacy and went to shower and dress. She shampooed her hair, taking her time, massaging conditioner into it, then after the shower, she took her time drying herself and smoothing lotion into her skin.

She dressed in maroon bell bottoms and a caramel colored tee, straining to hear if Sun was still talking to Tae, but it was quiet. She returned to the living room and saw him on the balcony. She went out to join him and was horrified to see his tears. "Oh, Sunbeam…"

She wrapped her arms around him and let him cry as much as he needed. Then she led him inside as he told her what happened. As she suspected, he had an argument with Tae.

"He thinks I'm with another man. He wouldn't believe me when I said I'm alone, most likely because I suck at lying."

India was dismayed. "Oh, Sun… you should have told him you were with me."

Sun gave her a wan smile. "Indy, that would put you in danger, and Tae… he loves you, but he's actually insanely jealous of you and me. He knows I love you."

"But he knows you love him, too, right?"

"Yes, but Tae is the ultimate self-saboteur, and he's not as open-minded as you and I. He thinks as long as you and I are sleeping together, then he and I are not really a couple."

Indy stroked his hair. "Maybe he's right. I've been selfish taking you away, especially now."

Sun shook his head. "No, I wanted to see you. I needed to see you." He sighed. "Maybe…"

"What?"

"Maybe we're not meant to be. If I really loved him, I wouldn't feel this way about you."

"Sunbeam… I love you so much. It hurts me when you're unhappy. You and Tae should try again and I'll stay away, at least until you sort things out."

"You want to leave?"

It was heartbreaking. He was still a kid, and she was

playing with his heart. "No, and listen, you will never, ever lose me. *Ever*, okay? We're family, Sun. But listen, right now, you need to go fix things with Tae." She swept a hand through his silky hair, her heart thudding with sadness. To see him so distressed... Someone this beautiful should never be unhappy, and that's what she was bringing to him. *I'm a curse to everyone,* India thought.

"Don't go," Sun said softly, but there was hesitation in his voice, and she knew that what he wanted, what he really needed, was to get back with Tae.

"Sunbeam, I'm going to call Laz, have him arrange to pick me up and to take you to Tae's. Tell him. Tell him you were with me and only me, and that we needed to talk..." She smiled wryly. "Almost certainly, don't mention the sex."

"I don't regret a moment," his dark brown eyes intense on hers, and she stroked the soft curve of his cheek.

"Me, either, my darling, darling Sun. You are my angel, you know? My best friend, my confidante. You are the best thing in this world, and I will always love you." She leaned her forehead against his, breathing him in. "But I have to let you go."

She felt his arms tighten around her, his tears mingling with hers, but he didn't argue. "Promise me," he said, almost in a whisper, "promise me, even if you let me... you'll *never* let me go."

"You are my angel," she said again, nodding. "That will never change."

. . .

TWENTY-FOUR HOURS LATER, she was on Lazlo's plane again, her heart shattering for leaving Sun. He called Tae, told him he was coming home, and even though Sun was desolate that India was leaving, there was light in his eyes when he knew Tae was overjoyed that he was coming back.

India managed to hold her tears at bay until she got on the plane, and after a quick security briefing with Nate, she excused herself to the bedroom. Only then did she let herself break, burying her face in the pillow and sobbing. *Fuck this life...*

After she composed herself, she splashed water on her face and silently berated herself. *Stop being so fucking whiny and get a grip. Figure this shit out, woman.*

They were going to New York City, where she might be in greater danger on one hand, but better protected on the other. Lazlo would be around as well as Jess and some other friends. For the holidays, Lazlo invited Coco and Alex, their friends from California. India would have plenty of love and protection. It would give her some time to figure things out.

She opened her laptop and checked her emails, replying to a few. There was one from Jake, Massimo Verdi's publicist, checking on the dates for the video shoot. India replied in the affirmative.

PLEASE TELL *Massimo I look forward to seeing and working with him in January. Thanks for agreeing to letting him be in it. His time must be in demand and I appreciate it.*

. . .

Was that passive aggressive? Indy shook her head. Did it sound like a dig at his time being taken up by Valentina? She shrugged. She didn't really care and clicked *send*.

Afterward, however, Indy sighed. Is this what she's turning into? A passive-aggressive user of men? *Shit, girl, get your act together.* She got back on her email and made arrangements at a New York recording studio to create some new music. Her record company, Quartet, was understanding as she took her time working on each record, but it had been a couple of years since the last one was released. With the filming of the new video for "Hurting" in January, they'd want to know how things were moving along.

Being at home with Lazlo meant he wouldn't worry as much. Lazlo sacrificed a lot to look after her, to make sure she was pleased. She gladly did as he asked safety-wise so he wouldn't get another ulcer.

Indy went out to see Nate and ask him about the security arrangements at Lazlo's Manhattan dwelling, and he gave her the lowdown. "We'll be with you twenty-four-seven, Indy. We'll try not to crowd you, but your safety is paramount. Lazlo insists on it, so if you have a problem with—"

"—no, it's fine." Indy cut him off. "Whatever Laz says, goes."

No more acting like a scared little girl, though. We'll face this head-on. If Braydon Carter thinks I'm going down without a fight, he has another thing coming.

She went to the bedroom and checked her messages again. An email from Massimo himself.

Bella India, I'm looking forward to seeing you! Massimo.

Good. Friendly but not flirty. He was immensely fuckable and sexy as all hell, but she couldn't get involved with anyone. She didn't *want* to get involved. She couldn't risk their safety or her own heart. Leaving Sun was shattering, but it was for the right reason.

She gave in and checked Sun's group's Twitter feed. Her heart fluttered when she saw a selfie of a beaming, overjoyed Tae alongside a slightly subdued Sun. She pressed translate on the tweet.

Reunited with an emoji of a heart next to it.

That was good. Tae had obviously forgiven Sun, at least for now, and that meant no permanent damage. India was relieved, except…

…why did it hurt so much?

14

CHAPTER FOURTEEN - HUNGER

Manhattan, NYC

"Seoul? Where the fuck is *Seoul*?"

Braydon stared at the lackey who rolled his eyes, sighing at Braydon's ignorance. "South Korea, douche bag. We have intel Lazlo Schuler's private jet landed at Teterboro this evening. We were able to confirm it took off from Seoul yesterday."

"And you're positive India was on that flight?"

The lackey, whose name still eluded Braydon, nodded. "She was spotted getting off the plane by our people."

"Careless."

"Not really. Short of being covered by a blanket, which would have given her away anyhow, what could she do? The car had tinted windows. She was taken to Schuler's apartment. Before you get hopeful, it's like Fort Knox at that place. Your move, Carter." He threw another fat wad of money onto the table. "My boss will want to know something soon."

Braydon was staring at the envelope. "Tell him I'm going to Los Angeles. To get to India, we need an indirect way in. Like her west coast publicist, for example."

Lackey-boy smirked, nodding at Braydon's head. "Hence the new look."

"Hence."

"Fine, I'll tell... Stanley. In the meantime, enjoy SoCal."

BRAYDON WAITED until his visitor left and then grabbed the envelope. He smirked. A couple of hundred thousand dollars. Really, money was no object to this guy. Braydon considered —the longer India stayed alive, the longer this cash would keep flowing in.

But the urge to kill her was making him edgy. He had been squirreling away enough of what Stanley had been giving him, so when India was dead, he could make a clean getaway. He had no illusions Stanley would keep him alive after Indy was dead. He was a loose end.

Well, fuck that. His life was on *his* terms. He wouldn't be erased by a rich boy with a grudge against India Blue. Which led him to question why this man wanted Indy dead as much as he did. Was he a jilted lover? A rich old billionaire rejected by her? He couldn't believe Indy would go for him. She was no gold-digger. After what Braydon did to her, he knew everyone she had been with.

Everyone. Which amounted to a couple of guys—Indy did not sleep around. So, what was halfway around the world in Asia?

He opened his laptop and typed 'India Blue, Seoul, South Korea.' It brought up mostly pictures of several concerts she played in the city over the years. There were selfies with fans and some of Korea's biggest celebrities. Braydon scrolled down the page, almost losing interest until he saw it.

India with a group of exquisitely pretty young men. Laughing, joking for the camera. His eyes narrowed. India and the handsomest of the young men looking at each other. He opened another browser window and went to a video streaming site, punching in India's name and the name of the group, adding 'backstage' to the search.

The video was the first on the list, a shout-out to their mutual fans. He didn't understand what they were saying. Instead he watched the body language of India and the young man, saw the way their hands kept touching, their eyes meeting, bodies leaning into each other.

Connection. Attraction. Longing.

Braydon unclenched his jaw, realizing he was grinding his teeth. So, she was fucking the pretty boy. Shame on him. Braydon looked him up. Sung-Jae, twenty-three years old. A kid. Braydon had to admit—he was fucking *attractive*. It made him angrier. If India was with him...

Calm down. Focusing on the kid wouldn't get him closer to India, especially now. Maybe they broke up. A glance at the

K-pop group's Twitter account told him the kid was probably fucking his group mate, too. To each his own. It was another link to India if he needed it. For the pretty boy's sake, he hoped he wouldn't. Pity to waste so much beauty. Braydon snorted. On the turn, Brady boy?

And being worried about wasting exquisiteness when your plan is to kill the most beautiful being you've ever known? Yeah, right.

He closed his laptop and, grabbing a bottle of Scotch, stepped out onto the balcony of his apartment. It was bitterly cold here in December, but he didn't care; the alcohol took care of his body heat. He stayed outside until the cold started to get to him, then went to bed and dreamed of making love to India as the pretty boy watched. As Braydon took out his knife to kill her, India smiled over at Sun and held out her hand. Sun came closer as Braydon drove the knife into her, and as Sun got spattered with her blood, he smiled at Braydon as India screamed...

~

Manhattan, NYC

Lazlo got the news that India had landed and was transported to his loft without incident. The relief was palpable. By the time he greeted Massimo Verdi in his office, he was more relaxed than he'd been in weeks.

Verdi obviously picked up on his good mood. "How are things?"

Lazlo smiled. "My sister is fine, thank you."

Massimo laughed. "I'm that obvious, huh?"

"You and she made a connection in Venice, and she asked you to be in her music video." Lazlo studied him. Massimo Verdi was spectacularly handsome—and knew it—but Lazlo was surprised the man didn't come across as arrogant. In fact, he seemed nervous.

"I'm happy to say it's arranged for January, but you know that already, don't you?" Massimo chuckled. "Look, this may seem strange but lately, the press has been playing around with some falsehoods about me."

"I saw the photos."

There was a silence. "And so did India, right?"

"Yes." Lazlo sighed. "Look, I don't know what to tell you, Mr. Verdi."

"Massimo."

"Massimo." Lazlo inclined his head. "I'm not my sister's keeper; she makes her own decisions, so I'm not sure why you're here." He hesitated. "At the moment, we're dealing with a safety issue. A serious one."

Massimo frowned. "Serious? Like death threats?"

"Sounds like you've had experience."

He nodded. "Since my break-out film. They're usually from internet trolls or fans who feel slighted." He looked at Lazlo. "But your expression tells me it's more than that."

Lazlo nodded. "It's as serious as a heart attack. The FBI is on it and we know who it is. There's history, shall we say?"

He noticed Massimo's smile disappear, and the man leaned forward, obvious concern on his face. "Is there anything I can do to help?"

Lazlo looked away for a second. "Massimo... I do not feel comfortable telling you more without consulting India and at the moment, given the gossip about you and your ex..."

"Valentina manufactured those photographs. We are not together."

"Still." Lazlo smiled to soften the rebuke. "I have to protect my sister. I will tell her about your visit, and if she wants to get in touch, she will."

"She can call me anytime, or email, or whatever. " Massimo sighed. "I may seem to be a player, Lazlo, and I have been. But the night I met India, I found something I'd never experienced—that indefinable link to someone else. That doesn't happen much in my industry. I don't just mean physically; I sensed we really connected emotionally. I sound like *Cosmopolitan*."

Lazlo laughed along. "I understand, but India's private life is her own. I'll tell her you came to see me but it's up to her."

"That's all I can ask." Massimo handed him a card with his contact details, then stood, offering Lazlo his hand. "Thanks for not throwing me out like the creep I must look like."

Lazlo grinned, shaking his hand. "For what it's worth, you don't come across as a creep. You obviously care about my sister, and believe me, the more friends she has around her at the moment, the better. I hope she calls you. If not, I guess you'll see each other in January."

"Thanks, man."

"Thank you, Massimo, and it's good to meet you."

"You, too." Massimo turned to go, then looked back at Lazlo, his expression serious. "Lazlo... is it bad?"

Lazlo nodded slowly. "The worst. The very worst."

Massimo looked sick. "Anything you need, Lazlo, and I mean, *anything*, just ask. I'll help you protect her even if she doesn't want me around. I'll help in any way I can.

"I believe you would. Thanks, Massimo. Goodnight."

"Goodnight."

15

CHAPTER FIFTEEN - WAITING GAME

Stepping into his loft and calling out, Lazlo chuckled when he heard India's whoop of happiness. She jumped into his arms, and he hugged her tightly. Lazlo was a huge bear of a man, six-foot-six and broad, and India felt tiny in his arms. *Too* tiny. "You lost weight, boo."

"I wish. I ate quite well in Seoul... you know Sun's cooking. It's so good."

But she was skinnier now, and she knew it. Stress always wrecked her health-wise. "I'm ordering pizza."

"Already done. Extra everything. And I got two! I'm starving."

That was a good sign. India looked tired, but there was determination in her eyes. When Indy was down, it was hard to drag her out of the pit, but clearly she had made a decision not to be passive in her situation.

"Give me a sec to change and get comfortable, then we can chat."

"Take your time."

Lazlo ruffled her hair. She might be twenty-eight, but he will always think of her as a kid. She poked her tongue at him and he grinned. "Brat."

Lazlo felt lighter when he went to shower and change. Optimistic Indy was always a good thing. By the time he changed, the pizzas had arrived, and they both jumped on them like they hadn't eaten in a week. India gave him a rundown on what she planned while in New York.

"Don't worry," she said, "I've worked the security out with Nate and his team." She finally stopped eating, holding her belly. "Carbs! So, so good. Hey, when are Coco and Alex coming?"

"Day after tomorrow. Coco's slammed, and Alex has meetings all day tomorrow so they couldn't make it sooner. Jess will be here, though."

India grinned. "Tell me you and she are closer to realizing you're perfect for each other?"

"Ha, keep on dreaming, sis. Jess is way out of my league."

"*No one* is out of your league, Laz." India ran a hand through her hair. "You know I'm right."

"Jess is seeing a lawyer from Beach, Fuller and Hoskins."

India gave him a look. "Meh, merely a placeholder."

Lazlo laughed, shaking his head. "Talking of relationships, guess who came to see me today."

"Who."

Lazlo watched her to gauge her reaction. "Massimo Verdi."

Indy's cheeks flushed and a smile twitched at the corners of her mouth. "Really?"

"Yes, really. He seems to like you, and he wanted to clear up any misunderstandings regarding the photos of him and his ex."

India looked away from her brother. "Laz..."

"Seems like he's a good guy. He wasn't asking to pursue you, he just wanted to make his case. I liked him."

India nodded but said nothing. Lazlo patted her shoulder. "I told him I would pass along his wishes. He's looking forward to see you in January for the video."

India seemed unsure and Lazlo shook his head. "It's just a music video, and he's an actor in it. I don't think he's expecting more. You made the commitment, Indy, and he made time. Professionally, it would be unfair to scrap it. Everything is in place, money has been spent, and dates have been set."

A small shy grin appeared on her face. "Actually, I'm looking forward to it. If nothing else, he'll be a beautiful distraction."

"I thought you just had that with Sun."

Her smile faded. "It was wrong of me. Sun is in love with Tae, and they need to work things out."

"What a shame they can't go public."

"It really is. In this day and age..." She shook her head. "He's just a kid, and he's confused. I made things worse."

"He loves you."

"And I love him, but Tae is... Tae is his destiny."

They sat in silence for a moment, then Indy got up. "I'm

turning in, Laz. I'm so glad to be back. You think it's dangerous for me to be back, but I feel safe when I'm with you."

Lazlo returned her fist bump. "I'm glad you're here too, sis. Love you."

"Love you, bro. Goodnight."

"Night."

Los Angeles, *California*

Coco Conrad was almost done for the day, and she half-regretted the meeting she squeezed in at the last moment with a prospective client. But business was business, and Coco was a notorious workaholic.

The client was punctual, and as Coco's assistant, Mark, showed him in, Coco stood and shook his hand. He was in his late forties, handsome in a rugged way, with watchful dark eyes, swarthy olive skin, and a ready smile. "Ms. Conrad? Dimitri Panza." His accent placed him from somewhere in Europe, somewhere on the Mediterranean.

She nodded and offered him a seat. "Mr. Panza, thank you for being punctual. I don't have a lot of time, but please, let me know what I can do for you."

He smiled, straightening his pants. "I'm starting a production company, mainly focusing on high quality music videos, and I need representation on the West Coast. I'm currently in negotiation with some directors, but we need to liaise with a recording company. My preference is Quartet, and you have strong links to that firm."

Coco nodded. She tucked a long strand of her blonde hair behind her ear. "I do, but Mr. Panza, Quartet already has a roster of trusted video directors, some of whom they've worked with for years."

"I assumed that, but we can bring fresh vision and new ideas. Some of Quartet's artists are the biggest in the world: 9th & Pine, Ebony Verlaine... India Blue."

Coco giggled. "You really want 'in' right at the top, huh? I like your ambition."

"Aim for the stars and you might land in a tree. That's what my mamma always said." He smiled at her. Coco nodded. She liked this man; he was no bullshit, and she appreciated that in this business.

"I don't commit to a new client without testing the chemistry. I'll reach out to Quartet and ask if they would collaborate for one video. It won't be a major artist at first; they'll want to see what you can do. Don't expect Ebony or India at first. They have a big say in who directs them. It's the result of their success and hard work. But for what it's worth, you're more likely to get some help with Quartet. They're more open-minded and collaborative than many others."

Panza nodded and stood. "That's all I ask for now. Thank you, Ms. Conrad." He handed his card. "I'll be in LA only for today and then to Manhattan for the holidays."

Coco stood up, offering her hand and smiled. "Ditto. I can't deal with having summer at Christmas."

Panza laughed. "It's somehow wrong, isn't it?"

"Jimmy Stewart would have never approved."

"Never." He seemed to hesitate for a moment. "Ms. Conrad, thank you for seeing me. I'm grateful. Maybe, if you have some free time in New York… I could take you out to dinner?"

Coco was surprised but flattered. Her love life was a wreck or more like a deserted ship because of her work ethic. Yet here was an attractive man offering to take her out…

"I'd like that. Here," she took a card from her silver case and gave it to him. "I'm slammed for a few days but should be free the week before Christmas. Call me."

Panza took the card. "Thank you." He smiled. "It was really good to meet you, Ms. Conrad."

"Coco, and you, too."

COCO WENT HOME and began to get her things ready for New York. Her best friend and roommate, Alex, got home an hour later. They had supper as they discussed the trip.

Alex Rogers was one of the most sought-after record producers. A strikingly handsome Canadian, Coco and he bonded at their first meeting. As an openly gay man, he was between lovers at the time, and their friendship blossomed to where they were inseparable. They met India simultaneously when she signed with Quartet, Alex's employer. Although he struck out on his own, he remained close and India always insisted on having him produce her music.

Now, they're were travelling together to spend the holidays with their friends in New York. "I can't wait," Alex said, wiping his mouth, "I need this break."

"Same here." Coco got up and put the empty Chinese food boxes in the trash compactor. "Oh, someone asked me out today."

"Really? How cute was his seeing-eye dog?"

"Ha ha, funny." Alex was smirking as she passed him, she clipped his shoulder as he ducked. "Actually, the guy was okay. Good-looking. A bit older than me... *ancient* actually. He must be his in his forties."

"*Now* who's being funny?" Alex, who was forty-two, flipped her the bird, and she laughed.

"Anyway, a dinner invitation when we're in New York."

"Who is this guy? Do I need to give him the talk?" Alex was protective.

Coco rolled her eyes. "For one dinner? I think not. Who knows if he'll even call? Anyhoo, enough about that. I'm going to finish packing."

"How many suitcases are you taking this time?"

Coco was a known fashion maven, and she looked somewhat guilty.

"Less than Rachel Zoe would, so hush your mouth." She flounced into her bedroom, leaving Alex chortling.

She spent the remainder of the evening packing, and it wasn't until she showered and was slipping into bed that she checked her messages. Among the usual work ones, a note from Dimitri Panza.

Looking forward to seeing you again, Coco. All the best, Dimitri.

Coco felt a flush of pleasure. It was nice to be desired, even if it couldn't get serious. Still, she went to sleep with a smile.

BRAYDON LEFT the meeting with a smile on his face. Conrad bought his act hook, line, and sinker today. If he could infiltrate India's record company and gain the trust of those associated with her, the opportunities to get to her would be infinite.

Satisfied, but not smug, he carefully removed the false beard and washed his face, sloughing off some of the tinted moisturizer. His natural olive skin didn't need much sun to darken, but being in New York in the winter wasn't optimal. Maybe a couple of days in Los Angeles and the sunny California winter would help.

He snagged a beer from the fridge and flicked on the television, watching it, but not concentrating on it until he recognized someone.

Braydon turned up the volume and listened to the man speaking on the television. After a few moments, he began to laugh.

He laughed because the man on the television giving the impression of being a philanthropist was the same man who was paying Braydon to hunt down, stalk, and murder India Blue.

The man on the television was the man he knew only as Stanley, and he laughed because now, without a doubt, Stanley wasn't even close to his real name.

16

CHAPTER SIXTEEN - SCARED TO BE LONELY

India thought long and hard about calling Massimo. She made the decision not to see him until after the holidays, at their planned meeting in Venice, but she was seriously debating calling him, seeing if the chemistry they built up virtually in Helsinki was still there.

She was almost at the point of calling when she heard voices in the lobby. She stood as Gabe came into the room, followed by Lazlo. Gabe tried to smile at India. "Hey, boo."

"Hey." India felt awkward. Gabe looked clean, at least. His eyes were clear and bright—the only thing that was odd was the wariness. India's heart went out to her brother. "Are you good?"

"Are *we* good?" He came closer, and she studied him. There was something different about him. "Indy, I can't even begin to apologize for screwing up so badly. If anything happened to you in Helsinki…"

"It didn't though, Gabe. It's okay. We're good."

"We're good?"

She nodded, and he hugged her a little awkwardly, but India squeezed him tightly. "This isn't a time for us to be at loggerheads, Gabe. Really. Let's find a way back to each other."

"I swear," he whispered as he buried his face in her shoulder, "I will do everything in my power to protect you. Everything."

"I know." India felt tears spring into her eyes. They always had a fractious relationship, being closer in age then she and Lazlo, but they were adults now and rebuilding their kinship.

They hugged it out for a couple more moments before Lazlo cleared his throat. "I have some things, Indy, we should go through. Gabe?"

Gabe smiled. "Sure. Can I come back later?"

Indy squeezed his hand. "Please do."

"Thank you, boo. Look, I'm going to airport to pick up Coco and Alex later, so I'll see you then."

Gabe kissed her cheek, clasped Lazlo on the back, and said his goodbyes. Lazlo and Indy soon settled at the kitchen table to get through some work. After a while, and a cup of strong coffee, Lazlo sat back. "Your dad called. Again."

Indy rolled her eyes. "He doesn't get the message, does he?"

"Did you see him on The Today Show this morning?"

Indy shook her head. "Nah." Even the mention of her biological father's name made her chest tighten with unease.

"He wants you to help endorse him."

Indy gave a bark of laughter. "For what? 'Father of the Decade?'" She shook her head in disbelief as Lazlo chuckled.

"No. He's about to announce he's running for president."

Indy gaped at Lazlo. "You're fucking kidding me!"

"Nah." He echoed his sister and they both laughed in bemusement. "He thinks the endorsement of a liberal-friendly, biracial celebrity, especially his *daughter*, will sway the New York public. He's already running the 'this is what I learned as a deadbeat dad' angle."

"At least he's not pretending he raised me."

"No, he knows that can easily be disproven, and he doesn't want to come across as a liar. He's hoping a reunion will pull at the heartstrings." Lazlo calculated her expression. "Shall I tell him no?"

India sighed and rubbed her eyes. She may not have had a relationship with her father since *birth*, but he had tried to reach out over the past few years. India wasn't interested, not then, but maybe... No. Having someone so powerful in her life might help push the FBI to find Carter a lot quicker, but after Sun, she never wanted to use anyone again to assuage her ache.

And the truth was... her father wasn't someone she liked. He was a politician and a narcissist, someone she wouldn't pay attention to if he wasn't her blood.

But he turned her mother away when Priya was pregnant with India, destroyed her mother's life, and sent her down a path that eventually led to her death. She would never forgive him for that.

"Indy? You still here?"

She blinked and smiled. "Sorry, Laz. What's next?"

He gave her a steady look. "Should I tell him no?"

"Yes. Say thanks but no thanks." She sighed. "Tell him I wish him well, but I don't want to get involved."

Lazlo patted her hand. "I will."

"Do you think it's the right thing to do?"

"It's not my place to say, but you do what feels right. Trust your instinct."

She nodded. "I agree. So, no. Next?"

Lazlo grinned. "You asked me to find you things to do while you're here, and your wish is my command, blah... blah... blah. There's a charity auction at the Women's Center you'll want to be involved in, so I already said yes on your behalf. That's a couple days before Christmas. Then RAINN is asking if you'll do a couple of songs for their next concert. UNICEF, too."

"Yes and yes."

"Good. Then we're into January. First week, obviously, is the video shoot in Venice." Lazlo paused and chuckled. Indy tried to wipe the smile from her face. "You have terrible poker face. Massimo is forgiven?"

"I don't know that he's done anything to forgive," she said. "I'm trying not to be judgey."

"That's no fun."

They turned to see Jess walking in, a grin on her face. "Who are we judging and why are you trying to ruin my fun, gorgeous?" She kissed Indy's cheek.

India got up to hug her friend. "Girl, you get more gorgeous every time I see you."

"Oh, I know," grinned Jess, then stood back and assessed India. "And you get skinnier."

"I know," Indy rolled her eyes as Lazlo agreed, "but I'm working on that. I ate a whole pizza last night, and half of Laz's."

"And I never said she could have it," Lazlo complained. "She was like a wolverine. Just took it from my hand."

Jess snorted with laughter as Indy cuffed her brother's shoulder. Jess put down her bag and shrugged out of her coat. "So, kids, what's happening? Give me all the skinny. I'm out of the loop."

Massimo returned to Italy after meeting with Lazlo, but he was happy with the way the meeting went. He didn't want to crowd India, so he left New York.

Also, there was the matter of his pride. He wanted her, but he also didn't want to seem like a lovesick teenager. His ego may not be fragile, but he still maintained a certain level of machismo.

He flew to Rome, then drove down to his hometown of Apulia to spend the holiday season with his family. His parents, devout Catholics, always wanted their children around, and even a superstar like Massimo wasn't immune from his Mamma's wishes.

Also, he loved them dearly. His younger siblings, twins Gracia and Francesco, who were almost half his age, adored their elder sibling but never stopped ribbing him. It gave him a good sense of reality, which was rare. He usually brought his family to red carpet events—only his father, shy and introverted, would duck out, but Massimo never held it against him. His father was one of the kindest, most loving people he knew, and he was proud of his eldest son.

When Massimo was starting out, it had been his father who spoke to him for hours on the phone after auditions or when parts fell through. He encouraged his son to follow his dream, even if it meant waiting tables and living on pasta for weeks on end. "Anything that's worth having will not come easy. You're already ahead of the game, my boy. Your face will get you in the door. After that, it's all a matter of craft. Practice, practice. Learn. Grow. You will make it."

Massimo never forgot that. And when he fought, studied, and clawed his way to being Italy's number one actor, he made sure he paid his father and his mother back every euro they had given him and made sure they had the security they deserved.

He bought his parents the farmhouse they always dreamed of, and that was where he was heading to celebrate Christmas.

THE HOUSE WAS quiet when he arrived and he called out his greeting. His mother came hurrying in, giving a cry of delight when she saw him. She gathered her son in her arms and hugged him tightly, weeping some.

"Mamma, you knew I was coming." He dried her eyes with his handkerchief and then gave it to her. "The place is quiet. Where's Papa?"

He felt a pull at his heart when his mother's face fell. "What is it?"

"Come sit down, *piccolo*."

Massimo was the eldest child and over six feet tall, but she still called him her 'little one.' "What is it?"

Giovanna wiped her eyes. "Papa is... sick, my darling. Very sick. He's out in the garden as always, picking olives, but he's weak."

Shock filled Massimo's heart. "Sick? From what?"

His mother gave him a look and he knew. Cancer. His father had smoked his entire life, and now it had caught up with him. "Oh, Mamma... how long?"

"A few months. Darling, I'm sorry but Valentina knows. She called the other day to see how we are. It was an inopportune moment. I was upset and told her." She sighed. "She was very kind."

"Why didn't she tell me?"

"I told her not to."

Valentina could have easily used his father's illness to worm her way back into Massimo's life, but she hadn't. She kept her word to Giovanna and helped his mother with her kindness. Massimo felt new warmth for his ex in a way he hadn't for a long time. He got up, squeezed his mother's shoulder. "I'll go see Papa."

Giovanna grabbed his hand, an imploring look in her eyes. "Don't be shocked at his appearance, *piccolo*. It upsets him."

Massimo called on every acting skill not to howl with grief at his father's skeletal appearance. Both of his sons had inherited Angelo's good looks, but now his father's once handsome face was drawn, his skin grey, his hairline receding. Massimo greeted his father, trying to keep the emotion out of his voice.

"Hey, Papa, looking good."

Angelo snorted. "Those acting lessons paid off, my boy. Come here and hug your old man. Don't squeeze me too hard."

Massimo embraced his father. "Does it hurt?"

"Only when your mother thinks I'm a fragile weakling."

"Oh, Papa."

Angelo waved him away. "It comes to us all eventually, Massi." He looked his son up and down. "You look different."

"I do?"

"More relaxed. You got a new woman?"

Massimo grinned. Angelo didn't miss much. "Not as such but there's the promise of someone new."

Angelo rolled his eyes. "Son, don't waste time. If you like someone, let her know."

"It's complicated."

Angelo shook his head but said nothing more on the subject. "Help me out here."

Subsequently, Massimo spent the afternoon picking olives from the groves outside the house. When he and Angelo returned to the kitchen, he exchanged glances with his mother, who nodded gratefully.

Gracia and Francesco arrived in the early evening, rambunctious as always, and the family had dinner on the outside patio, lingering over Giovanni's delicious food and listening to the same stories Angelo had been telling them their whole life.

. . .

LATER, in the guest room Giovanni assigned him, Massimo got into bed and checked his phone. The signal was iffy, but he was surprised the connection was good. He toyed with calling Valentina to thank her but decided against it. He'll call her once he was back in Rome, so he wouldn't be vulnerable if she reverted to her manipulative ways.

On impulse, he sent a text to Lazlo Schuler asking for India's number. He was surprised when his phone rang a few minutes later.

"Hello?"

There was a hesitation on the other end and then, "Hello, Massimo."

Massimo sat up. "India?"

"Hi."

Massimo felt his heart jump. "Wow... um, I wasn't expecting... hi. *Hi.*"

He heard her chuckle. "Hello again."

"Thank you for calling me back..." He was flustered and laughed at himself. "I'm all Mr. Smooth this evening, aren't I?"

"Very smooth. And it's still afternoon here."

"Are you in New York?"

"I'm spending the holidays with Lazlo and some friends. And you?"

"In Apulia with my family."

"That's the heel of the boot, right? Southeastern Italy?"

Massimo was impressed. "That's right."

"Is it cold and snowy?"

"Hardly. It's mild and beautiful. Maybe you could visit one day?"

India laughed softly. "Maybe. How are you?"

"I'm good, thank you, *Bella*. Did your brother tell you about my visit?"

"He did." India hesitated again. "Look... the photographs of you and Valentina—"

"—they really meant nothing."

"I know that now. But even if they had, I had no right to be angry or jealous. There's something going on with me and innocent people should not be dragged into it."

Massimo bit his lip. "Lazlo said you're getting death threats. More than the standard crap in the entertainment industry."

India was silent for a while and Massimo wondered if she hung up. "Indy?" He said her name softly.

"I don't want to talk about it," she almost whispered. "Something, just one damn thing in my life should not to be about *that*."

How he wished he could hold her. "I can be that, Indy. For you. I'll be whatever you need. A friend. Someone who is just... here for you."

She was silent again and apparently conflicted.

"Look," he explained, "all I'm saying is... I'd like to prove you can trust me. I know my reputation. I'm not asking for anything else but your friendship even if that just means we talk now and again."

"I... want more, Massimo, with you. I've been thinking about you. But I don't know if..." She sighed. "But talking I *can* do. I'm texting you my number."

His phone bleeped, and he saved her contact details. "Don't save it under my name," she said quickly, and he gave it a temporary codeword until he could think of an appropriate name. "It goes without saying, please don't share it with anyone."

"It goes go without saying. Indy?"

"Yes?"

"I'm counting the days until I see you in January.

He heard her soft giggle. "Two weeks, Mass. Two weeks and we can see if that spark is still there."

"I'm confident it will be." He snickered at his cockiness and she joined.

"I hope so, too. Even if it isn't, we can be friends."

Massimo smiled to the phone. "You got it, *Bella*. I think we were destined to meet, regardless if we... you know."

"I agree. I don't often make that kind of connection... not with... anyway." She gave a nervous chuckle. "We have plenty of time to talk."

"Can I call you tomorrow?"

"I'd like that. Goodnight for now, Massimo."

"Goodnight, beautiful one."

HE SHUT his phone off and laid down on the bed, smiling. He really couldn't wait to see her. Two weeks. "Okay, Pa,"

Massimo said softly, "you got it. I'll stop wasting time. Let's see if I can make a life with this beautiful girl. Let's see if I have it in me."

17

CHAPTER SEVENTEEN - DUSK TILL DAWN

India dialed Sun's number, her heart beating hard. He's done it. He declared his love for Tae to the media in South Korea.

And Tae had denied him. After *everything*. Sun was humiliated. The call went to voicemail.

"Sweetie, Sunbeam, please, let me know you're okay. If you need me I can come over. Please—" her voice broke, and she fought back tears. "Tell me you're still breathing."

It was the day before Christmas. The heady week of having Coco and Alex around and her nightly chats with Massimo in Italy were shattered this morning by the news.

Despite not wanting to interfere, India called Tae. They argued with India yelling at Sun's lover. "You're a Goddamned liar, Tae. He gave up everything for you, and you do this? Shame on you!"

"Shame on *me*? You were *fucking* him! You knew he loved me, and you slept with him anyway. So, don't give me with your hypocritical bullshit, India! *Fuck you*." The phone went dead.

"Fuck!" India screamed so loud that Coco, Alex, and Lazlo came running to her room. She ranted until finally Alex put his arms around her. He looked at the others. "Guys, can we have a minute?"

After Coco and Lazlo stepped out, India looked at Alex guiltily. "Are you going to share your gay wisdom with me?"

Alex sneered. "You bet. Look, between you and me... what's going on with you and Sun?"

"Nothing."

"Indy."

"What?"

Alex sighed. " Come on. The way you two looked at each other?"

India rubbed her forehead. "All right. Yes, we had a thing. Recently and one time prior. We were both single at the time. *Both* times. Neither of us were cheating."

Alex said nothing, just held her gaze. After a moment, India nodded. "That's why I left Seoul. Sun wanted to be with Tae, to talk to him... What happened, Alex?" She dashed away a tear. "Sun is broken by this. He'll be harangued by the press because Tae wasn't brave enough to admit he loves Sun."

"You can't force people to come out." Alex said. "Believe me. I was lucky. I came out on my own terms. Remember, we don't know the circumstances between them. We don't know if Tae told Sun he wasn't ready, but Sun did it anyway. Is Tae the villain here? Neither of them are. Sun's in love—he wanted to shout it to the world!"

India listened to her friend with sadness in her heart. Alex was right. Tae was hurting, too, and she made it worse. Alex watched her processing this with his blue-green eyes. He wrapped his arms round her shoulders. "This will pass. They're one of the biggest K-pop groups in the world. No one will care in a few months. Look at all the people who came out over the years."

Indy leaned again him. "I just feel so protective."

"Which is a good thing. However," he kissed her temple, "stop fucking Sun. As much as you love each other, you're not his and he isn't yours."

"You're right." She smiled gratefully. "Alex, can I just say? The male gender is damn lucky to have you."

His beaming grin hitched up at the side of his mouth. "Hell, yes, they are." He kissed her forehead. "And stop hitting on me, you trollop."

India giggled. "Don't you know by now gay men are my thing?"

"Sorry, honey, but unless you can grow a cock..."

She laughed, batting at him. "Jerk."

They went out into the living room where Lazlo and Coco were talking, curious about what they discussed. India smiled. "Sorry. Mini-freak out. I'm just worried about Sun."

Her phone bleeped as she said it, and she checked the message. Relief swept over her. Sun's message was short but sweet.

I'm okay. Just taking some time. Don't worry. Sun.

"Oh, thank God," she said quietly and told the others. Coco and Lazlo shot each other a look.

Lazlo cleared his throat. "Okay... listen. It's Christmas. We're together. Let's enjoy ourselves, okay? We had enough stress this year."

India nodded. "Besides, we have to get Coco ready for her hot date tonight."

They all teased Coco who smirked. "You're all bastards. It's just a dinner, no biggie."

"You said this guy was trying to get into video production?" India asked.

Coco nodded. "Well, if he can come up with a good director with a vision, I'd be happy to give someone a shot."

"Really?"

"Sure. Everyone begins somewhere. I did. I'll be forever grateful to Bay Tambe for championing me. If it wasn't for her, I wouldn't be here today, so, of course. Pass it forward!"

Coco smiled. "I like that idea."

"As long as we can do a background check on them," Lazlo added. Both women rolled their eyes at him. "Hey, I'm the one who needs to have his feet on the ground. We're dealing with a very real situation."

India's smile faded and she sighed. "I'd like to make a wish. A wish that my life isn't built around what a psychopath wants to do to me. Fuck that shit." She grabbed her glass of milk and raised it. The others chuckled, raising their coffee mugs.

"Fuck that shit!" They chanted and laughed as they banged their cups together.

. . .

Massimo found his days were almost always scheduled around his calls with India. He waited until his family was already in bed, sometimes as late as midnight, and then he'd call her while he sat outside gazing at the stars. With so little light pollution, the romantic in him wanted to stare at the sky, knowing she was seeing the same moon he was.

He told her that tonight, on Christmas Eve, and she chuckled. "That's very sweet... I actually love that. Forgive me if I don't go outside to watch the stars, it's below freezing here when the sun goes down. I'll just sit at the window."

"Let's video chat, then we can see each other."

India laughed. "We sound like lovesick teenagers, you realize that?" But soon, he was able to see her, wrapped in a comforter sitting by the window. She waved to him, her sweet face breaking into a smile when the connection was made. "Hey, handsome."

"Hi, beautiful." He touched the screen, and she raised her finger to touch his image. Massimo couldn't help but smile. Here he was, a megastar, an international playboy, and his heart was melted by such a simple gesture. "I wish I could be with you right now."

India smiled. "Ditto. But I think for now, we're where we are supposed to be. Ten days, Massimo. That's all until we see each other again." She gave a shy giggle. "I'm... excited."

"Me, too, Indy. Listen, Lazlo sent over the synopsis... I love the concept. Dark," he added with a grin.

"I must warn you, my acting is nowhere close to being as good as you're used to. So, you'll carry me some."

"You'll be great."

They talked for a while about the video, and India seemed somewhat more relaxed. When he mentioned it, she nodded.

"Talking to you helps. You've become a very dear... friend to me." She hesitated before she said the word *friend* and then giggled afterwards. There was more than friendship here and they knew it.

Massimo traced a finger down the image of her cheek. "I'm honored by that."

India smiled at him. "I wish you could be next to me right now."

"I wish that, too, baby."

India looked slyly at him, then slowly dropped the comforter and shrugged out of her sweatshirt. She was naked underneath, and Massimo drew a sharp breath of arousal. "*Mio Dio*, India..."

Her cheeks flushed, and Massimo could see she was nervous, but she stood up and walked over to her bed. She set the laptop on the nightstand and stripped for him.

Massimo pulled his own shirt over his head and went to his own bed.

"I want to see all of you," India said in a soft voice as he set his laptop down and kicked out of his pants and underwear. He heard her gasp of desire and felt warm. He moved his hand down to his cock, already half-erect.

Naked, India was sensational, her soft curves and

gorgeous honey skin making him yearn for her. "You're making me hard, beautiful Indy... I want to be inside you."

"I *want* you inside me," she whispered. She picked up her laptop as her hand moved down her body, stroking her own belly, then dipping into her clit. "I'm imagining this is your hand," she murmured, "stroking me, caressing me. And my fingers are on your cock, tracing the length of it... show me, Massimo... let me see you..."

His hand was wrapped around the quivering length of his cock as it hardened. "Spread your legs for me baby..."

She did as he asked and the glistening, pink folds of her labia were uncovered as her fingers worked on her clit. "Wow, you're so beautiful..."

His cock was rock-hard now as he worked on it, imagining sinking it deep into her, feeling how soft and wet she was. "God, I want you so badly..."

"I feel you inside me," she gasped. "I feel your skin on mine, your mouth on my lips...God, Massimo... *Massimo...*"

"Can you feel me sliding inside you?" He wanted her to put two fingers inside herself and she seemed to understand, slipping her forefinger and middle finger into her vagina, mimicking his action.

He was sliding his hand up and down his cock now, wanting so badly for it to be her hand or her *yonni* enveloping him. Pleasure exploded as they gasped and whispered to one another.

"Show me your face," he panted as he neared completion, "I want to see you come..."

India was flushed with dewy sweat, her eyes huge with

desire. She smiled at him the moment before she came, arching, her head tilting back, her eyes closing, and as he listened to her long moan of pleasure, he came, too, groaning her name over and over...

They lay on their respective beds, breathless and laughing. "That was incredible," India said, panting. "I've never done that before."

"Well, you sure made a great debut," and he chuckled. "*Mio Dio*, India, have you any idea how much I want to be with you right now?"

"I do, I really do..." She laughed along with him. "Ten days, Massimo."

"Too long," but he grinned. "Anticipation."

India gave him a wicked smirk. "We have a video to shoot... first."

"About that? Any chance you could write a sex scene into it?"

India threw her head back laughing. "That would be something. I can't see MTV playing it if we fuck."

"Don't say 'fuck' like that, you're driving me crazy."

"Fuck," she purred again, her mouth close to the microphone, then giggled as he groaned.

"India Blue?"

"Max Green?" Her smile was mischievous.

"Oh, ha ha. It *is* weird that our surnames are colors; it never occurred to me."

"Actually, Blue is my middle name. I don't use my surname. Anyway, what were you going to say?"

"India Blue, in ten days' time... I'm going to fuck you into the middle of next year."

She moaned with desire, and they began again where they had left off, talking and touching way into the night. They made each other come again and again, and then, when dawn began to break, Massimo looked out of the window as the morning winter sun streamed in.

"Indy?"

"Yes, baby?"

And he touched the image of her face. "Merry Christmas, my darling."

India smiled at him, her eyes soft. "Merry Christmas, baby."

And at that moment, Massimo knew he was in love.

CHAPTER EIGHTEEN - HARDLY WAIT

Coco thanked Dimitri Panza for a wonderful dinner and asked the waiter to call a cab for her.

"Of course, ma'am."

Dimitri smiled at her. "I could take you home."

Coco smiled. The dinner had been... interesting. Dimitri was erudite and seemingly charming, but there was something she couldn't quite get a handle on, and it was bugging her. On the surface, he was good-looking and pleasant, but there was something off, and it wasn't until the end of the meal that she figured what it was.

He told her absolutely nothing about himself. *Nothing*. He talked about her, her work, her clients, what his ambitions were for his company, but nothing private. He deflected almost every personal question and, in the end, Coco gave up.

Besides, even as he was so amiable, there was no chemistry, and soon Coco wished she had turned down his invitation. So, when he offered to drive her home, she shook her head. "No, thank you."

He didn't press the matter but escorted her outside to her waiting cab. He kissed her hand. "Thank you, again, Coco. It's been a pleasure."

"It has. I may have some news about work in the New Year but leave it with me."

"Thank you. Have a good Christmas."

"You, too."

SHE TOOK THE CAB HOME. Lazlo was out and Alex was alone in the living room reading. Coco fondly swiped the back of his head, and he smiled at her. "How was the date?"

"A bust but at least a polite bust." She flopped on the couch beside him. "Where's Indy?"

"Talking to Massimo, I expect. She's been in her bedroom for hours."

They exchanged a sly smile. "Ah."

"I've heard some definite nonverbal… noises."

They both giggled. "I tried turning up the music but that seemed to spur her on."

Coco laughed. "Hey, if she's happy…"

"Exactly. So, the dude was just okay?"

"Meh," Coco shrugged. "Probably best to keep it professional. He seems committed to his work." She frowned. "Between us?"

"Always."

"I'm not comfortable handing him India's new music video. I love her for what she said, but we know nothing about this guy. Lazlo was right. We need to check everyone's background and, I don't know, there's just an off-vibe coming from him. Until we know more..."

"You didn't talk backgrounds over dinner?"

"No."

Alex made a face. "Strange, for a first date."

"Right? It's weird." Coco sat back. "But who cares? I doubt there will be a second date."

At that moment, they heard a muffled cry and they laughed. "Unlike India and Massimo— Clearly there will be a first, second, third..."

"Good. I'm glad." Alex sighed. "Personally speaking, coming off a bit of a drought... I'm jealous."

Coco laughed. "If you can't score a date, no one can, Rogers." Alex Rogers epitomized what it was to be man: tall, deep-voiced, well-toned, and with the face of a Roman god. When they first met, Coco had no idea he was gay, but Alex never hid his sexuality. He told her once, he'd never come out because he's never been in, and Coco loved that about him. Of all of them, everyone always turned to Alex when they needed an honest opinion. Even Lazlo, a strong man except for his latent guilt from not protecting India back when she was a teenager. Then he wasn't impartial nor reasonable. And when India needed him to see both sides of the argument, she went to Alex.

Even Coco, a feminist and a kick-ass publicist, asked for his advice, trusting him more than anyone else. Now, she crawled over to him on the couch and he looped an arm around her. Everyone feels safe around Alex. "Lex?"

"Yeah, babe?"

"Wanna run away with me?"

"Always," he chuckled and kissed her temple. "Would you settle for this old man?"

"You're not someone who is *settled*, Rogers. People should fight to the death for you." She snuggled to his chest, feeling his laugh rumble through his body. He stroked her hair.

"Sweet talker."

Coco grinned. "If only I had a cock."

"A big cock." Alex amended and she laughed.

"You know I would. The biggest cock. I'd be a tripod." They both laughed when a very flushed, slightly sheepish India appeared. She shot them an embarrassed glance before heading to the kitchen.

Coco and Alex leered at each other, got up, and followed India. They stood at her side and stared until she started laughing. "What? God, you two are so damn childish."

"Uh-huh." Coco said, poking her friend's side. "And you just had some radical phone sex. Deets."

India's face burned bright pink, but she couldn't stop the grin that spread across her face. "Video chat sex, actually. And it was glorious."

"We heard."

"Jealous."

"Yup." Coco started to laugh. "I'm assuming that was the Italian actor?"

India just picked up her glass of water. "Good night, guys."

"Night."

"Sweet dreams, Indy."

Both of them sighed. Then looked at each other and laughed. "We really need to get laid." Alex said and Coco agreed.

"Yes, we do. In the meantime, would you settle for a cuddle buddy? I hate waking up Christmas Day alone."

Alex looped his arm around her. "Come on, let's snuggle."

"Lex?"

"Yup?"

"Don't poke me with your morning wood."

Alex grinned. "You should be so lucky."

'Dimitri Panza' followed the cab back to where Coco Conrad got out. It was the building with Lazlo Schuler's penthouse loft. So, she was staying with India and Lazlo. The dinner was… okay. Although Coco was a beautiful woman, he had to watch everything he said to make sure he didn't seem more interested in India than the rest of her clients.

Braydon grinned. He thought he had pulled it off, but he was certain that Coco wouldn't clamor for a second date. No problem. He made sure she knew he was all business and seemed willing to hook him up with some work. Great. It gave him cover.

He told 'Stanley' what he planned when he saw him a few days back, and the man seemed to be enthusiastic. "Good. The more you can be trusted within her circle, the closer you'll get to India. Take your time, make her feel the worst kind of pain before she dies."

"What did she do to you? Did she fuck you and dump you? Doesn't seem like India."

Stanley's eyes grew so cold they made the normally unflappable Braydon shiver. "My relationship with India is none of your business, Carter. You want her dead as much as I, and that's what I'm paying you for."

"And it'll be my pleasure. Just curious."

Stanley said nothing more and left soon after, but Braydon wondered again why this bordering-on-elderly, on-the-surface respectable man would want a twenty-eight-year-old pop singer dead. Maybe he was as obsessed with India as Braydon was? He would hardly blame him.

Braydon took another look at the building, then drove home. He opened his laptop and looked through his alerts. India's were pretty dull, mostly old news, but he had also set an alert for the young Korean singer, and that one was very interesting.

He came out? He's gay? "So, you *weren't* fucking him, Indy?" But they cared about each other. How much would it torment her if something happened to the kid? He smirked. Was it worth it? If something happened to Pretty Boy, she might go underground and he'd lose his advantage. Not worth the trouble.

Unless the kid wasn't gay, maybe bisexual, and he fucked

India? Then it would be worth killing him. Braydon's hands were itching to slaughter right here, right now—it didn't matter who.

Still, South Korea was a long way to go to scratch an itch. Instead he changed into black sweats and a hoodie and went out into the city. It was bitterly cold, but he didn't care. His adrenaline was pumping, his mind a shrieking noise of bloodlust and desire. He'd search all night if he had to, but he got lucky.

He took the subway to a rundown area in Queens and went to a bar he knew. He saw her as soon as the bartender brought his drink. Dark hair curling down past her shoulders, a sweet face, beautiful golden skin. Not as breathtaking as India, but she would do. He already had an erection. She was sitting with a group of friends, chatting and laughing, but after one a.m., she went out on her own to smoke. Dumb mistake.

A hand over her mouth, the knife was out of his pocket in an instant. She never saw it coming. One... two... three... four... and he let her body drop, blood gushing from her sweater. He heard her gasp one last time, her eyes faded, and her last breath sighed out of her. India's face transposed over hers in his eyes. It would have to do, but India wouldn't die this quickly.

He jogged away from the body as people begin to spill out of the bar and took the subway back to Manhattan, stripping off his bloody clothes and throwing them in the washer. He showered, jerking off at the memory of the kill, shuddering and grunting as he came. The anticipation was killing him, but he had the memory of what he did to India last time. It was twelve years ago. That remembrance fed him for over a decade, and he knew he would get to relive it soon. So soon.

Braydon went to bed and dreamed of India screaming, begging and pleading him for her life...

19

CHAPTER NINETEEN - PILLOW TALK

Christmas Day, Manhattan, NYC

INDIA ROLLED over in bed and opened her eyes. Christmas Day. It was after ten a.m. Lazlo and her friends were already up. She stretched her body. She hadn't slept this well in years, apart from...

...apart from when she was with Sun. She wondered how he was. She hoped he was with his family at least. She grabbed her phone and sent him a message.

ANGEL BABY, You are loved and cherished. Tae loves you, he's just scared. You're very brave, my darling. Happy Christmas, I love you. I xx

. . .

It would be four p.m. in Korea so she wasn't surprised, but elated, when a message came back.

I'm okay. With my family. Being loved and cherished, don't worry. I love you, too. Tae and I will figure things out. Believe it or not, we're both adults. I miss you, Happy Christmas to you and Lazlo. Sun x

India smiled as she re-read it. "Angel," she whispered and flicked to a selfie she took when they were together and sent it to him. *Friends forever*, she wrote. In a second, he replied with a heart emoji.

India sighed. She was nervous about the next message she was sending, which was ridiculous given what happened last night. Should she call instead?

Before she talked herself out of it, she pressed 'call' on Massimo's number. The second she heard his voice, she knew she had made the right decision.

"*Principessa*," he purred, and arousal flooded her body in an instant, "Merry Christmas, *Bella*."

"Merry Christmas, Massi." It was strange how quickly they had fallen into using nicknames for each other. She loved that about their relationship; they were like real friends as well as potential lovers. "I'm being lazy. I'm still not out of bed."

He gave a low, throaty chuckle. "That's good because that's how I'm picturing you. But I'm there, too."

"Soon, baby."

She heard his sharp intake of breath. "*Si*. Soon."

They talked for a while longer then said goodbye. "I'll call you later, *Bella*, if that's okay."

"It's very okay," she said with a smile.

She showered, got dressed, and then went out to see her family. "About damn time," Coco said, her mouth full of food. India grinned and hugged them all.

"Gabe is on his way over," Lazlo told her, a question in his eyes, but she smiled back at him.

"Good. We should all be together today. Is Jess coming?"

"Later. She's visiting her new girlfriend's parents today."

India chuckled. "So, it's just us sad singles today?"

"Yeah," Alex tapped her shoulder. "You sure didn't sound single last night."

"Huh?" Lazlo looked confused, and India glared at a giggling Coco and Alex.

"Never mind. Let's get this party started..."

APULIA, *Italy*

MASSIMO PUT HIS PHONE DOWN, and his brother nudged him with the shoulder. "I know that smirk. Who is she?"

They were sitting in the kitchen of his parent's farmhouse, the table filled with the food his mother and sister had prepared. They returned from church this morning and now, duty done, they could relax and enjoy the day. The three children were persuading their mother to sit down and rest, but it was a losing game. Angelo chuckled at their efforts, knowing from experience that Giovanna wouldn't rest until everyone had eaten their fill.

She looked at her eldest son. "A new woman?"

Massimo hesitated. Giovanna and Valentina were incredibly close, and his mother had been devastated by the split. Still... that was in the past, and he couldn't keep India to himself if they had any kind of future.

"She's a singer. And American. India Blue. I met her in Venice a few months ago, and we've been talking."

"Do you like this girl?" Angelo was interested.

"I do. Very much." Massimo shot his mother a look. Giovanna had a terrible poker face, he decided. She wasn't happy. "Mamma... I know you love Val, and she'll always be my family, but we're not getting back together." He decided not to mention Val's recent behavior—why make this more difficult?

"You never know." His mother waved her fork at him, but then relented. "Tell us more about this other girl."

So he told them about India's career, her sweet nature, their mutual friends, and by the end, he noticed a little warming to the idea from his mother. *Very* little.

They lounged around for hours, enjoying the day together. Massimo learned from his younger siblings they were thinking of going into video production together.

"Maybe your girlfriend could hook us up? We have a ton of great ideas."

Massimo leered. "It might be too early to ask for favors, but if you enroll in film school, I'll pay the expenses. Afterwards, you can intern at a film company—we'll get you in with someone—then, when you're ready I'll finance your company. But you have to work hard first."

Gracia and Francesco gaped at their elder brother. Massimo had always been generous—he bought their house in Rome, after all—but this was beyond what they ever expected. "You would do that?"

"Of course I would!" he chuckled, noticing tears in his mother's eyes. "You may be the biggest pains in the butt, however, you've never asked for a thing from me. I know you can do this because you proved it. This is an investment for me, too. An investment in your future."

"*Wow*..." His siblings were astounded, and his mother started sobbing. But Massimo noticed that his father had gone very still and quiet. Later, when Angelo was out on the porch, he approached him.

"What is it, Pa?"

Angelo gave him a wry smile. "It's dim-witted.... It's a great thing you're doing for your brother and sister. I just... wish I could have done it."

Massimo put his arm around his father's shoulders, trying not to wince when he felt the bones beneath his shirt. "Papa, you and Mamma gave us everything. That's all that matters. Sure, money can buy opportunities, but I wouldn't have that money if it weren't for your support, even when we ate dry pasta. Gracia and Frannie wouldn't have the mad dog spirit, work ethic, that joy of life without you. They're great kids, Pa, and that's because of you and Mamma."

Angelo looked away from his son's gaze, his eyes red. "Thank you, Massi. That means everything to me." Suddenly he grasped Massimo's hand. "Promise me you'll take care of them after I've gone. I know you will, but it would ease my heart to hear it."

"I will always take care of Mamma and the twins, Pa. Always. And don't talk like you're going anywhere. We Verdis are immortal."

Angelo chuckled. "I'm not afraid of dying. Just of leaving you all behind."

Massimo leaned his head against his father's. "Papa, we'll always be together, whether in body or spirit."

They stood in silence for a while then Angelo nodded. "Let's go inside. Enjoy the rest of the evening."

Massimo was last to retire to bed, then he snagged his phone. He saw a message from Val.

Merry Christmas, gorgeous. Please give my love to your family. I have an exciting new project I'd like your input on. Don't worry; it has nothing to do with 'us.' I got the message...finally. I'm sorry, I wish things could have been different, I'll always regret letting you go, but it was the right thing. All my love, forever. Val.

. . .

Massimo re-read the message. Was this another of Val's games? Being that it's Christmas, he could give her the benefit of the doubt.

Merry Christmas to you and yours, Val. We'll talk in the New Year. Mass.

Short and sweet...*sort of*. If he were any gushier, Val would use it against him. *Could* use it. *Benefit of the doubt, remember?*

Then he forgot about Val as his phone screen lit up with an incoming call. His heart—and his cock—immediately responded.

"*Bella* India..."

"*Bella* Massimo," she giggled, and he laughed.

"Are you drunk?"

"A little," India said, then chuckled. "A lot, actually. A day of food, friends, and board games mixed with copi... copulative... whoops, not that... copio... *lots* of drink."

He laughed at her muddling her words. "Crazy *Bella*."

"Crazy about you... oh God... I am drunk."

"Ha, and I'm crazy about you, too."

"This whole thing is fanatical... We've spent less than a few hours in each other's company several weeks ago, heck, months ago now. So why do I feel so close to you?"

Massimo grinned. India, his lovely India was a love drunk. He should have expected it. "Because of our chemistry, baby."

"Ah. *Science*." She hiccupped. "And then there are reasons, of course."

"Reasons?"

"Just reasons. I wish I was in your arms right now."

"I wish that, too. India?"

"Yes?"

"Are you alone?" He lowered his voice and heard her gasp of arousal.

"I am."

"I want to touch you."

He heard her moan. "You *are* touching me."

Massimo smirked, slipping his hand down to his cock and beginning to stroke. "Where is my hand, Principessa?"

"You're stroking my nipples, Massi... now my belly..."

"Yes, your belly... can you feel my tongue circling your belly button? My lips against your skin?"

"Oh, God, yes... Baby, your cock is so thick and heavy in my hand, can you feel my fingers caressing it?"

Massimo's breath caught in his throat. "I can," he said gruffly. "It feels so good, Indy, so good... my lips are moving downward, my tongue is on your clit."

India groaned louder. "Turn around, baby, I want to suck you, too."

Massimo closed his eyes and imagined her beautiful mouth closing around his cock. "*Mio Dio*, India..."

She moaned. "You taste so good, baby, so good..."

"My tongue is buried deep in your cunt now, beautiful girl, so deep inside your velvety warmth. I want to eat you forever, your honey is so sweet..."

She gasped as she climaxed, and a moment later, he groaned as he reached his peak. "India, you're making it very hard for me—um, so to speak—not to get on a plane right now..."

India, panting for breath, chortled. "Tell me what you'd do to me if you were here, right now."

"I'd pin you to the bed and fuck you until we were exhausted. I'd bury my cock inside you again and again, India Blue, until you begged for me to stop."

"I'd beg you to *never* stop," she said, her voice breaking, and then she laughed. "Massimo, how the hell are we going to get any work done?"

Massimo chuckled. "Anticipation, remember? I'd say the video will have more sexual tension than any other in music history. We might even get banned."

India laughed. "That would be a first for me. And my detractors. I think most of them think I'm Little Miss Purity."

Massimo was surprised. "Really?"

"I don't play the red-carpet thing. I never had a relationship in the public eye. I might have to call on my limited acting skills to hide how crazy I am about you."

Massimo smiled. "Don't hide it. I'm not going to."

They talked for hours until both were exhausted, then said goodbye. "Nine days," India whispered.

"I can't wait."

CHAPTER TWENTY - ALL THE STARS

New Year's Eve, Manhattan, NYC

Lazlo read the newspaper article three times over before he pushed it aside. Coincidence, that's all, he assured himself, but he couldn't stop looking at the photograph of the murdered girl. Her resemblance to India was unquestionable, plus the way she was killed...

...this victim's injuries are so similar to the ones Carter inflicted on India years ago. That wicked knife attack. He felt unwell.

"Hey, what's with the face?" India, barefoot and dressed in a beige turtleneck with a long brown skirt, her hair shoved untidily into a bun, sat down opposite him. She tugged the paper to her but Lazlo reached over and grabbed it.

"You don't need to see that."

India's smile had faded. "I saw it already." She met Lazlo's eyes and nodded. "Yeah, I know."

Lazlo sighed. "It may be a coincidence. It's not like stabbings are so rare."

Subconsciously India put her hand over her stomach and looked away. Lazlo's heart ached. "Oh, Indy..."

"Let's change the subject," she said in a hurry. "It's been such a wonderful week."

He smiled. "It has indeed."

"I wish Coco and Alex could have stayed for New Year's."

Lazlo laughed. Their friends unenthusiastically returned to Los Angeles to fulfill their commitments between Christmas and New Year's, and since Indy had interviews lined up, she and Lazlo couldn't go with them.

Lazlo looked at Indy. "Do you want me to find a party safe to go to?"

She shook her head. "Nah. I'd rather just stay in with you—if you're not going out, that is. I don't mind being alone if you are."

"I'm not."

"Laz... I feel like you work too hard. Actually, scratch that, I *know* you work too hard. You're a catch! Why aren't you dating?"

Lazlo shrugged. "I manage."

"With one-nighters?"

"Occasionally. I'm really not looking for love."

India got up and made them both some coffee. "As long as you're not denying yourself because of... God, Lazlo, can I be frank? This may sound narcissistic but I worry that you think your job is to protect me and you don't want any distractions."

"It *is* to protect you."

India brought the coffee over and sat down next to him. "No, Laz, it isn't. It truly isn't. What happened back then..."

"I told your mom he could be trusted," Lazlo said quickly, not looking at her. "I didn't see a problem with both of you getting a ride from him."

"Laz... you were a kid yourself. What the hell was Mom doing asking for advice from..." She sighed. "Mom... I loved her, but she got us into that state of affairs. She trusted people she shouldn't have. Even if you said no about Carter, she still would have gone with him."

Lazlo reached for her hand. "You're sweet to let me off the hook, but—"

"The world does not revolve around me. *Your* world does not. At least it shouldn't. If you curtail what you could do with your life because of what happened... he's won. That way Carter has power over *more* lives. Fuck him. *Fuck* him."

India was fuming, her usually warm dark eyes flashing with vehemence. She got out of her seat, pacing. "He won't get to do that anymore. Promise me, now, on New Year's Eve, that next year, you'll make a life outside all this bullshit. I'm going to. I'll be in Venice in five days, and I'm going to—sorry—*fuck* Massimo Verdi's brains out and have a good time with him and love every minute of it. I'll also go to Seoul and make sure Sun and Tae are in high spirits. I'm sick of this death watch. If Carter comes for me... fucking let him. I'm not some poor victim... If he comes near me, I'll fight him until one of us is dead. But that's my responsibility, not yours, Laz."

She stopped, took a breath, and laughed. Lazlo snorted. "Where did that come from?"

"Twelve years of being trapped." India sat down, looking sheepish. "I'm not running any more. I want roots, Laz, and you do, too. That's my goal now."

She took Lazlo's hand again. "And I want everything first-class for you. And Gabe. I want you to soar, Lazlo, and not just for me. I don't figure into this. Live. Please."

Lazlo chuckled. "If you insist, Indy."

"I do." She gave him a wicked grin. "I mean, there's Jess..."

"Ha. You wish. I doubt that will happen." Lazlo shook his head. "But who knows who I'll meet if I put myself out there?"

"Then go to a party tonight, Laz. You got a bunch of invites." She patted his hand. "Okay?"

"Fine." He got up. "You'll be all right on your own?"

"Yes. I have a fridge full of food, Netflix, and a phone call to Italy." She batted her eyelashes suggestively and Lazlo chuckled.

"Well, maybe I should go out then. You two will have some privacy... and my ears will have a rest. I think you made them bleed last night."

"Lazlo! Gross!" But she started to laugh, flushing red. "I'm not sorry, though. He makes me happy."

. . .

LATER, alone in the penthouse, she tidied up a little and then grabbed her phone. Before she called Massimo, there was someone else she wanted to talk to. She scrolled down her contacts list then pressed 'call.' She waited nervously, not knowing if he would pick up or not.

"India."

She let out a sigh of relief. "Hi, Tae."

A silence. "What do you want?" The question was brusque but there was no malice in his voice.

"I wanted to say I'm sorry. For yelling, for...complicating things. I'm not sorry for loving Sun—*and* you—but for using him the way I did—when I knew his heart belonged to you."

Another silence, and then "Okay."

"Have you seen him?"

Tae hesitated. "He's with me right now."

"Oh, thank God," she sighed, the relief palpable. "Is he okay? Are you both okay?"

"We're talking." She heard him moving around wherever they were. "Look," his voice lowered, "I'm not dumb, India. You love each other, and there's nothing to be sorry for. He made the decision to come out, not me. He didn't even discuss it with me and... I wasn't prepared."

A pang of sadness went through her. "I'm sorry, Tae."

Tae sighed. "The management called us both in. They were pretty supportive. They never asked us to deny fraternizing, but they were annoyed that Sun didn't discuss it with them. They're talking about suspending him for a while until it all dies down."

"Oh, no, Tae." India was dismayed.

"It's just talk right now; they know the group won't carry on without Sun."

"How is he?"

"Prepared to accept any reprimand they deliver. He even offered his resignation." Tae sounded amazed and bemused. "He told them he wasn't sorry."

"Because he loves you, Tae. He's *in* love with you." India said it gently. "In the end, that's all that matters."

"Thank you, Indy. Look, I'm sorry about before… I didn't mean what I said."

"But you were right. I've been selfish and careless. Please know, I love you both, and I want to be a good friend. If you need anything…"

"I know. I love you, too. We'll get through this."

She wanted to ask him whether he was ready to come out but knew it was inappropriate. They said goodbye and India went to her room. Standing at the window, she looked out at the night sky. It was just before midnight, and she flicked on the television to watch the ball drop. As she listened to the countdown, she gazed up at the moon and smiled. "Happy New Year, Sun and Tae. Happy New Year, Massimo."

She was determined it would be.

CHAPTER TWENTY-ONE - HURTS

Venice, Italy

INDIA FORCED herself to get ready for the shoot without getting overly excited. In less than an hour, she'd see Massimo face to face for the first time since that earlier dinner, and she could barely contain herself.

All she wanted to do was run into his arms and tear off his clothes, but it wouldn't be the most discreet thing to do with all the dozens of people on the set.

The location was one of the lavish palaces on Venice's beautiful piazzas; the setting was a masquerade ball for the first part of the video. Knowing she would be costumed in fancy clothes for the shoot, India chose a lavender tee and her favorite blue jeans. She knew she looked good in them, and as she showered, she carefully shaved her legs and underarms, quivering with excitement about what would happen later.

On route, she checked her phone and giggled when she saw a one-word message from Massimo.

Today.

Her stomach fluttered with excitement and nerves, and as the car pulled up to the set and her bodyguards stepped out, she spotted a car pull up behind them, and Massimo stepped out from it.

He saw her immediately and for a moment, time stopped as they gazed at each other. Massimo's smile matched the desire in his eyes, and India's tension melted away. In seconds, they were in each other's arms, not caring what anyone else around them thought.

Massimo stroked her face. "Hello, beautiful."

"Hello again, Massimo. At last."

"*At last.*"

Then they realized they were not alone and although desperate to kiss, Massimo took her hand and they walked into the palace together. Hair and makeup was first as they sat side-by-side, eyes never breaking contact as people fussed around them.

The director came by and talked through the scenes they were about to film. "We'll start with you, Massi, at the party, talking to some other women, surrounded by them. India will be searching through the masked crowds and will come across you just as you take your mask off. India looks at you —that's when your track comes in, Indy—and she begins to run away. We'll film Massi pushing through the crowd as he tries to catch up, and then he'll spill out onto the street filled with partygoers. The feeling is, we'll keep you apart as long as possible."

Massimo and India exchanged a knowing glance. *We're used to that.* India eyed his trim body. The temptation of being so close to him was both electrifying and frustrating. She wanted to rip those clothes from his body and fuck him right there, crew be damned.

When they were finally alone for a moment, Massimo reached over and drifted his hand up her thigh, stopping before his fingers reached her yonni. "A foretaste," he whispered as she shivered with desire.

"Tease," she leered. "I'll make you pay for that."

Massimo chortled. "I look forward to it."

India looked furtively around to make sure no one was watching and then quickly squeezed his cock through his pants. He groaned. "Devil woman."

It was India's turn to smirk. "This will be fun."

They were called to set, a vast ballroom full of extras dressed in evening gowns and tuxedos. Massimo looked spectacular in a blue velvet jacket and a dark, elaborately beaded mask, only his bright green eyes visible.

India was dressed in all white, a figure-fitting dress, which would make it easy to scurry away in during the second part of the video where Massimo pursues her through the dark streets of Venice, over bridges, and along the canals.

India and Massimo shared one lingering look before the shooting started. India hoped she would be able to hold her own acting alongside Massimo's talent—she had been nervous about that all week—but found it pretty easy to pretend to be hurt and jealous when Massimo was flirtatious with another woman. In this scenario, she could be jealous, could let her pain show, and she did. As she came across her beloved about to kiss another woman, it felt quite real, and she flinched with a sharp knot of agony passing through her, and as directed, she turned and fled just as Massimo noticed her and set off in pursuit.

India lost herself in the role to such an extent it shocked her when the director called cut. Massimo came up to her, grinning widely. "Wow," he said, obviously impressed, "Wow... You're a great actress, Indy!"

India flushed with pleasure and leaned into him, his body. "I'm not. It's you... You make it easy for me to be..." She swallowed and gave an embarrassed giggle. "For me to...feel... all those emotions. Want, need, jealousy..." She met his eyes. "Love."

They gazed at each other for a moment before they were called back to set once more, but something had shifted in their relationship, something palpable, and it was as if everyone nearby was affected by it. The set became charged with an erotic tension, and the director was delighted how India and Massimo played their parts.

As the day drew on, the video shoot progressed efficiently, and when it came to filming the bridge of the song, a moment where the two lead characters stood on a bridge and kissed each other, India was trembling so much that Massimo had to steady her.

"Action!" The director, Luke, called out, and Massimo gently pressed his lips to hers. God, it was heaven, the feel of his mouth on hers, his tongue gently caressing hers. The kiss went on until they were breathless, and Massimo pulled her closer to his body. She could feel his cock, hard, thick, and long against her belly. India looked deeply into Massimo's intense eyes and saw her own reflection.

When the crowd, directed by Luke, swelled around them and forced them apart, it wasn't hard to despair at being torn away from him. As the crowd dragged her away and surrounded her, India had to remind herself this was just an act.

Then came the murder scene. The story was that the crowd, so turned on by their own decadence and abandon, was baying for blood, and India was their sacrifice as Massimo tried desperately to reach her.

As the wardrobe people fussed around her, soaking her white dress with fake blood, India began to feel a little queasy. Although the narrative was typical of the tragic love story, she still felt a little anxious about murder being a part of it. She glanced at the props.

"I know this is a stupid question," she said quietly to one of the prop head guys, Alan. "Those knives are all fake, right?"

Alan, who knew what happened to her, patted her shoulder. "All of them, Indy, don't worry. We checked and double checked. Even if you accidently get caught by one of them, it'll retract into the hilt, no problem. You won't get a scratch."

She smiled gratefully at him. "Sorry for being a wuss."

"You're not." Alan smiled at her and then she was alone again.

"*Bella.*"

Massimo came into the room and winced at the fake blood on her "I should be used to the red corn syrup by now... but it just looks terrifying."

She chuckled. "It's grim, huh? But it suits the story. I'm more worried about you picking me up and carrying me afterward. You'll wreck your back."

Massimo laughed. "Nonsense." He came closer. "After all, what I'm going to do to you later on will be *much* more strenuous."

She groaned in anticipation, and then he was kissing her again, this time with a feral need that turned her on so much she could barely stand.

"Damn, I wish this filming was over..."

"Anticipation," he grinned and she laughed.

"There's anticipation and then there's plain torture."

STILL THINKING about Massimo and his cock buried inside her, India went out to film the death scene. The director wanted unsettling, jerky, quick shots of the vicious crowd and India to show complete bewilderment as she was 'murdered.'

India barely needed to act as she caught sight of the crowd-wielding knives. God. She swallowed hard. *This is make-believe. This is pretend.* But the flashbacks started. Blood, the screaming, Braydon Carter's face, bloodlust in his eyes as he stabbed her again and again...

The panic attack started but no one noticed that India was not acting. The extras slashed at her with the prop knives and India's eyes whirled in her head, all the breath leaving her body. *No, no, stop it, please, stop, stop...*

She couldn't breathe. Her eyes couldn't focus on anyone, and she didn't even see the extras fall back, their faces shocked as someone shouted at them to stop.

Massimo grabbed India as she began to pass out and hugged her tightly to him. "Indy?" He whispered it urgently to her. "It's all an act... Indy..."

But she was back there, back when she was a teenager, in the middle of nowhere in Tennessee... Braydon was killing her... she turned her head and saw her mother staring at her with dead eyes, not able to protect her... *Momma... Momma...*

"Give her some air!"

India closed her eyes and willed herself to calm down. She turned her head to bury it in Massimo's chest. He comforted to her while rocking her slightly.

"Is she okay?" Luke, the director, was concerned. India wanted to reassure him but she couldn't talk.

"Listen, she's not an actress. It can be overwhelming to film such a violent scene, even for an experienced actor." Massimo told everyone. "This isn't extraordinary."

He was covering for her, and India felt a warmth flood through her. "I'm okay," she said, opening her eyes. "Just got a little panicked. Sorry, everyone."

Massimo helped her sit up, and she grinned sheepishly at all of them but holding Massimo's hand tightly. "Sorry," she said again, "you must think I'm a drama queen." She attested to the extras. "You were really convincing."

That made everyone relax. Alan was watching her and he raised his eyebrows. *Are you okay?* his expression asked. She nodded, smiling at him appreciatively.

"Come on, let's give these two some space for a bit," Luke said. "We'll set up for the final scene tonight, if that's okay. Indy, are you good?"

"I'm good. Thanks."

Massimo swept her up into his arms and carried her to a quiet spot. He cupped her face with his hands. "That was more than a panic attack," he said. "You might not be ready to talk about it, but listen… I'm in this, Indy. You and I. When you're ready… I'm here."

He kissed her tenderly, and India knew she was in deep, too. This was more than sexual attraction. It exhilarated and terrified her, but she pushed aside her fears and kissed him back with just as much passion as he.

"Indy…" He drew her closer and his fingers tangled in her hair and their breath mingled as they kissed. "I fell for you the moment I saw you," he said when they finally broke apart, "and now, I cannot imagine my life without you."

"Nor I," she replied, her eyes serious, "to me you are special, very special, Massimo. I hate being apart from you."

He kissed her again until both their heads were whirling. He leaned his forehead on hers, and then they both laughed. "There's so much more I want to say," he said, "but not here. Not now."

"I know."

They heard Luke calling for them, and they walked back to join the others, hand-in-hand. There was an unspoken agreement between them now—they weren't going to hide anymore.

The filming went on without incident, Massimo carrying her 'dead' body to the center of the now-empty piazza, slowly sinking to his knees as he lamented over her passing.

Massimo was so convincing that Indy's closed eyes filled with tears and one slipped out, dripping down her cheek. Massimo's hand was on her face and then his lips kissed the tear.

"Cut! That was phenomenal! Thank you guys. Wow, loved that tear at the end, Indy, great job."

Indy opened her eyes and chuckled, gazing at Massimo. "Thank Massi," she said, "his performance made me cry."

Massimo hauled her to her feet. "You were amazing."

"Right back at you," she said, surprised she sounded so calm. Filming was done. They could be alone at last...

Massimo nodded as if reading her mind, and they went through the process of thanking everyone and saying goodnight.

"We'll finish off the interior scenes tomorrow," Luke said, "and I'm wondering if you would be up for filming some bed scenes? Nothing explicit, but the chemistry is so good between you two."

Indy nodded not trusting herself to open her mouth without giggling, and Massimo squeezed her hand. "Yes, that's cool," he said with amusement in his voice.

Finally. They got into the car and the driver set off for

Indy's hotel. India and Massimo, holding hands, just gazed at each other before Massimo leaned in and kissed her. "Guess what we're about to do?"

India smiled at him. "At last..." she breathed and pressed her lips to his. "*At last...*"

Braydon returned to his own hotel, exhilarated. How easy it was to infiltrate the film set. Masked and with a blade in his hand, he got so close her he could smell her sweet perfume. He saw her panic and the same terror in her eyes as she had twelve years ago: the same surprise and the same torment.

It was *stunning*.

And the temptation to just plunge the blade into her, to kill her for real in front of those people, in front of that bastard she was fucking...

Little Miss Purity wasn't so pure. First, the pretty boy in Seoul, now this Italian actor. When Braydon saw the admiration the guy had for India... he wanted to gut her in front of him.

She's mine... she's mine.

Braydon dragged his mind back to why he was there. It was a test of her pathetic security detail and they failed —spectacularly.

He tugged off his clothes and went to jerk off in the shower. He was doing that a lot lately but today, he'd been the closest to India in twelve years, her life literally in his hands. And she was so beautiful, even more so than before. Those large soft brown eyes, that creamy skin, that perfect mouth lathered in red corn syrup...

He came just as the image of her and Massimo Verdi kissing blasted into his mind and ruined it for him. Yes. She was a whore, clearly—fucking two men. He wondered if they knew about one another. How would one react seeing India's grief when the other was killed? Pity? Jealousy? Anger?

Maybe he should find out. Maybe he should...

CHAPTER TWENTY-TWO – 8 LETTERS

Venice, Italy

INDIA HELD Massimo's hand as they took the elevator up to her suite. Neither of them spoke, but the mood was so charged up that India could hardly breathe.

She opened the door and they stepped in. Massimo hung the *Do-Not-Disturb* sign on the doorknob and locked it before turning back to her and smiling. He kissed her softly.

India smiled, her lips curving up against his. She had changed into a tee and jeans, but her body was sticky from the fake blood and she chuckled.

"I need to shower."

"Want some company?"

She laughed. "Like I'd say no at this point."

Massimo laughed and she was glad he was someone who didn't things too seriously. She was not shy while undressing in front of him nor could she take her eyes off his sleek, impressive body. Even though she had seen him naked over the video call, it was nothing compared to seeing him in the flesh. His broad, firm shoulders, thickly muscled arms and flat stomach, and his cock—thick and long, already hard—standing proud against his belly.

Massimo smiled lazily, appreciating her analysis. She grabbed his hand and slid it between her legs. "You make me wet, so damn wet," she whispered as he began to stroke her.

"You're so fine looking," he confided and moaned as she took his cock in her hands. "Jesus, Indy…"

Somehow they made it into the shower, touching and caressing as the water poured over them. Massimo helped her wash off the sticky corn syrup blood and noticed the jagged scars on her belly. He looked at her questioningly. She shook her head. *Not now. Don't make me explain them right now.*

Massimo lifted her from the shower and carried her, still dripping wet, to the king-size bed. He laid her down and covered her body with his. They both sighed with relief from all the tension, from waiting all those months and then they giggled. Massimo grinned. "*Finally,*" was all he said and she nodded.

India helped him roll a condom over his straining cock, and he hitched her legs around his waist as he pushed into her. India whimpered at the feel of him filling her entirely, tightening her thighs around him as he began to thrust. His lips were on her neck, his hands on either side of her as he buried his cock deep inside her with every slam of his hips. "*Mio Dio*... India... India..."

She pulled his face down to hers, her tongue eager to explore his mouth as they kissed, and Massimo hitched her legs up on his shoulders and spread her thighs wider as his pace quickened.

As they made love, India felt her body catch fire—every touch of his igniting new flames. She couldn't get enough of him, her hands roaming over his muscled back, digging her fingernails deep into his buttocks, urging him deeper, harder, wanting to be wholly taken by him.

She climaxed, losing control of her body to the pleasure he gave her, arching her back, pressing her belly against his as she cried out his name over and over, and feeling him tense and climax, his cock pumping deep inside her.

They collapsed on the bed, gasping for air, not wanting to disconnect yet. Massimo kissed her tenderly. "There are no words," he said, panting, then chuckled, "just these five: I love you, India Blue."

"*Ti amo,* Massimo," she grinned back at him, making him laugh.

"Touché, my darling... how the hell could we wait so long?"

India shook her head. "I don't know, Massi, but we'll make up for lost time, right?"

"Hell yes."

They were giggling and smooching for a while before Massimo reluctantly withdrew and excused himself to remove the used condom. India stretched. Her muscles ached pleasantly, her petunia still throbbing and sensitive from the pounding of his cock. She put her hand down and lightly touched her clit, starting when she felt another jolt of pleasure pass through her. She giggled when she saw Massimo watching her, leaning against the bathroom door. His sleepy eyes were filled with desire and awe. "Don't stop on my account," he insisted, slowly walking over to the bed, "I like to watch you touch yourself."

He lay down beside her and ran his hand down her body, splaying his fingers over her belly. He traced one of the silvery scars that bisected her navel. "Who did this to you?"

"A horrific man. A long time ago." Somehow, she didn't mind telling him now, and even speaking it aloud wasn't as painful as she supposed.

Massimo traced another scar. "Is he the reason you left Venice back then?"

India nodded. "They let him out of prison. On a technicality."

"And he's still on the loose? Looking for you?"

She nodded. "He is. He wants to finish the job."

Massimo embraced her. "He'll never get the chance." He snapped.

India snuggled into his arms. "I agree. Massi... when I'm with you, nothing can hurt me. Nothing."

"You better believe it."

She gazed at him. "That is why we can't go public. We need to be one step ahead of him. It's why I went to Helsinki... and Seoul for a while."

"Random choices."

She looked away, hoping he wouldn't see the guilt in her eyes. "Yes. But it keeps him guessing."

"So who is this psychopath?"

India gave a snort of derision. "A redneck asshole that nevertheless can be charming." She bit her lip. "He charmed my mom for a time."

"What happened? I mean what happened for..." He touched her belly again. "For him to do this to you?"

India hesitated. Did she really want to burden him on their first time together? Massimo slid his thumb under her chin and tilted her head so she could meet his eyes. "Indy... this is it for me. You and I. Tell me. Tell me everything."

And so, she did.

CHAPTER TWENTY-THREE - FRESH BLOOD

T*welve years ago...*
Rural Tennessee

"Mom? I don't think we should go with him."

Priya gave a sound of frustration and turned to her sixteen-year-old daughter. India was edgy, her long hair down, hiding her face as always when she was unhappy about something.

"Darling, it's just a ride to the city to play a set at the bar. You love music and singing."

"I'd rather stay home."

Priya shook her head. Lately, Indy had been reluctant to go out with her mother, preferring the company of her pseudo-brother, Lazlo. Whenever he was home, the two of them would hole up in Lazlo's room to read, and laugh, and play music. Indy's shyness disappeared when she was with her brothers, even Gabe, who was younger than Lazlo and more fractious.

Priya, however, knew if India were to have a future in music, the future Priya wanted for her talented daughter, she would have to work hard. India's voice was a phenomenon, her mom often told people, the maternal pride for once not exaggerated. Coupled with her daughter's ethereal beauty, Priya knew she still had to work hard to get noticed—pretty girls were ten-a-penny in the music industry and even an exquisiteness like India's would need to network and build a reputation.

Having raised Indy by herself, Priya was determined to help her daughter have the life she never had. An immigrant from the subcontinent, she had come to America, following the man who got her pregnant, and when he rejected her, Priya resolved to keep the baby.

She and India always were close. When she joined the commune and met Hanna, Lazlo's fiercely protective mother, they found a family.

Lately though, Priya felt a distance between them, and she knew it was because of Braydon Carter. Carter saw one of India's gigs a few months back, and as far as Priya was concerned, was a Godsend, offering them rides to gigs farther away.

But India loathed the man—and that was unusual. Indy was shy but also kind and loving and rarely took exception to people unless they were rude.

Carter rubbed India the wrong way. She kept her distance

from him and hated it whenever he looked in her direction—which was quite a lot. Priya didn't see anything untoward in his study of her daughter—India's startling beauty meant people often stared—but India told her many times how uncomfortable he made her.

Priya wondered if her virgin daughter was feeling an attraction to a man. Carter was a good-looking guy with dark eyes in a swarthy face; it would only be natural for India to have a crush on him.

INDIA GAZED at her mother's reflection unhappily. There was no telling Priya something once she made up her mind. She simply would not listen about Carter.

Carter, whose dark eyes followed India every moment she was near him. Carter who made her feel dirty as he watched her. Carter who she loathed with every inch of her being and did not trust in the least.

Carter who terrified her in the daytime and haunted her dreams at night.

India turned away to get dressed. She'd be damned if she were dressing up tonight; her jeans and favorite tee would do —a small rebellion against her mother. She kept her hair down, covering her face, and looked for Lazlo.

Her older brother smiled as she knocked on his open door. "Indy, come in, you know you don't have to knock."

She perched on the end of his bed. "Laz... what do you think of this Carter guy?"

Lazlo put his book down. "He seems okay. What's up?"

"I hate him," she admitted. "He gives me the creeps."

"He's harmless," Lazlo shrugged. "He's just a bit of a weirdo, is all." He looked at her carefully. "You okay?"

India nodded. "Yeah." She sighed, and wondered if she should say more. Everything in her was screaming not to go with Carter tonight. Was she being irrational? Why should tonight be different? It's going to be fine.

"Indy, if you really don't want to go..."

"No, it's fine. Ignore me, I'm being... just a little annoying..." She half-smiled. "Nah. I'm good."

"You sure? Because I can come with."

"Don't you have a term paper due tomorrow?"

"Yeah." Lazlo acknowledged in resignation, and India grinned, throwing a pillow at him.

"Then I guarantee you'll have a worse evening than me. Laters."

"Laters."

INDIA STARED out of the window in the back seat of Braydon's car. Her mother was up front, chatting to Carter about the upcoming gig, and it wasn't until Braydon slowed down at an unfamiliar house, that India noticed they arrived in a different part of the city from where the club was.

"Why are we stopping?"

Carter sneered. "Just picking up a friend. He's eager to watch you play."

India's stomach knotted, but Priya seemed unconcerned. "A new fan, Indy. How about that?"

India met Carter's glance in the rear view mirror and a wave of nausea overcame her. "Why didn't you mention that before?"

"Forgot."

The rear passenger door opened up and a man got into the backseat with her. Indy caught a stench of rust and salt and edged away. He scoffed. "Hey, pretty girl."

"Bud, this is India and her momma, Priya. Ladies, this is Bud, an old friend of mine."

Bud smiled and India felt sick. Something seemed very wrong here...

Before she could reach for the door handle, Carter began to drive again, and Bud leaned over and locked her car door. "Can't have you falling out, can we?"

India tried to sit as far away from him as she could. "Momma?"

Even Priya was quiet, sensing a change of tone. "You're going the opposite direction of the club," she commented, but Carter ignored her. She turned around to see her daughter with panic in her eyes. India reached for her mother's hand from the side of the seat and Priya took it, squeezing it to reassure her.

"Carter, it's quicker the other way," she said and this time Carter smiled.

"We're not going to the club, Priya. Not tonight."

"Where are we—" Priya didn't get the rest of the words out before Crater punched her viciously in the temple, knocking her against the window and rendering her unconscious. India screamed, grabbing at the door. In her panic, it took a moment to feel cold metal press against her belly. She turned to him and saw the pistol in Bud's hand. "Hush now, beautiful. I wouldn't want this to go off by mistake."

Sheer, blind terror filled her. Oh dear God... they were going to die, she knew it now. She looked at Carter's reflection in the mirror, her eyes pleading, and he hissed.

"Yes, sweetheart. I *am* going to kill you, but you probably know that already. Stop struggling or your pretty momma will suffer the worst of it. Bud, tie her hands."

Smirking, Bud wound a cord around India's wrists. "I want to have a taste of her before she dies, Carter."

"The girl is mine, Bud."

"What about the mother?"

"A loose end."

India panicked. "No! Please don't hurt her... I'll do anything, go anywhere, just please..."

Carter pulled out his own firearm and without warning, brought the car to a halt. "Bud, get the mother out. She's coming around. Have your fun with her."

"No!" India screamed as Bud got out and dragged a semi-conscious Priya out of the car. Carter climbed to the back seat, stroking India's face. "I've been waiting for this moment for a long time, India."

She struggled with him, but he was too strong, and Carter did what he had planned all along. Priya had pushed Bud off her and leapt up to the open car window. She was screaming for her daughter and India was crying, and eventually Carter had enough.

"For fuck's sake, shut up!" He shot Priya in the chest.

Slowly, she sank to the ground, her blood spilling, her gaze never leaving her daughter's. India was unhinged with grief as she watched her mother die.

Carter just cackled, pushing India back down and ripping her top open. Through her despair and terror, India didn't care, and when he began stabbing her, she gave up, closing her eyes, wanting the horror to end. The last thing she remembered was the searing pain of the knife ripping through her belly again and again, and Carter's almost orgasmic laughter…

A MONTH LATER, she woke up in a hospital in New York. Six months later, she began to speak again.

24

CHAPTER TWENTY-FOUR - NEVER LET ME GO

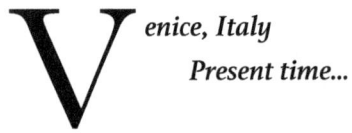

enice, Italy
Present time...

MASSIMO STARED AT her in dismay. "India. *Mio Dio. Mio Dio.*"

"That's it, that's the whole story. Except the judge who put him away was corrupt and had all his cases thrown out, and Carter got released. He's been stalking me ever since." She uttered a humorless laugh. "He somehow traced me to Helsinki."

Massimo paled. He slid from the bed, pacing up and down, softly cussing to himself. India watched. "If this is too much for you, Massi, I understand. It's a lot to deal with."

He walked up to her, cupped her face in his hands, his eyes fierce. She truly loved this man. "India Blue, never say that again. *Never* doubt me. I love you. We will fight this together and prevail, you hear me? Whatever it takes."

He kissed her, his arms tightly around her. She felt safe. "Are you sure?"

"Always," he reassured. They made love again and again, long into the night, and chatted for hours about their future.

DESPITE ONLY HAVING HAD a few hours of sleep, they went back to complete the video in the morning. On set, there was a different mood than yesterday. Because of the nature of the scenes they were filming, only a few people were around. To her surprise, she felt no embarrassment being butt naked in front of a crew. Massimo shielded her with his own body anyway, and it was strangely erotic to be filming a scene like this in front of others. She wore her panties and Massimo wore boxers, a white sheet wrapped around their hips as they acted out the love scene. She could feel his erection as the scene went on, and they shared a look only the two of them understood.

Massimo seemed to question her with his eyes, and she nodded, trying not to grin as Luke directed them, and while the lighting people worked out their methods, she and Massimo rolled a condom over his cock. India shimmied out of her underwear and hid it.

"Right, kids, make it look as real as possible." It took all their self-control not to laugh. Luke called action and Massimo thrust into her.

India didn't give a crap twenty strangers watched them.

She was making love with her man and only that mattered. When she orgasmed, she let the sensation flood through her body without holding back.

When Luke called cut, he looked as hot and bothered as everyone else on set. "Great, guys... wow, um...okay. Sure you don't want a new career, Indy? Like acting?"

"*Method* acting," Massimo whispered, making her giggle and blush. The crew gave them some privacy to get dressed, thankfully. India and Massimo couldn't seem to stop smirking at each other. "We just made a porno. That's basically what just happened." India was laughing, shaking her head, while she tugged her jeans on.

"Ah, I bet you they won't use much of that. That was just for us."

"Yeah, I'll ask for that tape," India giggled, then stopped him, putting a hand on his chest. "I never thought I'd be so adventurous. *Ever*. Thank you."

"For what?" Massimo looked surprised.

"For setting me free," she said and kissed him. "I am so in love with you, Massimo Verdi."

"From now on, it's you and me, okay? For always.

"For always."

BRAYDON STAYED in Venice just to watch their hotel and was surprised they didn't go out more. He suspected India kept them from public view—that was par for the course for India. But they were in Italy, and Massimo Verdi was the country's biggest star. No way they could go out together and not be followed by paparazzi. Which meant, once again, India would insist on going somewhere and he would have to follow them... again.

Braydon ran a hand through his hair. Maybe he should stay undercover for a while, see if he could lull them into a false sense of security so they could settle somewhere. He researched Massimo Verdi on the internet last night, found he had family in Southern Italy. That meant he would go back home to visit and would no doubt take India along if this was more than a fling. Jealousy churned in his gut. He wanted to lash out, to hurt her. He decided to save that guy in South Korea until later if he did it at all. Something to keep in the bank if he grew frustrated—a way to distress India some more.

That evening, he went out, intending to find someone to kill, to find another girl who looked like India, but that would only draw attention and alert her of his presence. He strode around the dark streets for a while, then gave up and walked into a bar to drown his sorrows for the night.

Fuck it. He was at an impasse. He couldn't figure out a plan until he knew what was going on with the Italian guy. Where would the relationship go? If they were in love, it would complicate matters, but would also be all the sweeter to know he'd be devastated by her death.

Braydon growled in frustration. 'Stanley' and his crowd complicated a simple plan. All he wanted was India's blood on his hands and for her to know that he has always been her destiny. To think that she was in love, that she was happy, made his rage boil over.

It made him even more frantic to kill her.

MASSIMO GENTLY DREW his fingers along the soft flesh of her inner thigh as India sleepily smiled at him. They were laying on the hotel bed, sheets and pillows strewn everywhere, the aftermath of their lovemaking. The video was in the editing room, the cast and crew disbanded, and all there was for Massimo and India was time. Time to be together, time to talk, to make love—for four long days.

Massimo was almost forty years old, but he had never felt like this about anyone, not even Val.

"You make me feel like a teenager again," he said to India and she chuckled.

"Same here. Can we just stay here forever?"

Massimo shifted so he could kiss her. "There's nothing I'd like more." He gently rolled her onto her back and covered her body with his. Her skin, soft and glowing in the sunlight streaming through the window, made his senses reel. He felt he could devour the scent of her clean skin, her doe-eyed loving gazes. "You are the most gorgeous woman on this Earth," he purred, "even if your face wasn't so exquisite, you would still be the loveliest creature ever. I love your heart."

Tears filled her eyes. "Thank you… that means a lot to me." She kissed him, and then made a face, pointing back at it. "This… It's all a matter of preference, but I'm not naive. Society deems this "beautiful." When I look in the mirror, all I see is the same doofus. I get sick of being judged solely by my face. You know what that's like, don't you?"

"Yes. People will see what they want and it's up to them, unless it negatively impacts you."

"Exactly." India laughed. "First world problems, though."

"Indeed." He studied her. "Was it because of your looks that he…"

"I don't know. It might have been my age." She shuddered, and then looked at him guiltily. "If I had the chance to kill him… I wouldn't hesitate. And I hate that he made me into someone who could slay another person."

"He made you watch your mother's murder. No one would blame you."

India nodded. "But then again I'm nowhere close to perfect. I've made mistakes, huge mistakes, and I've hurt people. I try to learn, but I can be selfish." She smirked wryly. "And jealous, too, apparently."

Massimo stroked her belly. "Nothing was going on in those photos of Val and I. She orchestrated it. She wants us to reunite and wasn't happy when I refused." He kissed her. "And she is jealous, too. I told her about liking someone else. That didn't go too well."

"You were together for a long time."

"And she'll always be my family. But I am in love with you, India."

India smiled. "And I love you, but I had no right to be resentful of you and Val. There's no problem with you and her being friends, I swear." She was quiet for a long time. Massimo drew her closer.

"What are you thinking, *Bella*? I'm still learning to read you."

India shook her head. "Nothing. Just thinking people are with who they *ought* to be with."

Massimo didn't quite understand, but she said nothing else. They made love again before falling asleep exhausted and sated, wrapped in each other's arms.

THE NEXT DAY, Massimo flew with India to New York, accepting her invitation to come and meet her family.

25

CHAPTER TWENTY-FIVE - HIM & I

New York, NY

INDIA WAS RELIEVED when Massimo and Lazlo greeted each other like they were already friends. The fact that Lazlo approved of him was even more of a blessing. "I told him everything," she announced to her brother when they were alone for a moment. "He's aware of the extra security, and he's okay with it."

Massimo was talking quietly to Lazlo when he thought she wasn't listening. She heard her lover say he would do anything to protect her. She knew Lazlo would be happier now that she found someone.

On the trip over, they had avoided the paparazzi at the airports, especially in Italy. They had managed to sneak in when no one expected, and they flew coach to throw people off. This was their time—just theirs—and the longer they could keep their love private, the better.

It was early evening, and they waited for Gabe and his new girlfriend to come over. Dinner was on, and India, Massimo, and Lazlo all pitched in as they prepared a fusion of Italian and Indian food. India taught Massimo how to make naan bread. "It's a whole new world of flavors!" he exclaimed.

India grinned. "I have so many nationalities in my DNA that fusion is just regular food to me. I try to make things that will complement each other. You like spicy, right?"

"Oh, yes." He winked and she giggled.

"Dudes." Lazlo made an exaggerated gagging sound, and India laughed.

"Laz, how come you're not bringing a date?"

"I like being the third wheel," he said dryly. "It's a comfort."

Massimo snorted at the other man's sarcasm, but then noticed India's attention was fixed to the newscast on the television.

A tall, elegant white-haired man stood at a podium, smiling with his two rows of sparkling white teeth. He wore a skillfully made suit and was using careful gestures to make his point. The tagline read *'Philip LeFevre, Senator."* Massimo was confused. Lazlo turned up the sound.

"So, it is with great humility but also great pleasure that I announce my candidacy for the Presidency of the United States!"

"Oh, fuck *no*." India said darkly, and Lazlo gave out a somber bark.

"He's delusional."

India rolled her eyes. "Now we know why he's been calling me. He wants an endorsement. Fucker."

"What am I missing?" Massimo asked, and India smiled, motioning to the TV.

"Philip LeFevre. He decided he's running for President, and he wants a wonderful little photo op with me to help his cause."

"With respect, why would a politician need *your* endorsement?"

India gave Massimo a strange smile. "To rewrite history. To give the impression that he's a changed man, that he can relate to family values."

"Family values?"

"Yeah," India sighed as she looked at the screen with surly eyes. "Because he doesn't want to be the man who abandoned his pregnant lover. Or the man who didn't claim his child when her mother was murdered or even visit the child when she was stabbed and in a coma. He wants my endorsement, Massi, because then he can paint a picture of reconciliation and forgiveness. He wants my support, darling, because he's my father."

MASSIMO WAS MULLING over India's newly revealed estranged father when the other brother Gabe arrived later. When he saw who Gabe's date was, his heart sank, and all other thoughts fled his mind.

Fernanda Rossi. His one-night-stand from a year ago. *Oh, damn it!* She stood behind Gabe as Lazlo introduced the men, her expression smug and vengeful. She looked at him steadily, then turned her gaze to India, examined her slowly, and then looked back at Massimo with a look that said *Really? Her? Instead of me?*

Shit.

He waited for the bomb to explode, but Fernanda was clearly going to make him suffer because all she said was, "Massi, how nice to see you again," and kissed his cheek, lingering for only a beat too long.

However, India didn't seem to notice, and Massimo was relieved. The last thing he needed was Fernanda starting a pissing contest. He also wanted to get a read on the younger brother. India told him that Gabe's loose tongue and drug dependency caused Carter to find her in Helsinki. Massimo tried not to let that color his perception of Gabe, but it was hard not to, especially coupled with the fact he was dating Fernanda. How the hell did they meet for Chrissakes?

"So, how did you two find one another?" India seemed to have read Massimo's mind as she smiled at Fernanda.

They were sitting at the large table in the kitchen for an informal dinner with everyone dressed casually, except Fernanda, of course; her spectacular body was poured into a slinky red dress. She was tasting some of the vegetable curry India prepared, her nose turning up as the heat of the spice hit the back of her throat. She delicately dabbed at her mouth with a napkin before answering.

"It was a fundraiser, a Christmas charity ball. *Vogue Italy* invited me to emcee the party. Gabe was one of the folks they put me in touch with." Fernanda possessively touched Gabe's neck. By the surprised look on Gabe's face, Massimo would bet all the money in the world this was the first spontaneous gesture of affection Fernanda had ever made. Massimo knew she wasn't one for PDA. For effect, Fernanda was showboating—trying to make him jealous.

Gabe shot a confused glance at his date, then shrugged. "We hit it off. We've been out a few times while Nanda is in the country." He smiled at Massimo. "You've worked together before, I hear?"

Massimo nodded, rattling off the name of a movie they finished a year ago. "It did okay, but not one of the best either of us have been involved with."

"Maybe you'll get to work together again?" Bless India, she really had no idea about Fernanda's spitefulness. Fernanda was staring at her now.

"Of course, we dated for a time afterward, didn't we, Massi? Wasn't meant to be."

There it was. Massimo kept his expression neutral as India glanced at him. Gabe's eyes grew colder. "Briefly," he nodded. "The Italian press was trying to bring us together and sometimes it's hard to resist the pressure and the promise of publicity. At the end of the day, we weren't compatible as a couple. Much better as friends, don't you agree, Fernanda?"

He held her gaze, daring her to argue, but she inclined

her head gracefully. India smiled at Massimo, patting his thigh under the table that she was fine with it. "Everyone is with someone who they are *supposed* to be with," she said again, and Massimo leaned over and kissed her cheek.

"Damn right," he said. He shot a look at her brother. Gabe's face was like stone and he didn't say anything. Ha. It wouldn't be Massimo and India fighting tonight—Fernanda's plan had backfired.

THE REST of the dinner passed without incident. Later, when Gabe and Fernanda had gone, Massimo braced himself for India's questions. He had to bring it up himself. "You're not curious about Fernanda and me?"

"You explained it all, and it's none of my business what you did before we met."

Massimo smiled. "It was just a one-night stand and the absolute worst."

India smirked. "That is a little satisfying, to be honest. I didn't care for her either way, but Gabe's a grown up."

"If it makes you feel better, Fernanda is very anti-drug and a teetotaler, so..."

India relaxed. "If she keeps him sober, I'll be her biggest cheerleader."

They were in the bedroom, India slowly discarding her clothes while Massimo lay on the bed watching her, enjoying the striptease. He knew every inch of her honey skin already, every mole and every dimple, the smooth curve of her belly, the rounded buttocks, and the full, ripe breasts.

He had memorized the taste of her and the clean scent of her skin.

"You have *dirty* in your eyes," she murmured as he blatantly lusted after her, and he laughed.

"I'm only human. Come here, *Bella*."

"Patience, boy."

She slowly shimmied out of her panties, letting them fall to the floor. And she stood in front of him like a goddess.

"*Mio Dio*, Indy..." His cock was in his hand, hardening quickly. India smiled mischievously.

"I'll come to you, Massimo Verdi, but you cannot touch. You can just...watch... and feel what I do to you."

He groaned. "You're such a tease..."

"You know it." She slowly walked to the bed and crawled onto it. "Lay back, Massi. Put your hands behind your head." She straddled him, waiting until his hands were away before taking his cock into her mouth. She sucked and teased him with her tongue, and Massimo groaned with pleasure.

"I want to touch you, *Bella*..."

She shook her head never letting it out of her mouth, slowly turning so that her pussy was in his face, provoking him even more. His cock was ready to explode as he watched her cunt begin glistening; it was all he could do to restrain himself.

He came hard, shooting thick creamy cum onto her tongue, and no longer able to restrain himself, he plunged his tongue deep into her sweet spot as his hands gripped her ass. His thumb worked her clit, determined to give her just as much pleasure, and she didn't stop him. He quickly brought her to a shuddering orgasm, and then he grabbing her roughly, turned her onto her back, and wrapped her legs around his waist.

His cock, already hard, slipped hotly inside her, and he fucked her, almost ruthlessly, pinning her hands to the bed, his eyes never leaving hers. India's eyes were full of fire, excitement, and arousal.

"Fuck me hard," she whispered, "make me scream, Massi… fuck me until it *hurts*…"

Her whisper flicked a switch in his head and he became an animal: carnal and feral in his desire, and they bit, clawed, and fought each other, enjoying the physical challenge as they screwed all night long. At one point, he had her against the wall-to-ceiling window looking out over the city, her wrists bound behind her back, his tie blindfolding her.

They had each other on the floor again and again, India straddling him and riding him as he caressed her breasts, then finally in the shower, he eased into her ass and they moved more slowly together.

Finally in the wee hours of the morning, they collapsed back on the bed, sated, panting for air. "Wow," was all India could say. "Just wow."

Massimo looped his arm around her neck. "You are quite the little animal, Miss Blue."

"For you, always." She kissed him and tucked her arm around his waist. He stroked her hair.

"So…"

"So?"

"You know my romantic, or rather, sexual history."

"Some of it," she said with a grin, "I'm sure there are hundreds more. I mean, look at you."

Massimo laughed. "Not hundreds, but yeah, there have been a few. What about you?"

"You wouldn't believe me if I told you."

"Try me."

India looked up, met his gaze and half-smiled but there was nervousness in her eyes. "Two."

Massimo's eyes bugged. "Two? Two and me?"

"*Including* you." Her face was flushed now, and he touched the beautiful pink of her cheek.

"How is that possible? I mean... have you seen *you*?" He threw her words back at her and she chuckled, but her face got redder. "Who's the other lucky guy?"

She shook her head. "It's... I'd rather not talk about him. It's complicated, and I... I made a mistake. I mean I... God, can we talk about something different?"

Massimo was curious but could see she wasn't comfortable with the subject. "Of course, baby."

They talked a little longer before falling asleep in a tangle of limbs.

IN THE MORNING, they showered together, then India chuckled as they dressed. "Better go apologize for the noise last night. Laz will be traumatized."

But when they went into the kitchen, Lazlo wasn't in a jokey mood. His face was set and grim, and India frowned. "What is it, bro?"

"Your father," Lazlo said nodding to the television news, where Philip LeFevre was being applauded by a roomful of paid lackeys. "He's just announced a huge charity concert where he and *his daughter* will be reunited—and *his daughter* will be the headline act."

"What the actual fuck?" India gaped at her brother, and Massimo made an angry noise. "He announced I'd headline a concert?"

Lazlo nodded, his jaw clenching. "He's forcing your hand. The charities honored will be Action on Violence against Women and Single Mothers."

India laughed but there was no mirth in it. "So he can spin his story of a repentant deadbeat dad and if I say anything else, I'm the bad guy?"

"Basically."

"*Fuck!*" India exploded and Massimo locked his arms around her to calm her down.

He looked at Lazlo. "Is there anything we can do?"

Lazlo sighed. "We can say no, say we're holding our own gig for the charity, that we don't endorse any political figures, and that Indy's relationship—or lack thereof—with her father isn't up for public debate."

"Which will immediately ignite interest in it and the press will go a-hunting."

"Exactly." Lazlo sighed. "Which means they'll stalk you, Indy, which could lead Carter right to you. I hate to say this, but..."

"The safest route is to quietly do the gig then go away after he's used me to further his political ambitions." India said this in a dead voice, and she shook off Massimo's hug and went to the window.

She felt them watching her as she put her face in her hands. She desperately didn't want anything to do with Philip LeFevre. He had abandoned her mother when she was pregnant and not once did he visit India in hospital after she had been abducted, raped, and almost stabbed to death.

Not once. The only sign that he even acknowledged what had happened was that he had paid, through an intermediary, her hospital fees. *All* of them. *Guess you didn't want that to come back and bite you in the ass, Pa, hey?* India had no doubt he would use that in his spinning of their story, and it just made her…tired. She was tired of fighting all the time.

She turned to Lazlo and nodded. "Call his people. Call his people and tell them I'll do the concert. I'll pose for press photos, but no interviews, and I will not give a statement endorsing him. I'll give the impression of reconciliation, but I don't want it in reality. I want to meet him once, before any of this starts, to say what I have to say to him. Tell them that and I'll do it."

Massimo and Lazlo looked unsure, glancing at each other. "Are you sure, Indy?"

She nodded. "I am. But this is the last time Philip LeFevre gets to dictate anything in my life. The last time."

CHAPTER TWENTY-SIX - FAKE LOVE

Massimo was due on the set on his new movie in Italy. He offered to stay with India as she met her father for the first time in years, but India shook her head. "No, darling, it's okay. This will not dictate our lives, and I'm sure your contract won't allow time off to support your girlfriend when she meets her shitty dad. That's probably not standard."

Massimo was amazed at her ability to make a joke out of something that was clearly traumatic for her. She hadn't been sleeping well since the announcement of the concert, and he toyed with the idea of breaking his contract, even knowing it would cost him a lot of money and reputation. She was worth all of it.

But India wouldn't hear of it. They had a long goodbye, both agreeing it wasn't safe to see him off at the airport. Massimo felt the terrible wrench of leaving her, glad his schedule after this film wasn't set, and he could arrange things around India's commitments.

MASSIMO WAS LOOKING FORWARD to his brother and sister meeting him at the airport in Rome, and when they greeted him at Arrivals, he couldn't wait to tell them about India, but he never had the chance.

"We do have some bad news. Papa's in a bad way. Real bad." Frannie said with a grimace,

Massimo's heart shattered as he saw the anguish in their eyes. "How long?"

"Mamma says it could be days."

"Oh, *Mio Dio*..." Massimo sat down heavily. "We should be there."

Massimo's publicist, Jake, was with them. "I've arranged some personal days with the film studio, Mass. They're fine with it because Patricia declined the role, and they're scrambling to fill it. So, we have a few days. You should go to Apulia today."

It turned out that instead of going to the movie set in Rome, Massimo set off for his parent's home in Southern Italy with his younger siblings. Although his brother and sister tried to keep the atmosphere as light as possible, by the time they were almost there, the mood was somber.

Gracia peered out of the window as they neared the estate. "Someone's here."

Massimo saw a Ferrari parked outside, and his heart sank. Valentina was here. As Francesco pulled up alongside it, she appeared in the doorway. "Darlings." She embraced them, lingering over Massimo.

Massimo sighed. This was the last thing he needed, but to her credit, Valentina immediately switched into caring mode. "He's awake now if you want to see him."

"Of course."

They followed her inside, and the twins went upstairs immediately. Massimo paused, holding Valentina's arm, halting her until they were alone. "Val... what are you doing here?"

"Your mother called me. She wanted another woman here, one who could look after you kids while..."

"We're not kids."

"The *twins* are still children," she amended, and he could see no malice in her reproachful look. "You and I know about life and death. They... will need everyone they can around them."

Nausea rose in his throat. "Papa?"

She shook her head. "He's in and out of consciousness. It's almost time, my love. I'm so sorry, Massi."

Massimo wanted to break down, to scream that it wasn't fair, that his papa had so much more to give. But he didn't dare, especially not in front of his ex, however good her intentions might be. "How's Mamma?"

"Being a rock, of course. She'll be glad to see you, Massi."

They went upstairs, and his siblings made room for Massimo at their father's bedside. His father was shriveled, his cheeks hollow and sunken, but he attempted a smile. "Hey, Papa."

Angelo held up his hand, and Massimo took it, feeling the papery skin. *Oh, damn it...*

Massimo's mother, who put a hand on her eldest son's shoulder, gently shooed everyone from the room. "We'll give you two some time to talk."

When he was alone with his father, he allowed himself to break down a little. "Papa."

"It's okay, son. I'm ready, you know... ready to meet my maker." Angelo's eyes were alert as always. "You look different. Relaxed. Is it this girl?"

"India." Massimo couldn't help a smile that spread across his face as he spoke her name. "Papa, I wish you..." He couldn't say the words 'I wish you could have met her.' He didn't want to acknowledge the truth that, even if India got on a plane this moment, she probably wouldn't make it in time. Massimo's father would never meet the love of his life.

Angelo squeezed his hand. "She's the one, eh?"

"She is. Papa, you would love her. She is everything that is perfect."

"Do you have a picture?"

Massimo showed him the lock screen of his phone, set to his favorite picture. Angelo whistled softly. "*Bellissimo.* She's exquisite."

"Inside and out, Papa."

"And she sings?"

Massimo nodded. "She does."

"I'd like to hear her someday." Angelo stretched. "I need to sleep again now, son. I'll feel better in a few hours."

Massimo got up and kissed his father's cold forehead.

"Get some rest, Pa. We'll talk more later." As he moved toward the door, his father called him back.

"Massimo? Don't let her get away. Your India. Hold her close. Never let her go."

Massimo smiled at his father. "I promise, Papa. I promise."

Seven hours later, at three a.m., Massimo's mother woke him to announce his father passed away.

Lazlo asked India once more if she wanted him to go with her when she met her father, but she shook her head. "There are things I want to say to him that you shouldn't hear, Laz. Stuff about... what happened. Things I never told you, but that fucker will know every detail of what Carter did to Mom and I. Since he forced me into a corner, I'm going to say all the things I ever wanted to say to him. *All* of them."

Lazlo hugged her. "Angry Indy is Scary Indy."

She shrugged. "I just want to see if any of it is true, if anything about that time affected him at all. If he truly cares. I suspect not, so I'll make him feel as uncomfortable as possible. I know it's petty..."

"It's not."

"You are a sweetheart, Lazzie. You are the only family I've ever known, so the fact this man shares my DNA is beside the point. I'll meet him, I'll do the concert, but after that, fuck him."

Lazlo hugged her. "Good luck, boo. Remember, I'm only a phone call away."

IN THE CAR to her father's Manhattan office, India tried to quell the nerves inside her. She checked her phone for messages but the one person she wanted to hear from was silent. It was odd that Massimo hadn't called, but then again, there's was six-hour time difference and filming can be intense as well. *Trust*, she told herself.

At her father's office, she was met by someone she recognized. Howard 'Howie' Black tried his hand at being an entertainment lawyer back in the day, and India gave an inward sigh. They had a history. Howie relentlessly pursued India for a few years, not taking her firm 'no' for an answer. Now he was working for her father? Jesus. LeFevre certainly knew how to surround himself with the worst people.

More reason to hate both of them. "Howie." Her tone was cool, and she dropped the proffered hand quickly. She hated even being in the same city as this man.

Howie smiled, snaky and almost victorious. "India, how charming to see you again. Fate has kept us apart for too long."

"If you say so." She didn't feel like encouraging further chatter as he escorted her into the elevator. She stood as far away from him as she could, answering his questions in monosyllables. His eyes were on her, roaming over her body, and she was glad she wore a bulky suede pancho and yoga pants, no makeup, and thick, black-rimmed spectacles. She refused to dress up for her Goddamn father.

As the elevator door opened, she stepped out to see Philip LeFevre waiting, a wide smile on his face. "Darling."

He held out his arms to hug her, but India sidestepped him, shoving her hand out for him to shake instead. The fake smile wavered, then became a rictus again. "Come in. It's wonderful to see you."

Asshole. India thought. When she stepped into his office, her heart sank. Apparently, this wasn't going to be estranged-father-and-daughter time. Around a large table sat various besuited men, all looking at her curiously. "India, this is..." LeFevre ran through each of them, but India didn't listen. So, he wants to bully her some more? She sat where he indicated, sighing when he and Howie flanked her. This was clearly going to be a coercion.

Well, fuck you, Philip. "I don't appreciate being railroaded into a concert I never agreed to, Mr. LeFevre."

"India, I'm your father. Please call me Dad."

"No, I don't think so, *LeFevre*."

He flushed angrily. "So, you're not interested in helping out women in this state? In this country?"

India glared. "Right... Because *you* care so much. Mr. LeFevre. I am very interested in helping woman. I'm just not inclined to help *you*. And please, don't paint this as anything but a pathetic grab for votes. You have never given a flying fuck about women."

"I think we should discuss the concert," Howie interjected

as LeFevre's face grew redder at India's compete dismissal, "if we could."

India and her father stared at each other, both furious, each hating the other. She wondered how she could ever be related to this pig. "I'll do the concert but if you think I'll campaign for you or give joint press calls, you're mistaken."

"We only ask for your participation in the concert. You'll be the headliner, of course."

India glared at Howie, who had the most annoying, simpering smile. "There are plenty more qualified artists to headline."

"But we chose you, India." Her father finally added. "This could be quite a prestigious event for your career."

"I thought this was about abused women and single mothers? That's who the focus should be on. You're only saying this because you want to tell the world it's *your* daughter headlining. Not going to happen."

Her father was silent for a moment, then looked at the others. "Could you give us some time alone, please? You too, Howie."

Everyone quietly shuffled out of the room, Howie, the last, closing the door behind him. Philip got up and paced around the room. "Alright. What do you want?"

"From you? Absolutely nothing except to leave me alone."

He shook his head. "Not going to happen. We need to reunite, India, and yes, alright, I admit, that will look good for my campaign."

"But you couldn't actually give a crap, could you?"

There was a smirk on his mouth. "Do you want me to care?"

"No. Because why now? Why not after Braydon Carter killed Mom in front of me? Why not when he raped me, stabbed me, and left me in a burning car to die?"

Philip sat down, and India was gratified to see guilt in his eyes. "I will regret that every day until I die, India. I paid your medical bills, yes, but I should have... Your brothers stopped me from seeing you. I tried."

"Not hard enough." He reached out a hand to take hers. India shook it off. "No. I don't want to reconcile with you, Philip. I do not want *anything* from you. Stop using me to help your campaign."

"I cannot do that. You are incredibly admired by the younger voters—being associated with you with help me immeasurably."

"That won't happen."

Philip smirked. "Oh, to the contrary, I think it will." He stood and walked to his desk, pulling out a folder. "Because there's someone else you want to protect from public knowledge, isn't there?"

He dropped the folder on the table in front of her. India stared at it, not wanting to know what was inside. "What are you playing at?"

"Open it." His voice was cold, and India shivered at the malice in it. Reluctantly she opened the folder and felt her stomach tie up in knots.

"I hear Carter was released and left some pretty explicit

letters detailing how he'll finish the job. What could that crazy fuck do if he found out about this?"

India hands clenched into fists as she stared at photographs of a family. Mother, father, pre-teen child.

"She's eleven now," Philip continued, "and apparently very bright. She's at the top of all her classes. Her mother, to all knowledge, is intelligent as well. Enough to realize that if the girl's true parentage was revealed…"

India's hand flew and struck her father hard across the face. He laughed, merely shrugging off her rage. "As Carter was driving that knife into your belly, I imagine he thought you wouldn't survive. That him raping you without protection could never result in a pregnancy. That even if you survived your wounds, a baby couldn't." Philip leaned into India who was rigid with shock. "But she did, didn't she, India? Your daughter… *his* daughter… the child you gave away but fully finance on the condition she never learn she was adopted. Could you imagine what she would go through if she learned her father is a murderer and that her famous mother didn't want her?"

India choked back a sob, and Philip chuckled. "I thought so. Consequently, India *Blue*, your self-righteous indignation… it's a little hypocritical, don't you think? Your fans would certainly think so."

"Fuck you! Fuck you all to hell, LeFevre! You're a monster, and the world is going to find out. Your campaign will be over before it's begun."

Abruptly, Philip grabbed her hair and yanked her up, throwing her across the room. He was on her before she could recover, grabbing the letter opener from his desk and holding it against her throat. India froze. Philip sneered. "You think I wouldn't do it?"

"I know you would," she whispered, finding her voice. She pressed closer against the tip of the blade. "Go on, do it. Then try to explain my blood on your hands... *again*. I blame you for Mom's murder because you didn't have the guts to face your responsibilities. But I *do*. That's why I send money for my daughter. That's why she has a caring home. She's not fucked up in the head like me because my father is an abusive, selfish asshole. So, go on, kill me, right here, right now. You think all those guys out there will defend you?"

Philip threw the letter opener across the room and pulled her to her feet. He walked away, brushing down his suit, calming himself. India didn't straighten her own clothes or hair. She wanted to walk out of here looking like he got violent with her. No word was ugly enough for what he is. She picked up her bag and headed for the door.

"You will do the concert. That is all I ask in exchange for my silence about your bastard child."

His voice was cold, and India stopped. She turned to face him. "I'll do the gig. For all the women and the kids who know what it is to be abandoned or abused by the very person who is meant to protect them. I'll do it for them. And my daughter. But I won't appear on a stage with you."

"Fine."

India opened the door but again her father called her back. "What was it like?"

"What was what like?"

She almost gasped at the coldness in his eyes. "Being stabbed. What did it feel like?"

India's jaw set. He was getting off on the thought of it. She felt sick. She tugged up her pancho to show him her scars. "It was torture. Mindless, unimaginable agony. And yet I'd take it all over again rather than watch my mother being murdered."

Philip nodded and turned away, and India left the room, slamming the door behind her. She stormed past the waiting lawyers and assistants, who were watching curiously. She punched the elevator call button, ignoring their stares, but as she stepped in, Howie jumped in behind her. India groaned and attempted to leave, but he shoved her back against the far wall as the doors closed.

"My turn," he sneered nastily. He forced his mouth onto hers as she struggled with him. India slammed her knee into his groin and pushed him away as he cried in pain. "Fucking little bitch!"

He came at her again as India swung her bag at him, hard, but he knocked it out of her hands and rammed his fist into her stomach. India dropped to her knees. Howie grabbed her hair, forcing her head back and kissed her again. "Little tiger. I know you whore singers all want it rough. Come on, give it up. I've always wanted you, India..."

This time, India was ready. As his lips smeared her cheek and neck, her hand found her bag, and she fumbled around in it. Her fingers closed over a pencil she kept in her notebook. She yanked it out and plunged the sharp point into his balls. She heard the fabric of his pants tear and felt the soft, vulnerable flesh give way as the pencil stabbed him.

Howie screamed just as the elevator doors opened, and India pushed past him, half-sobbing, and half-collapsing as she stumbled into the lobby. Some people rushed to help her as the elevator doors closed, and Howie's hunched form disappeared from view.

They offered to call the police, but India declined, hoping they wouldn't recognize her. "Was that Howie Black?" A woman asked as she helped India wipe her tears. India nodded and the woman sighed.

"He's a creep. I'm surprised it's taken him this long to show his true colors. What did you do to him?"

India told her and the woman smiled. "Good for you. If he tries to press charges, you call us as witnesses. He won't stand a chance."

They kept trying to persuade her to call the police, but India politely refused, thanking them for their compassion. They called her a cab and as soon as she was driven away, the adrenaline drained from her body. Fresh tears came, but she dashed them away impatiently. She decided to wait to see Lazlo in person to tell him, after she calmed down.

The penthouse was empty when she returned, and India took the opportunity to take a long soak in a hot tub to relieve some of her anguish. She took her phone to the bedroom afterward, and after drying her hair and putting on fresh clothes, she checked her messages.

There was one from Massimo, and she frowned. His voice

sounded strange, and she called him back. "Hey, baby, are you okay?"

"No... no, I'm not." She heard his voice crack. "Indy... my father died."

India was filled with dismay. "Oh no, Massi! I'm so, so sorry. When?"

"This morning. We've been... well... we've been dealing with it ever since."

"Oh, darling... I can get on a plane right now. I'll come."

"No... it's not safe."

"Screw safe," she said, "I love you and you need me. I'm coming."

CHAPTER TWENTY-SEVEN - YOU AND ME

Howie Black had difficulty explaining to the emergency room staff what exactly had happened to his bruised, swollen testicle, and he was absolutely certain they were laughing at him behind his back. Worse yet, his medical insurance was declined. He ordered them to try again, and again it was refused. When he called the campaign, he was informed that he was no longer on the payroll, and that his medical insurance coverage was no longer valid. Howie demanded to be put through to Philip immediately, and to his surprise, he was.

Philip, however, made short work of his dismissal. "You assaulted my daughter, Black. You tried to rape her. It's all on the security cameras in the elevators... you did know about them, right? Or are you really that stupid?"

He appeared to be more upset about the effect the scandal would have on him and on his campaign than about the insult to India. "Look, I'm sorry... we have history, your daughter and I. She led me on. I was just collecting."

"*India* led *you* on?" he responded, laughing. "I doubt that, Black. I highly doubt that. Do you think, just because my contact with her is limited, that I haven't kept an eye on her all these years? You wouldn't even figure into her imagination! You tried to rape her, and she got the best of you. Very careless."

Philip hung up without waiting for a reply, and Howie was left mouthing like a fish into the silence.

Bastard.

Well, Howie *wasn't* as stupid as India, but it was clear Philip thought so. He'd been siphoning off money from the campaign for a couple of years now, and though it pained him to use some of it to pay these medical bills, he would have to. Thankfully, it was simply a bruised testicle needing only some ice and rest. As he left the hospital, he decided to stake out India's place. He wanted payback and would be patient for the opportunity, but when he arrived, he saw her getting into a cab with a suitcase. He followed her to the airport, frowning. "Why the hurry, my dear?" he muttered to himself.

He pulled the wool hat he kept in his pocket down low over his ears as he followed her through the airport departures. Italy? Why the hell was India in such a rush to get to Italy of all places?

What... or *who* was there?

No matter. He edged close enough to learn of her other destination, an unfamiliar name to him: Bari Palese. He learned that the next flight wasn't for four hours. He had enough time to go home to get his passport. He'd follow her to this Bari Palese place and find out what the hell she was doing there.

India finally boarded the plane, bidding goodbye to Massimo. She could tell he was relieved she was on her way. *God, poor Massimo...*

It put the fight with her father and Howie into perspective. She's never known what it was like to have a father she loved, but having watched her mother die, she knew the agony. The trauma of dealing with her own mess of a family left her thoughts. She called Lazlo to tell him she was on her way to Italy, and although he expressed concern, he didn't try to stop her. "But at least take Nate."

"I already have. He's here with the bags."

"Good. How did it go with your father?"

She gave a dry, humorless laugh. "It went. That's all I can say. I'll do the concert but no press. He agreed."

She would fill Lazlo in on the rest when she got back, but for now Massimo and his family were her priority. Though it was already dark when the plane took off, India couldn't sleep. Her body ached with sorrow for her love, and she couldn't stop thinking about him as the plane glided over the Atlantic.

She finally fell asleep as the plane passed over Ireland and woke a couple of hours later as they came in for landing.

She never saw the man tailing them through Bari Palese, Apulia's main airport.

To her delight, Massimo was waiting for her and Nate. He wore dark glasses, but it was obviously him, so she was surprised at the lack of press around. Massimo drew her into his arms right away, his whole body trembling. He buried his face in her hair. "Thank you," he murmured in a broken voice that made her heart shatter. "Thank you for coming, my love."

Nate drove so India and Massimo could sit together in the back seat. Massimo gently pressed his lips to India's. "You don't know how much this helps," he exclaimed, leaning his forehead on hers. He looked shattered and exhausted.

"I love you so much," she whispered, stroking his face, "and I'm so sorry about your Dad, Massi. "

"Thank you." He closed his eyes, rubbing them. "Mamma's trying to be strong, but it's been really rough. The twins try to cheer us up, and I feel useless. I'm the older brother. I feel frozen. I don't know what to do. I don't know how to be in a world without him."

"Oh, Massi..." India wrapped her arms around him, feeling his body shake with silent sobs. She held him all the way back to the farmhouse in the countryside, murmuring her love to him, consoling him.

As they neared the farmhouse, Massi suddenly remembered something he'd forgotten to tell her. "Indy... God, I forgot." She was surprised to see guilt in his eyes as he spoke. "Valentina is here. My mother called her a few days ago, even before I got here. They've been close since Val and I... well, you don't just end your family when a romance ends..."

"Massi, it's okay." India interrupted him gently, caressing his face, soothing him. "It's okay. Of course she was and *is* close to your family. It's fine. Please don't worry about anything. Come on, let's go see your family."

MASSIMO HELD India's hand tightly as they entered the farmhouse. The first people they found were his siblings, who hugged India and welcomed her as if they had known her forever. He felt a deep relief when he saw India relax into their friendliness and seeing her with his brother and sister lightened his heart. He saw her warmth as she hugged each of them, asking them if she could do anything to make them feel better. His sister, Gracia, especially, seemed enamored and Massimo saw his sister slip her hand into India's and India smile back at her.

Valentina made her appearance a little while later, but none of them noticed her watching them until she spoke. "Hello."

They all looked up, and Massimo watched Val and India size each other up. Finally, Val smiled. "It's so good to finally meet you, India. Massimo is crazy about you."

India approached Massimo's ex-girlfriend. She hugged a surprised Val. "And you, Valentina. It's an honor, really. Massi has been telling me just how much you've helped the family over these difficult days."

Massimo coughed back a laugh. He hadn't, but he was

grateful for India's white lie, and the trust she had given him. In fact, Val had been a great help; Massimo had wondered if her charity had been anything but another ploy to get him back. It distressed him to think this way, so he attempted to play it off as a symptom of his grief, but...

There were just so many little possessive manipulative moments. Nothing that couldn't be explained away as merely caregiving to an outsider's eye, but Massimo knew Val better than that. He knew her machinations.

He scolded himself for thinking this way with his father ready to be buried in the morning and his mother leaning so heavily on Valentina. He wondered what Giovanna would make of India. Val was so much closer in age to his mother than India was, his new love sharing more in common with his younger sister. And his mother adored Val... he had to admit, the idea of how his mother would react to his new love was worrying him.

In the end, his mother retired to bed without coming down to meet the newcomers. After Massimo had shown Nate to his private room, he took India back to his own bedroom, closing and locking the door behind him.

He took her in his arms and kissed her, feeling his entire body relax at her touch. "You have no idea how good it is to hold you, *mia amore.*"

India stroked his cheek. "Do you want to sleep, my love?"

He shook his head and slowly they began to strip each other, each movement soft and slow, and their lips moving against each other as if for the first time. They lay naked on his bed, and Massimo moved down her body until he took her clit into his mouth, tasting her sweet honey.

India buried her face in his pillow as he made her come, then returned the favor, sucking his cock until it was iron-hard. Massimo drew her up, turning her onto her back and thrusting deep inside her. They made love quietly, intensely, their gaze never faltering as they rocked and moved with each other.

Massimo smothered her moan of ecstasy with his mouth as she came, shivering and gasping as he pumped creamy white cum deep inside her. It only occurred to them afterwards that they'd forgotten to use a condom, but neither cared at that moment. They'd deal with whatever happened later; for now, they needed to be skin-on-skin, as close as humanly possible.

They made love again, each time Massimo feeling some of his grief lift. When finally, sated and exhausted, India fell asleep in his arms, Massimo lay awake, gazing down at her, stroking her soft skin. His heart ached knowing she would never meet his beloved father, but he believed with all his heart that his father would look down upon them approvingly. This girl in his arms, this woman, *his* woman, his love... she would heal him, of that he had no doubt.

He stroked her face. There were dark violet shadows under her eyes, not surprising since she'd been traveling, but there was also a tension in her he wondered about. She told him next to nothing about the meeting with her father, but he had seen the strain in her eyes. She tried to hide it for his sake, he knew, but it was there. How very different each family was.

He prayed his mother would like India, but he knew it would be a difficult meeting. If Val wasn't here, it might be easier, but…

India mumbled in her sleep and turned over. Massimo saw the bruise on her shoulder. What the hell? He touched it, noticing it looked disturbingly like fingerprints. Had he been too rough when they were making love? But the bruises were already blue and black… He frowned.

Upon closer inspection, he noticed for the first time, the small red mark at her hairline, and another, smaller near her left eye. He pushed the sheet back and examined the rest of her. India grumbled at the cold breeze on her skin and opened her eyes. "What is it?"

"Where did these bruises come from?"

Now he saw another shadowy bruise on her stomach. "Who did this to you?"

He felt panic well up deep inside, and he sat up, pulling her to him. India wrapped her arms around him. "Ssh, darling, it's nothing. I'm fine. Ssh."

He squeezed his eyes shut, trying to calm himself. Everything seemed heightened just now, and the thought of anyone hurting India was making him crazy. But she kissed him. "It was nothing. I handled it."

"Was it him? Was it Carter?"

India shook her head. "No, darling." She took a deep breath in. "I went to see my father."

"And he did this to you?"

"Some of it. The worst is from a man named Howie Black who thought he could take what he wanted. He couldn't as it turned out."

Massimo stared at her in horror. "So, he *beat* you?"

"Some. Then I burst his ball with a pencil. End of fight."

Massimo stared at her for a long moment then he saw her mouth twitch up in a smile. He laughed then, shaking his head. "India Blue, you are a force of nature. But I wish people would stop trying to hurt my beautiful baby."

India grinned at him. "Ah, it was nothing, I've had worse. Seriously, Massi, I'm good. Please don't worry about me. We need to focus on you and your family."

He gently pressed his lips to hers. "I feel stronger with you, Indy. Promise me we'll always be together."

"I promise." She smiled up at him. "I love you, Massimo Verdi. Don't ever forget it."

Massimo leaned his cheek against her soft one, breathed in her clean scent. "You are the love of my life, India Blue." He leaned back to meet her gaze. "Remember that. You might need it in the next few days. Val may seem sweet and accepting of you but she is sly. Remember the photos she manufactured?"

India's mouth hitched up on one side. "Oh, don't worry. I didn't buy the act. A woman knows when someone is jealous, but I'm not going to be the one to start something. I don't play that game. I trust you, Massi."

"And I will never betray that trust."

CHAPTER TWENTY-EIGHT - THE LIMIT TO YOUR LOVE

As it turned out, it wasn't Valentina who made India feel unwelcome the next morning as she and Massimo went downstairs for breakfast. It was his mother. Giovanni nodded slightly at India as Massimo introduced her to his mother, but otherwise ignored her.

India saw the irritation on Massimo's face as his mother turned to Valentina, but India put her hand on his arm and shook her head. It didn't matter right now. Today was about burying Angelo, and India wouldn't cause the family more stress if she could help it.

Massimo held her hand tightly as the funeral procession made its way to the small church in the village. She saw, and felt in her own heart, the devastation in his eyes. Her heart thudded against her ribs in sympathy for them all. During the service, Massimo went to sit next to his mother. The twins took his place next to India, Gracia slipping her hand into Indy's.

The ceremony was beautiful, achingly melancholy. Afterward, for the wake, everyone went back to the farmhouse, and India helped Giovanna, Valentina, and Gracia serve the food to the guests who looked at her with curiosity. Massimo introduced her as his girlfriend, his love, and some of the younger ones even recognized her, but India kept to the background.

The sadness that pervaded the family deeply affected India. When she saw to it that everyone was occupied and had full drinks and food, she quietly slipped outside for some air.

It really was a beautiful place. Along the cliffs, wildflowers grew, and below, the sea crashed up against the rocks. The sea was a tranquil, deep blue-green. Peace, India thought. This place was one of peace.

"Taking a moment?" India turned to see Valentina smiling at her as she approached. She nodded. "I don't want to intrude."

"You're not." Valentina came to her side and hooked her arm through India's, looking out to sea. "I always loved this place."

It was on the tip of India's tongue to ask if she missed it, but she didn't want to ruin this détente or feed into whatever Valentina was up to. Not now and not today. She would go along with whatever fakery Valentina peddled today.

Valentina sighed. "I hope Massimo can get past this. He adored Angelo." She looked at India. "You have family?"

Ah. Valentina obviously knew about her family. "Two brothers."

"No parents?"

"My mother is dead and my biological father has never been in my life."

"I see."

Do you? India smiled. "It's wonderful to see a family like Massimo's come together, even if the circumstances are awful. I wish I could have known Angelo."

Valentina studied her carefully. "He would have liked you."

India said nothing. "Perhaps we should get back."

"Of course."

They strolled back towards the house, but Valentina stopped India before they could go in. "From a friend, some advice."

And... here we go. India steeled herself against what was to come. "What's that?"

"Massimo. He gets involved and commits quickly. I can't tell you how many times I've had to slow him down in our relationship. In the end, though... he gets bored. He doesn't realize it, but when things start to go wrong, he panics and tries to fix it by going too far. Like proposing. Just a warning. Take things slow."

India tried not to roll her eyes. "Duly noted," she said evenly and half-smiled at her lover's ex. "Should we go in?"

THAT NIGHT AFTER THE WAKE, and after all the guests had drifted away, Giovanna kissed all of her children, and Val, and then announced she was going to bed. When she reached the door, Massimo spoke out. "Mamma? You're forgetting India helped out today."

India nudged him, shaking her head at him, flushing bright red, but Massimo was unrepentant. His mother wasn't a cruel woman, but she *had* gone out of her way all day to ignore India's existence and participation, and Massimo couldn't let that slide.

Giovanna turned but didn't look directly at India. "Thank you for your help today. I appreciate it."

"It was no bother," India said carefully. "It's an honour to be here with your family."

Giovanna nodded stiffly, then said goodnight. Val, a telltale smirk on her face she just barely suppressed, soon followed. The twins went outside to share a joint.

Massimo drew India close, with his body and his eyes. "My mother will come around."

"It's been an emotional time, and she doesn't know me. Don't worry about it."

Massimo leaned his head against hers, breathing her in, feeling the soft touch of her lips on his cheek. "I love you, you know? All of today I was thinking about how much my dad would have loved you, Indy. He would have adored you."

India smiled her eyes warm. "You'll never believe this, but Valentina said the same thing."

"She did? When?"

India nodded. "I had a moment with her of 'what are you up to?' but then I decided to take the high road, so I took it at face value." She stroked his face. "How are you, my love? You look tired."

He nodded. "I am I think, with the worry over my dad, over you, over everything that has happened recently. I have to go back to Rome the day after tomorrow to start filming."

"I could come with you, at least while my schedule allows it. I have to be back by next Monday in New York." She sighed deeply. "And then there's this damn concert. But after that, I'll clear my schedule for as long as you need me."

Massimo combed his fingers through her long dark hair. "I don't want to stop you from working."

India sighed and leaned closer to him. "I can write songs anywhere, Massi. Do you want me to come with you?"

"I want to be with you every moment, Indy. We still have so much to learn about each other, and I don't want to miss a thing."

She slid her arms around his waist. "And we won't. We have time, baby. There's no rush. Let's just be with each other whenever we are able."

He tilted her chin up with his finger and kissed her. "Let's go to bed, beautiful. I want to be inside you."

JUST A FEW MINUTES LATER, he *was* inside her as they moved together quietly, their gazes locked, their bodies undulating as they made love. His grief dulled as he looked down at her, his lovely India, and his heart pain eased. He wanted to be with her for the rest of his life, he knew that beyond a shadow of a doubt. She was the one for him: his person, his love, his destiny. Who cared what anyone else thought? Massimo Verdi, movie star, was deeply in love with India Blue, and the way he felt right now, in this moment, in this endless delicious delightfully delirious moment, no one could ruin it.

Through the dark Italian night, a small rental car drove from the farmhouse back to the nearest town and then to nearest small hotel. Howie Black could hardly believe his luck. India was with Massimo Verdi? They obviously intended to keep it quiet and discreet. Ha, he laughed to himself, aloud to no one but himself—not a chance. He knew exactly the reasons they were keeping it to themselves.

Braydon Carter. The insane psychopath who had raped and stabbed India twelve years ago. The father of her daughter. The man who was hunting her down now, singularly desperate to kill her. The man who was being *paid* to kill her. What would he do if he found out she was fucking Massimo Verdi? Or that she was in Italy?

Howie grinned. Payback's a bitch, isn't it, India? He could only imagine what Carter would do to her—it was horrifying and arousing at the same time. Howie checked the time, and then made a call.

India and Massimo were about to be outed—to the world—and there was nothing they could do about it.

CHAPTER TWENTY-NINE - STRANGERS

Two days later, Massimo and India said their goodbyes to the family. Gracia and Francesco hugged India tightly, making her promise to email and phone them and visit them in Rome. She promised them all that and more—it wasn't hard. She adored the twins and felt almost maternal about them. She didn't say that to anyone, of course, not wanting to be any more annoying to Giovanna. Massimo's mother hadn't thawed any, but at least she was civil. As they said goodbye, India risked kissing Giovanna on the cheek. "If you need anything, please call. We can be here in hours."

Giovanna nodded stiffly, then seemed to realize she had been nothing but rude to India since her arrival. She patted India's arm awkwardly, even a bit apologetically. "You are a good girl."

That was closest she'd get to acceptance right now, India realized, but it still made her feel better. She smiled sweetly at the family as she stepped into the car, but then stopped in mid-motion when she saw Valentina pulling her own suitcase out of the farmhouse. India shot a look at Massimo who looked just as confused as she felt. "What's going on?"

Val was kissing Giovanna's cheek. "Darlings, it's just confirmed. I'm taking Patricia's part in the movie."

Massimo blinked. "*My* movie?"

"The very one. Darling, I'm sorry to have to leave you like this."

"Don't be silly. Go, go." Giovanna waved her away. "I'm a grown woman, and I have to go on with my life."

Valentina looked apologetically at India and Massimo. "I'm sorry to be the third wheel, but I managed to snag the same flight as you."

"Don't be silly," India said smoothly, "the more the merrier." *There you go, try and use that against me.* It was crystal clear what Valentina was up to and she resolutely refused to be the jealous girlfriend, especially not in front of Massimo's mother. "We'll meet you at the airport."

Once in the car, Massimo phoned Jake who confirmed that Valentina had been cast in his new movie. "That's the bad news. The good news is that it isn't a romantic role," Jake said, sighing. He knew Valentina's games as well. "Her part is limited. She'll only be on set for two weeks max."

"It's okay, Jake, thanks." Massimo ended the call looking at India. "Say the word and I'll break my contract."

"Don't be silly," India said, shaking her head. "It's two weeks and I trust you. I don't trust *her*, but I trust you," she added with a grin.

Massimo looped his arm around her. "I love you."

"And I love you. This isn't a problem, Massi."

AND IT WASN'T, although Valentina seemed a little disappointed that neither India or Massimo kicked up a fuss about her presence. In fact, they seemed to be enjoying flaunting their love, although always out of sight of the press, of course.

India flew back to New York the following Monday for a prior commitment, but she and Massimo called each other every day, sometimes many times in a day, and when the following Friday, she flew back to Rome, Massimo cancelled everything to be there for her, even going undercover at the airport to pick her up.

They enjoyed a dinner together, chatting and catching up, flirting, then went directly to his apartment and stripped each other naked before even reaching the bedroom. India giggled as he tumbled her to the carpet and began to kiss every inch of her skin, making her squeal as he nipped at her clit with his teeth before sucking it so hard she almost came straight away.

They fucked on the floor of every room, then the guest room, then his bedroom—which was now their bedroom, he insisted, and then on the roof under the stars.

Afterward, they lay side by side, catching their breath and looking up at the night sky. India remembering something she had thought about a while ago, chuckling softly to herself. Massimo grinned at her and inquired of it. "What?"

"You'll think I'm cheesy."

"Cheese away."

India laughed. "Well, I think it was at Christmas. I was just staring out at the moon, you know, having a hipster-slash-emo moment, and I was thinking about the people I loved, and what you said about how we all share the same moon."

Massimo snorted. "Oh, I really said that?"

India giggled, poking his side. "I told you it was cheese."

"*Le Grande Fromage.*"

"Your French sucks."

Massimo grinned. "It was in the region. So, tell me, India Blue, who were you thinking about?"

India looked at him and made a decision. "You. My brothers. My friends. And a boy called Sun."

"Sun?"

"Korean."

"Ah. So, I assume he was a lover?"

India studied his eyes and saw no jealousy in them. "He was. And the last time I slept with him was... *after* I met you."

Now there was curiosity. "Okay."

"We weren't together, you and I, and I thought we never would be. After Helsinki, I had to get away and I went to Seoul just to stay with him and get some space. But it turned into something else, something at the time that we both needed. So, I feel extra bad about giving you a hard time over the photos of you and Valentina." She rolled her eyes. "And now I feel worse by bringing it up like I'm trying to make an excuse. No. Here's the truth. I love Sun and he loves me. Sometimes we needed each other physically, but mostly... we are soulmates. We love each other, but we're not *in* love. He's in love with another man, Tae. And I'm in love with you."

She stopped then and waited for his reaction. Slowly, Massimo nodded, gathering his thoughts and emotions into one place. "I get it. I do. And I'm kind of jealous."

India grimaced but Massimo shook his head. "No, not that way. What I mean is I've never had that kind of relationship with a woman, except with you. We were friends first and that is something I never had. So, I guess I'm a little jealous that you had it with someone else first. But listen, I actually think it's wonderful."

"You do?" India couldn't keep the amazement out of her voice and Massimo laughed.

"I'm amazed myself, to be perfectly honest. I'm a provincial guy, stupid male pride and all that comes with it. But with you... I don't know, things are different. I'm learning to see the world differently and relationships differently. I'd like to meet him."

"You will *love* him." India said, feeling choked up with emotion. She had been worrying so much about telling Massimo about Sun, but she knew she had to. There was no way she was giving up either of them. "I have to warn you—he might well seduce you. He's the prettiest creature on Earth plus his heart is the biggest. Sun is easy to love." She chuckled. "He might even turn you—he's that beautiful."

Massimo grinned. "I'll be okay. I'm already in love with the most perfect being."

"Ha, far from that, but I'll take the compliment." She rolled on top of him and kissed him on the mouth with full confidence in her disclosure and in his response to it. "You know what else I'll take?"

"What?"

She grinned mischievously down at him. "Your cock. Fuck me senseless, *Signor* Verdi."

And laughing, he complied.

THE PHOTOGRAPHER SITTING on the rooftop across from Massimo Verdi's apartment was unsure that the shots he was taking of Verdi fucking the gorgeous girl would be exposed clearly enough, but it was worth a shot. He'd been following them for days now at the behest of Howard Black. He didn't particularly like Black—he found him obsequious and slimy, but he paid well, and it was no struggle following India Blue and seeing her naked. God, she was so fucking *sexy*, he had a permanent hard-on, but the thought of the money he was earning for these shots also helped.

Her cry of ecstasy carried supremely across the rooftops, and he grinned. Massimo Verdi was well-known for being an exceptional lover and clearly, India Blue was enjoying his gift.

He took a couple more shots but since the light really was getting bad with the moon disappearing behind clouds, he gave up and went for a tasty dinner and some wine to celebrate. He knew he'd gotten the shots he came for.

New York City

. . .

BRAYDON CARTER HAD BEEN WATCHING Lazlo Schuler's apartment for days now, and there had been no sign of India. She'd managed to evade his scrutiny and disappeared again and even his contacts with 'Stanley' had come up with nothing. He was frustrated with not knowing where she was.

He had grown tired of waiting. He'd accrued enough money now to make his escape once India was dead, and now he just wanted to finish the job. He wanted to kill her.

At his own apartment, he powered on the television and mindlessly flicked through the channels. At an entertainment channel, he stopped short, recognizing the man on screen. It was the Korean boy, the pretty one who India had fucked. He turned up the sound, loud as it would go, so he would not miss a single word.

"AND FOR THE *first time in K-pop, two members of the band Midnight Snow have announced that they are in a committed romantic relationship. Kim Sung-Jae and Cho Taehyung, both twenty-three years old, were outed when Kim Sung-Jae, also known as Sun, revealed his bisexuality and declared his love for Cho. Since that announcement, Cho has confirmed the relationship and Midnight Snow's other members and management have tweeted their unconditional support for the couple.*"

. . .

Braydon stared at the two beautiful men on screen. *How fucking sweet.* And yet an idea was forming in his mind.

What would draw India out? Surely, the death of a dear friend, a lover? Braydon smiled. He called his contact.

"Fine. We'll have someone meet you in Seoul, but I should warn you. That band has serious security."

"This is why I asked you for a long-range rifle."

"You can shoot?"

Braydon didn't bother to answer that one. "Just get it done."

There was a pause on the end of the line, and when his contact spoke again, his voice was ice cold, clearly warning him to not overstep. "Remember you work for us, Carter. Don't push it."

The contact turned to his boss as the line went dead. "He's going to Seoul. He thinks murdering India's ex-lover will draw her out."

'Stanley' shrugged. "It might."

"It'll be international news."

Again, his boss was unaffected "At this point, I just want her dead. I don't care how he does it." He lit a cigarette. "And everything is in place for afterward? Your men are ready to dispose of Carter as soon as India is dead?"

"They are." He studied his boss. "You really want her dead that badly?"

"I do. She's become a serious problem, one who doesn't

mind saying what she thinks to the public, to the press. Her death will provide the requisite outpouring of sympathy."

"And that all-important bump in the polls."

Philip LeFevre smiled. "Precisely. Who wouldn't give their vote to a grieving father? And the fact that Carter's letter will be released to the press, that he'll be shown to be the obsessive stalker that he is, all the better. We just have to make sure nothing ties us to him."

His assistant nodded and left him alone. He wouldn't want to be the boss's estranged daughter when all this went down. She wouldn't just be murdered… it would be a slaughter.

PHILIP LEFEVRE FINISHED SMOKING his cigarette and then lit up another. It was all coming together. When India was killed, he would play his part, the devastated father. He would reach out to Massimo Verdi. The Schuler man, Lazlo, would be a problem but a 'suicide' could always be arranged. Stories about Lazlo and India's relationship could be planted, insinuations of an 'incestuous' obsession on Schuler's part. Philip had always wondered about their closeness.

No matter. None of it mattered until India was dead. Philip had never wanted children, and when Priya had told him she was pregnant and would keep the child, he made it abundantly clear he would never have anything to do with either one of them.

When Priya had been murdered and the sixteen-year-old India had been so badly hurt, there was a fleeting moment of responsibility. That's why he'd paid her medical bills. That's how he'd come to know about the child. A month later, with India out of her coma, she'd complained of nausea. A pregnancy test proved positive. Pregnant, sixteen, alone, and facing months of recovery at the same time. He had to hand it to India, she was a survivor.

The child had been given up at birth to a couple vetted by the adoption agency. India did not meet them. She hadn't wanted to. She only wanted to know where to send money.

Philip followed his daughter's budding career, curious about her life. He traced the adoptive parents of her child and discovered his granddaughter was well cared for, and that India regularly sent lots of money for her, all the while knowing nothing more about her than her daughter was well loved. That's all she cared about: that she was loved and cherished, despite her paternity.

The child would never know that the famous rock star who had been dreadfully murdered was her own mother.

Philip smiled. He loved the sheer tragedy of it all, looking forward to it with pure anticipation.

CHAPTER THIRTY – RUNAWAYS

Rome, Italy

INDIA LOOKED up as Massimo came into the room and giggled when he spread his arms wide yelling. "Ta-da!"

India grinned. "What's the celebration?"

Massimo kissed her first before answering. "We've wrapped."

"Early?" Her eyebrows shot up sharply and Massimo smiled.

"Yup. Well, my scenes anyway. They've rescheduled some of Olivero's scenes for later in the week, and as I only had a couple more, we got through them today. Thanks to your boyfriend's encyclopedic knowledge of his lines, and of course, his extraordinary talent!"

"Oh, of course." India stood and hugged him. "So, we get extra days together?"

His lips rested lightly against hers as they spoke. "We do... so I thought we could take a trip. Maybe East?"

India smiled, lips still touching. "Seoul?"

"I've been curious ever since you told me about Sun and Tae. I'd like to meet them—they're special to you and I want to know your world."

India pulled back just enough to scrutinize his eyes. "And you're sure you're okay with Sun and I?"

"Positive. Like I said, I'm intrigued by your relationship."

"You'll love him, and Seoul. It's stunning; such a vibrant city."

Massimo smiled, sliding his hand under her shirt. "Talking of stunning... I've been thinking about this body all day."

"This body?" India pointed at herself, pretending to be surprised. "This one? This saggy old thing?"

Massimo laughed as he picked her up in a fireman's lift. "This perfect body, your body, yes."

"This unfit, slack mess of a body?" She was still giggling as he dumped her on the bed and began to pull her clothes off.

"Mess, huh? Well, let's just check... hmm, thighs? Good and firm. Calves. Shapely." He ran his hands over both of her legs. "Feet. Perfectly shaped."

"Do *not* suck my toes."

Massimo laughed. "I'm not a masochist. Now, let's concentrate on the top half, and we'll get to the playground—" indicating her groin, "last." He unbuttoned her shirt and smiled. "Ah, the front-fastening bra today. All the better." He flicked it open with a deft movement and her breasts, heavy and full, sprang out of the bra. "Mm, tasty."

India giggled so hard her entire body shook. He took that moment to enjoy the undulation before latching his mouth around her nipple, sucking and teasing it, before turning to the other.

"Now," he said a while later, and his lips found her throat, and then trailed along her jawline, "the most exquisite face I have ever known." He kissed her cheeks, her nose, her forehead, and each eyelid before settling on her mouth.

India had stopped giggling and was lost in the pleasure of his gentle touches. She opened her eyes and smiled up at him.

His green eyes were soft with love. "You know," he whispered softly and she nodded.

"I know."

She helped him undress and they made love slowly and leisurely until it was twilight. They showered together and dressed in their casual sweats, unwilling to enter the city on a Friday night.

They made supper together, fresh salmon and a salad, and enjoyed it up on the rooftop, balancing their plates on their knees as they ate. Massimo salvaged a piece of arugula from her cheek and grinned. "Messy. So, shall we book tickets?"

"I'll call Sun first, if that's okay. I haven't mentioned visiting and at such a delicate time for them, I don't want to pile on." She ate the last piece of her fish. "Although I'm already dreaming of the food. Red bean mochi... God." She swooned and he grinned.

"I should be insulted on behalf of my country but I'm not."

India grinned. "You know me, food is good wherever. I even like English food."

"Sacrilege."

"Deal with it." She playfully stole some asparagus from his plate. "I could eat more. I don't know what's wrong with me. Probably contentment." She gave him a cheesy smile and he laughed.

Massimo stroked a long lock of soft brown hair over her ear. "Why don't you video chat Sun... then I can say hello in person?"

"That's a good idea. Break the ice. Sun's not a crazy jealous person so it shouldn't be awkward."

"Let's go for it."

India checked her watch. "But it's going to be after midnight in Seoul, so we might have to wait until tomorrow."

"Cool." Massimo laid back and ran a finger down her spine. India smiled at him.

"Babe?"

"Yeah?"

India hesitated. "I called your mom today."

Massimo was surprised. "You did? How did it go?"

"Okay, I think. I just told her we were thinking of her and that if she needed anything, we would be there for her."

"How did she react?"

India half-smiled. "It's hard to say, but she seemed... warmer."

"She's getting used to the idea of you. This also means Val hasn't been stirring the pot."

"How's Val been on set?"

Massimo shot an amused sideways glance at her as she lay back, making the question seem casual. "You've been dying to ask that, haven't you?"

India chuckled. "Only in a nosy kind of way."

Massimo threw his head back laughing. "Well, she's been friendly but not flirty. Always asks after you."

"In a *'how is she'* way or a *'is that hussy still around'* way?" India wiggled her eyebrows at him.

"Hard to say," he joked, "it could be both."

They went inside after a while and to bed. In the early morning hours, the sharp penetrating ring of the telephone woke them. It was Jake. "You might want to put the television on. Entertainment channel."

Wrapped in Massimo's robe, India switched the television and gasped. The photographs of herself and Massimo were of differing quality—the daytime ones of them walking around in his hometown in Apulia, holding hands, laughing, joking, kissing, were clear and conclusive. The distance shots of them making love on the rooftop of his Rome apartment were thankfully hazy, but seeing as it was *his* apartment, it could hardly be anyone else.

"Oh, fuck..." Massimo put his arm around her. "Darling, I'm so sorry."

India rubbed her face. "I don't care about the nude shots. It's just..."

"Now this isn't safe."

She nodded miserably then turned to him. "We've been outed. I suppose it was always going to happen except now it puts a timeclock on things." She looked up at him. "I'm not sorry the world knows I love you, Massimo Verdi. I've wanted to shout it from the rooftops for weeks now. I'm yours."

"And I'm yours. For all time, India. We'll figure this out." He ran his hand through his dark curls. "But the paparazzi, if I know them at all, will already be outside."

As he spoke there was a knock at the door. It was Nate coming to confirm Massimo's suspicions. "We have to get you both away from here. It's too dangerous with Carter on the loose."

THEY PACKED QUICKLY and then Nate managed to smuggle them out of the building through the basement. "We won't always be so fortunate. Luckily the paps are still gathering, getting their act together. We'll have you at the airport by the time they've figured it out. The private plane will be waiting."

"The plane's *here?*"

Nate nodded a ghost of a smile on his face. "Lazlo has been sending it to wherever you are in case you needed a quick getaway. We're going to flying to Vienna, then the Maldives, then Seoul from there."

"I haven't spoken with Sun yet."

"I have. He's the one who alerted me—the news broke in Korea first."

Massimo frowned. "That's odd."

Nate nodded. "I know. You would think it would break in Europe first... but who knows where they got their information, and who was paying someone to follow you. We're looking into it."

"What else did Sun say?"

"He told me to tell you to come there. You and Massimo. Their security team will keep you hidden for as long as you need."

Massimo sighed. "I hate to meet him this way."

Nate smiled. "It doesn't matter. Sun just wants you both safe."

They boarded the private plane with minimal fuss and were soon heading for Austria. India held Massimo's hand as they sat in silence for a while, then shook her head. "This life, hey?"

Massimo grinned. "This life." He leaned over to kiss her. "In spite of everything, I'm glad the world knows about us. I want to hold you, kiss you, without worrying if we'll be seen."

She cupped his cheek in her small hand and whispered sweetly, "I love you."

"*Ti amo, Bella* India." He nuzzled his nose against hers before kissing her again. "At least we can tell our kids that we had adventures, hey?"

India smiled, but there was a hesitation in her eyes, and

Massimo studied her. "Not that I'm presuming, darling. It's not something we've discussed."

She shook her head and looked away. "It's too early for that." She sighed. "Way too early." Her voice was barely a whisper; he could barely make out what she had said.

Massimo frowned. "What is it, *Bella*?"

India didn't say anything for a moment then turned to him. "Why did you and Valentina never have children?"

"It just didn't happen," he said, shrugging, "and now I am glad. We talked about it a lot and for a while I was almost desperate to start a family. I never thought I'd get to almost forty and be childless. But in the last few years of our relationship, I lived in terror that she *would* get pregnant." He half-smiled. "Because she and I weren't endgame, Indy. Fate knew that you and I were."

India leaned against him and he wrapped his arms around her. "It's too soon to talk about kids. Isn't it?"

"Maybe." He noticed she wouldn't meet his eyes. "What is it?"

But she just shook her head and didn't say anything else.

Seoul, South Korea

It was another day and a half before they finally, exhausted from travel and stress, landed in Seoul. Sun's security team hurried them through passport control and into a van with darkened windows. India felt whiplashed, but as the van carried them farther and farther away from the city, she felt nothing but gratitude for the efforts being made on their behalf.

At the same time, she felt tense and had a foreboding of trouble, like they should not have come to Seoul. A dread. A warning.

This was ridiculous. The van drove them to a compound—a luxury compound—where they had round-the-clock security, and plenty of it

Sun and Tae arrived together an hour later and Sun immediately wrapped his arms around India. They hugged for a long time before parting, and India introduced Massimo to them. Tae hugged India and shook Massimo's hand, but Sun threw his arms around Massimo in a bear hug. "Thank you," he said, "thank you for loving her."

Massimo chuckled, a little bemused while Tae rolled his eyes. "He's not always like this, I promise. It's been an emotional few weeks."

India squeezed Tae's hand. "Thanks to you both for this oasis. It was a shock when the photos came out. She tried to smile. "You know the rest."

"Well, you'll get some privacy here. There's even a beach we can all walk on. The company really helped us out."

"We can't thank you enough," Massimo repeated then smiled ruefully. "I've been looking forward to meeting you both."

Sun smiled but looked inquiringly at India who nodded. "He knows everything, Sun."

"Ah." Sun smiled. "Good. That saves any awkward conversations."

His sunshine smile broke the ice, and they all chuckled. "You must be hungry. Why don't you go relax in your room until it's time to eat? Sun and I will cook some food for you?"

THE ROOM, of course, was sumptuous in its decoration and comfort. "So damn soft," she said and her eyes closed. In a moment, she fell asleep, the dark circles under her eyes advertising how tired she was.

He couldn't sleep himself so he showered and changed and went to find his hosts. Tae was alone in the kitchen, chopping vegetables, and he laughed when Massimo told him how quickly India had fallen asleep. "I thought she might. I know the violet shadows from old. Definite sign. It's okay. We thought you both might need some rest so we're making food we can cook at the last minute." He wiped his hands. "Want some beer?"

"Sure." Tae handed him a cold bottle then motioned for them to sit. Massimo looked around. "Where's your man?"

"Flaking out on cooking," Tae grinned, "claiming he was suddenly inspired to write. He's in the studio." He nodded in the opposite direction of the bedrooms and Massimo laughed.

"This place really has everything, huh?"

Tae smiled. "You have no idea," He tapping his beer to Massimo's. "Cheers."

They chatted about nothing much for a few minutes, then

Tae looked at Massimo. "You must have questions. About Sun and Indy."

Massimo sighed. "I don't want to intrude, it's just... I never had that kind of relationship until I met India—where we were friends first. She's an unusual woman."

"And Sun's unique. I know. At first, before Sun and I were together, I couldn't figure them out. Sometimes they're like brother and sister. Sun's an only kid so I thought Indy was his sister substitute. Then I found them in bed together." He winced a little. "Sadly, for me, it coincided with me realizing I was in love with him."

"Ouch, I'm sorry, dude."

"No need. I was so deep in the closet that I was kind of grateful that it was taken out of my hands. But after that one time, it went back to being like siblings. So, yeah, if you can't figure it out, neither can I. It's been tough. Especially after the last year." He took a swig of his beer. "You know they had a fling last year?"

"I do. Indy's been very open with me about Sun and their relationship. She also told me how guilty she's been feeling."

"Looking back, now, there was no need. Sun and I were having major problems to the point where I had told him it was over. And India was scared. They needed each other right then." Tae looked at Massimo. "There's no news on where Carter is?"

"No. Wherever he is, whatever he's planning, he's curiously well-funded."

Massimo and Tae looked at each other before Tae asked, carefully. "How's her relationship with Philip LeFevre?"

Massimo nodded. "Yeah. That's the way my mind had been going, too. Who else would fund her murder unless it could be used for political gain?"

"Did you talk to India about it?"

"No. She's stressed enough."

"She's not dumb, Massimo. She's probably thinking the same thing."

"Who's thinking what?" Sun appeared and, not for the first time, Massimo thought how aptly he was named. His beauty was extraordinary, and given how his hair was dyed blonde and his sweater was yellow, he radiated light.

Tae scooted over on the couch as Sun sat down next to him, briefly touching his forehead to his lover's. They were such a beautiful couple Massimo found himself looking away, feeling strange. He was secure in his masculinity but these guys were so pretty, they didn't seem... human. He grinned to himself, and when they asked him what he was smiling about and he told them.

Sun laughed. "Yeah, Indy always tells us we're vampires."

"*Are* you?" Massimo laughed but he was only half-joking. Right now, it seemed a real possibility.

They talked about many things but avoided the subject of India's father, and when the lady herself appeared, ruffled and sleepy, her hair sticking up every which way, all three of them teased her until she was giggling.

Massimo felt some of his tension slip away. Here, in this luxury compound, with his love and her—*their*—beautiful friends, he could rest, imagining their problems were a world away.

. . .

It was interesting to see the dynamics at play as they sat eating the most delicious Asian cuisine Massimo had ever had. Sun and Tae told him that their agency had insisted on them finishing college and learning real life skills as they trained to become K-pop idols. Hence their cooking ability, and Massimo and India ate until they could eat no more

And so went their evening until the early hours of the morning. As they said goodnight, Sun hugged Massimo again whispering in his ear, "Thank you for making her happy."

CHAPTER THIRTY-ONE – ONE LAST TIME

Massimo told India what Sun had said when they had gone to their room and undressed. India slipped into the bed beside him and smiled. "You have. You have no idea how happy you have made me." She stroked his face. "I feel like we wasted all that time being apart."

"I think, looking back, things happened the way they needed to. But I love you. I think I fell in love with you the first moment I saw you on that stage. So, weirdly, I don't feel we were apart, simply on pause."

India chuckled. "That's a nice way to put it." She kissed him softly. "You know, Sun and Tae's bedroom is *way* over the other side of the compound."

Massimo grinned as she wrapped her legs around his hips. "Is that right?"

"Yeah," she drawled slowly, "so you can make me scream all night long. Ain't no one gonna hear a thing..."

Massimo gathered to him, tickling her and making her giggle before thrusting into her, his cock already rock-hard and throbbing. He moved his hips against hers, burying himself deeper and harder with each thrust.

India clung to him and somehow managed to roll him onto his back, straddling him and riding him with all of her energy until they were both coming and laughing. It felt so good, the release of tension and of desire.

India rolled off of him. "We didn't use a condom again."

"Nope."

"You bothered?" She propped herself up her elbow and studied him.

"Nope." He met her gaze. "We talked about this on the plane. Why don't you seem concerned?"

"I honestly couldn't tell you. All I know is... if it happens, it happens."

Massimo sat up. "Baby... this isn't like you."

India smiled. " Maybe I'm overtired but..." and to his shock, she started to cry. He drew her into his arms and let her cry herself out.

"I'm sorry," she hiccupped, trying to stop the tears, "I'm just so sick of all of it... coming here, being with the people I love, all I can think about is that at any minute it could all end and that terrifies me. It feels like if I allow myself to be happy... God, I'm sorry, but I just... I've had enough, you know?"

"I know, darling."

He held her for a long time before she spoke again. "Perhaps we *should* be more careful. Being pregnant right now is not a good idea. I'm messed up in the head."

"I have condoms." He kissed her temple. "It's not just you who's been careless. We need to get our act together. I've been thinking. When we get back to New York, I think we should sit down with the FBI, see what progress they've made. Look, I'm not bragging but I do have practically unlimited funds. We'll search the globe for Carter if we have to."

India looked unhappy but nodded. "I couldn't ask you to do that, but I can pay for it myself."

"We are in this thing together, baby. Money is nothing to me without you."

India sighed. "Can we talk about this when we're back home? I know this might sound weird, but just here, with Sun and Tae in this lovely place, I don't want anything to sully it. Can we just *be*, for now?"

"Of course, baby." He drew her close. They lay down again and tried to sleep.

IN THE EARLY HOURS, India slipped from the bed and padded into the kitchen for some water. She looked over the beach bathed in moonlight which gave the ocean an otherworldly feel. She felt an arm slip around her waist, Sun leaning his chin on her shoulder. "Are you okay?"

She leaned her head on his. "I am. Thank you, Sunbeam, for this, for allowing us to come here. We needed this."

"Of course."

India closed her eyes and leaned against her friend, her

beloved Sun. Thank God they had survived the mess she had made last year. "Are you and Tae really good now? You seem to be."

"We truly are."

It made India happy to see the joy in Sun's eyes.

"I'm so delighted for you, darling. You deserve to be happy."

"So do you, Indy. I adore Massimo! He is absolutely who I would choose for you if it were up to me. He can protect you."

India chuckled softly. "Feminism, Sunbeam."

He grinned his angelic grin. "I didn't say you couldn't protect *him*, too."

India laughed quietly. "Touché. I think he's a little taken aback by this world. Our little make-believe fairy-tale world."

"Anyone would be. We've been lost in it for way too long, Indy. It's time we realize we're adults already."

"Says the twenty-three year-old."

"Hey, I've grown up a lot. In the last year, in particular." He leaned his forehead against hers. "Not that I regret our time together."

"Me neither. Never. But it was a goodbye in a sense."

"But the beginning of the next phase of our friendship, too."

She smiled knowingly at him. "You *have* grown up. I meant it when I said I'm so happy for you and Tae. You belong together."

. . .

IN THE SHADOWS, Massimo listened to them talking and smiled to himself. He was glad India had found some peace after all, but he'd meant what he'd said. When they got back to the States, he would insist they go to the FBI.

This hell India had lived in for twelve years was ending now.

Right now.

CHAPTER THIRTY-TWO – SET FIRE TO THE RAIN

They spent the next few days with Sun and Tae, gradually beginning to relax again. They kept an eye on the situation with the reveal of their relationship, but to their relief the frenzy was short-lived, and the paparazzi had soon moved onto other gossip and other celebrities.

Still, they found themselves reluctant to leave their safe, happy haven. Sun and Tae made them feel completely and absolutely welcome, even encouraging them to stay as long as they liked, seemingly happy to make them part of their little family.

Massimo was still adjusting to the unusual dynamic, but he found peace in it. Sun and Tae were loving, inclusive, and fun, and he felt he had known them forever in the same way as he and India had bonded at the start. He felt it was serendipity the way he had met India and these two men—they were meant to be a family.

He was over a decade older than the three of them but he never felt it. With them, he felt a playfulness he had never felt before. He had been with Valentina for ten years from his late twenties and had grown up quickly, become sophisticated quickly, eschewing fun for elegance.

Now, with Indy, Sun, and Tae, he fooled around with them, teasing each other, playing games, running on the beach and feeling free. It was intoxicating.

Even so, the time came for them to return to New York. "We can't keep putting it off," India said with a bittersweet grimace, "and besides, there is my father's fake charity gig."

"Why did you agree to do it?" Tae shaking his head. "Just tell the press the truth about him. Organize your own concert for the charities involved."

"Agreed," Sun said, and Massimo nodded.

"Thirded. Tell him to suck it."

India smiled, but said nothing, and Massimo saw a flicker of something in her eyes for a brief second that he couldn't identify.

They spent their last full day with Sun and Tae on the beach outside their compound. India and Sun teamed up against Tae and Massimo in a game of volleyball. Rules were quickly thrown out of the window as they laughed and cheated their way through several games until eventually Indy and Sun victoriously proclaimed themselves the winners.

"No *way*," said Tae in mock-outrage, "you can't lift Indy up to knock the ball over and tell me that's not cheating."

Sun, his blonde hair in disarray, grinned at his lover. "Alright then,... death match it is."

India, who was out of breath, waved her hands. "I can't, I can't breathe."

Massimo also objected, and so Sun and Tae agreed to race along the sand for the match. "We'll be the referees." India sank down onto the sand, and Massimo joined her, looping his arm across her shoulders as the two men lined up.

"On your mark, ready, set," Massimo said, "GO!"

The two Koreans took off along the sand, and India and Massimo laughed, watching them bicker as they ran, tugging on each other, trying to get the advantage.

Then quite suddenly, with a distinctive cracking sound, Sun jerked backwards. At first, no one reacted as Sun stopped, a fine red mist enveloping him, then India screamed as Tae staggered to a stop and cried out as Sun crashed awkwardly to the sand.

They were running to him even before they could fully assess what they had seen and heard. All three of them rushed to help the fallen man who lay on his back, his eyes open, blinking rapidly, confused as the blood bloomed across his chest. "What...?"

His breathing came in panicked gasps as Tae, India, and Massimo knelt at his side unsure of what to do next. Nate and Sun's security team were racing to them to see what they could do. Tae was sobbing, holding Sun's head in his lap. "What happened? What happened?"

Sun had been shot. That was now clear to all. India,

unthinking, blind with tears of grief and despair, pressed her hand to the wound to stop the bleeding. In all the confusion, he felt someone's arms under her own ripping her away from her beloved friend, carrying her off down the beach and away. She screamed, clawing at her captor, but Nate was firm. "We have to get you inside, India."

"*Sun!*" She screamed and screamed as Sun was swarmed by people trying to save him.

THE NEXT FEW hours were nightmarish. Sun was airlifted to hospital and taken straight into surgery. At India's insistence, they went with him, and sat in a private conference room, India holding Tae's hand the entire time they waited for news. The room was surrounded by security staff and police. India tried to comfort Tae, but it was useless. He was hollow-eyed and broken.

"He'll get through this, I know he will." India knew her words meant nothing but she had to say them, to try to make them true. Sun, beautiful, lovely, kind-hearted Sun… how? *Why?*

She truly couldn't fathom who would do this to him.

Tae gave a cough of derision. "Plenty of people don't like the fact two men are in love," he said gruffly. "The world isn't at that place yet." He rubbed his eyes. "But why didn't they go for me, too?"

They got their answer in a few hours. A bouquet of flowers had been sent but was instead addressed to India.

Frowning, she opened the card and gasped, dropping it as if she had been poisoned.

Massimo picked it up. *"One down. Everyone you love left to go. Always yours, Braydon Carter."*

"No, no, no, *no, no*..." India broke down, her legs giving way, her head spinning, her heart breaking, and it took both Massimo and Tae to pick her up from the floor. Tae hugged her tightly.

"This is *not* your fault," he whispered urgently to a sobbing India. "It's the work of a madman."

But India was beyond consolation, and when the surgeon came to tell them Sun had been stabilized, the relief wasn't enough to comfort her.

Tae was pale and exhausted, but still he peppered the doctor with questions. "Will he recover?"

The doctor nodded. "But obviously it will take a long time, and we can't guarantee there will be no complications."

Tae was allowed see Sun after they'd operated, but Massimo and India held back to give them their privacy. "Just tell him we love him so much, and that I'm sorry. Please, Tae."

Tae held India tightly. "I will, I promise. But I know he'll want to see you soon."

India nodded and kissed Tae's cheek. "I love you both so very much," she said, her voice breaking, and Tae slowly nodded, gently wiping her tears away.

"We love you, too. Never forget that."

. . .

THE HOSPITAL WAS TOO quiet at night, Massimo decided. India had excused herself to use the bathroom, and he sat with Nate now, feeling drained. "Poor kid," he said. "I've grown very fond of Sun and Tae."

Nate nodded. "They're good people."

"The best." Massimo checked his watch. "Did you rearrange the flights?"

"I did. Left them open for whenever you and Indy want to fly back. I picked up your passports. I told India. Just in case we need to make a quick getaway."

Nate reached for the jacket he'd slung over the back of chair in the now-private conference room and reached into the inside pocket. He frowned, a bit perplexed, pulling only one out, and Massimo saw the cover. An Italian passport. "Where's India's?"

The two men stared at each other with unspoken understanding of the situation. Both stood simultaneously and lunged for the ladies' bathroom. Neither of them considered calling for a nurse to help, they both just burst in. Luckily, it was empty.

*Un*luckily, it was empty.

"Oh, God damn it, no..."

On one of the large mirrors, a note handwritten in make-up.

I'm sorry. I'm a jinx. Don't come after me. I love you. India.

"*Mio Dio*, no, no, no..." Massimo felt weak as he sank to his knees. Massimo knew what her plan was.

She was going home. She would put herself into the

hands of Braydon Carter to finish this thing off once and for all, and in doing so, keep safe the people she loved. India was sacrificing herself.

Massimo wanted to scream.

CHAPTER THIRTY-THREE – CLOSER TO GOD

ew York City

INDIA HAD LEARNED a few things while avoiding press and detection for so many months. The moment he realized she was gone, Nate would swing into action, but she hoped she could avoid him and his men long enough to board the flight to New York.

Luckily, because of her globetrotting and psycho-evasion over the last year, she now carried enough cash to avoid detection, although Nate would find out she used her passport and have people waiting for her at JFK.

So, she flew first to Rio de Janeiro, then Seattle, then back to Manhattan. Some of her security team was there, but she had disguised herself by then.

Where she was going? Somewhere *no one* would expect.

She took a bus to the Hamptons, her long dark hair stuffed into a blonde wig, huge sunglasses on her face. She asked the driver to drop her a couple of miles prior to the station and walked the rest of it.

At the gate of her father's summer home, the security guard looked skeptical when she told him who she was, but he had been told to let her through.

Philip LeFevre stood at the door of his house, looking somewhat surprised. "India. What are you doing here?"

India took a deep breath before she calmly explained, "I need to be where no one will look for me while I make a plan. For just a few days. I've never asked you for anything. But *this* I need from you."

Philip studied her for a long time. "And no one knows you came here?"

She half-heartedly shrugged as she pointed at the bad wig and the sunglasses. "I did my best. I took precautions."

Philip stared at her, wondering what to do next and then stood aside, gesturing for her to come in. India took a deep breath and stepped inside, suppressing her feelings of revulsion for this man. If her suspicions were correct, she wouldn't feel it for much longer.

She felt curiously numb as she was shown her room and absentmindedly unpacked the few possessions she had managed to bring with her: underwear, a toothbrush, and toiletries. India wondered how long it would take her father to call in the favor.

Well, you're getting what you wanted, Dad, she thought. *I've handed myself to you.*

At the same time, she needed this, this time to breathe, to heal. She pulled out her tablet and checked the news for any details of Sun's condition. No change. They were still saying he was stable but cautioned against hope. India rushed to the bathroom to throw up.

Oh, God, Sun... my Sunbeam... I'm so sorry for bringing this down on you, my angel...

Leaving him so sick and vulnerable had torn her up, but it was for the best. The further away she was from those she loved, the better.

And she knew her father would leak where she was, would use it to his own advantage. Which meant Carter would find her. Death was coming in the combined form of betrayal and revenge and ambition, and she knew it.

She doubted her father would mourn her at all. After she was dead, he would begin his sob story, the pity party. He would spin it every which way that suited his political goals. *Fuck him.*

India laid back and closed her eyes, waiting. *Good. Let's get this over with.* She had thought about ending it all herself, but she wanted the monster who had tried to kill her beloved Sun to pay for what he had done. She would not die quietly.

In all likelihood, he would kill her before she could hurt him, and she would never see anyone she loved again, even the child she had kept secret from everyone. But after her death, Carter would be satisfied, and they would all be safe.

India just wanted the pain to end.

A nervous-looking maid appeared at her door with a box. "Mr. LeFevre thought you might like to dress for dinner. I hope the size is correct."

India stared blankly at the white dress. It was soft material, not entirely dressy, and looked comfortable. "It's fine, thank you."

She showered and took her time getting ready. She had no makeup. She dried her hair, leaving it down. She didn't care.

STEELING HERSELF, she went downstairs to meet Philip who waited for her in the dining room. India nodded at him, accepting his offered drink, wondering what he'd put in it. Jesus, paranoia was not going to be helpful.

"How is this going to happen?"

"How is *what* going to happen?"

India smirked. "The spin. The story you're no doubt preparing for the papers."

"I thought you needed some peace. My home is yours for as long as you need."

India put her glass down and looked at him steadily. "Philip, drop the doting father act. It's just you and me. You need me for the boost in younger voters. I needed somewhere where no one could get to me, at least for a few days. Could we please not pretend we care anything about each other?"

Philip studied her for a long silent moment. "Fine."

The food was served, and India realized how hungry she

was. Hungry and exhausted. LeFevre noticed. "You look exhausted."

"Being under a death threat will do that."

"Braydon Carter."

India nodded. "He tried to kill my friend. An innocent kid. He shot him in cold blood. To get to me." Saying it aloud made her want to scream. "But Sun's a fighter." Please, God, let that be true...

"I'm sorry."

India knew he didn't care in the least, but it was strangely good to hear the words from him. "About Sun? Or about how you treated my mother?"

"Both. And I'm sorry about how I treated you when I saw you last."

Unconsciously, India touched the back of her head where he had grabbed her hair. "Why do some men think violence is the only way to handle a woman?"

"I'm sorry."

India looked away from him and shrugged. She hated this, hated being with him, but while she was here... "Why didn't you want us? Me. Mom. Was the idea so terrible?"

Philip sighed. "I never wanted kids. I told your mother that, just as I told her our affair could only be fleeting. I had a position in society to maintain."

India made a disgusted noise and Philip laughed. "You might think I'm a snob—"

"—no, I think you're an asshole."

Philip's smile disappeared. "Watch your mouth. I'm still your father."

India looked away from him. God, had this really been her best idea? "So, when's the leak?"

"No leak here. Your privacy is guaranteed."

India rubbed her eyes. Though she didn't believe him, she didn't argue. Her shattered heart could take no more. "Thank you. Please excuse me."

"Goodnight, India."

She managed to lock her bedroom door before she broke down sobbing.

Seoul

Massimo put his hands on Tae's shoulders. "Go grab some coffee, Tae. Get some air. I'll sit with him for a while."

Tae hesitated, loathe leaving his unconscious lover as he lay connected up to machines. He stood, bending to kiss Sun's forehead. He spoke softly in Korean to him.

"He's going to be okay, Tae." Massimo knew his words could not get through the layers of absolute grief. Outside of the hospital, thousands of Sun's fans were gathered, holding vigils for him. Sun's parents had only just left the hospital. They were a kindly couple, the same age as Massimo himself, and with Tae translating, he had told them he would do everything he could to find the man who had done this to their lovely son. "He'll pull through, I believe it with all my heart."

The heart that was broken into a million pieces. As he sat

with Sun now, he pulled out his phone and checked it for the millionth time that day. No messages. Knowing India had left them, had gone into hiding to keep them safe didn't help.

When Lazlo in New York informed him she'd gone to the States, but had since given them the slip, Massimo felt a deep panic set in.

And then he was angry. Angry and hurt that she didn't trust in him enough to stay. And when Lazlo asked him to stay in Seoul, he nearly went out of his mind.

Lazlo had listened to him rant, then spoke calmly, kindly. "Massi, what she did was reckless. I spoke to a psychologist. Sun's shooting might have triggered her PTSD."

"Where the hell has she gone, Laz? How could she stay this off the radar? She's freaking India Blue, for chrissakes!"

"And we're readying a story for the press. Tomorrow, I'm filing an official missing person report. The FBI advises me to make her disappearance public."

Massimo sighed. "I need to be there."

"You being in Seoul could be the one thing that persuades her to come out of hiding. She'll be grateful you respected her wishes to stay away."

"That makes no sense."

"None of this does."

There was a long silence. "Laz...her father. Do you believe he has something to do with Carter?"

"I do. I really do. I just haven't got any proof of that."

Massimo hesitated. "She wouldn't have... I mean, there's no way she would have gone to him, right?"

Lazlo gave a hollow laugh. "Philip LeFevre is the last person she would go to."

Now Massimo sat with Sun, watching the machines breathe for this young kid, this beautiful man barely out of his teens, and wondered if Lazlo was right. Because LeFevre *would* be the last person India would go to... and she would know no one would look for her there.

Massimo sat up. *I need to be there. I need to find her...*

When Tae came back, he took one look at Massimo's face. "Go," he said, hugging Massimo. "Sun will be fine. Come back when you've found our girl."

Massimo hugged him back. "I promise. We'll all be together again soon."

He was on the flight back to New York in less than an hour.

India slept fitfully, never fully giving in to the exhaustion but still, she didn't hear the bedroom door opening just after three a.m. The first thing she knew was the weight of another person's body on hers. She opened her eyes to her worst nightmare.

Braydon Carter.

She tried to scream, but he clamped a hand over her mouth. "Hello, my darling."

Panic and terror took over. She clawed and kicked, finally

freeing her mouth to scream. Braydon hit her hard enough to silence her.

"Careful." She heard her father's voice. "Don't get her blood on anything. I don't want this traced back to me."

In the midst of her fright, India wondered how something could be both a terrible shock and not at all surprising.

"You *bastard*," she gasped as Braydon hauled her to her feet. "Play the doting father. Even if he kills me…"

"Not '*if*', darling," her father said, his voice and his eyes cold. "*When*. Mr Carter has been itching to feel your blood on his hands. Tonight he will. There's no use in screaming. There's just the three of us here." LeFevre looked at Carter. "Make it painful, won't you? I'm so tired of this little bitch."

India felt Carter's breath on her neck. "*That* I can guarantee."

India felt the sting of a needle in her nape of her neck and the last thing she saw was the man who had fathered her smiling broadly at the man who was going to kill her.

34

CHAPTER THIRTY-FOUR – GONER

New York

Massimo wasn't surprised to find Lazlo waiting for him at the airport, clearly annoyed. Massimo held his hands up in his own defence. "Laz, before you start... she's with LeFevre. There's nowhere else she could have gone."

"We don't know that, Massi, and now you are in danger."

"Do you really think I care about that? Honestly? *Listen* to me. India was devastated about Sun's shooting, and she's angry. *Raging.* Who better to take that out on than Philip LeFevre while hiding at his place?"

"Wouldn't India have guessed we would think that, too, though?"

Massimo smiled grimly. "Remember, she wasn't in her

right mind. And we never discussed our suspicions about him with her."

"That was a mistake."

"I know." Massimo sighed. "By protecting her from that, we might have driven her right to him. I know it in my bones, Laz. India's with him, and he's got Carter on a leash. We have to get there."

Lazlo stared at him, and Massimo waited for him to resolve the conflict he felt. Finally, Lazlo nodded. "Fine. Let's go."

INDIA WOKE in the back seat of Carter's car. Her wrists were bound behind her back, her legs tied so that she could not move them. Flashbacks of the night twelve years ago flooded her mind. After her mother's murder, after Carter had raped India, she'd been tied in the backseat like this, too.

India shook her head. *No. Not again*. She strained against her bindings: sharp plastic ties that dug into her skin.

"There's absolutely no chance of you escaping, beautiful, so stop struggling. It's nearly over."

"Fuck you."

"Oh, you will. Over and over, my darling India, before you die."

"Try it and I'll kill you."

Carter's laughter enraged her. She kicked the back of the driver's seat. It just made his mirth increase. "Oh, little girl, there's a reason I'm crazy in love with you."

"Crazy is right, but it's not love. Love isn't abducting someone and trying to kill them, asshole. You're pathetic."

Part of her brain was screaming at herself to shut up, to not make things worse, but India was past the point of caring now. The animal side of her brain was spurring her on, her rage over Sun's shooting, the despair of being parted from Massimo...

Cause an accident. Change his plans.

She used her legs to pummel the back of his seat, eventually irritating Carter. He levelled a gun at her head.

India smiled grimly. She knew he wouldn't shoot her. His plans were much more intimate than a simple bullet to her head. But kicking the back of his seat wasn't doing anything.

She strained to loosen the plastic ties around her wrists, tugging so hard she felt blood drip from them and her fingers start to numb. She panted, exhausted, trying to figure out what she could do to cause an accident, then almost laughed aloud as the idea came to her.

Struggling into a sitting position, she grinned widely at Braydon in the rear view mirror. That freaked him out. "What the fuck—?"

She lunged at him, teeth bared, clamping down on back of his exposed neck, biting down as hard as she could. She felt flesh give way as Braydon screamed in pain and the car swerved violently. "Fucking bitch!"

Adrenaline pumped through India's body. *Yes... yes...* She was winning this. For her mother... for Sun... for herself... As Carter tried to regain control of the car, India rocked back and brought her feet up, slamming them into his head, feeling the satisfying crack of his head against the driver's side glass window through the soles of her shoes.

Braydon's head slumped forward. The car veered off the road and rolled, throwing her around like a rag doll for what felt like an eternity.

She heard her left arm snap at the elbow as the car finally came to a stop and for a moment there was nothing but silence and the tick-tick of the engine.

Pain. God, so much pain. Ignoring the agony of her broken arm, she managed to get her hands in front of her, screaming as she did. She smelled the salt and rust stench of her own blood.

In the moonlight, she could see Braydon was slumped over in the front, unconscious or perhaps even dead. She kicked open the door and managed to crawl out, moaning in pain.

She was alive and she was free. And now that she could use her hands, she found that he'd used rope to tie her legs. And then she found that untying a knot with a broken arm wasn't easy. Her head was thick with pain, but she loosened the knot enough to free her legs, and that's when she heard him.

"Fucking little whore. Do you think you get to dictate terms, India? I've waited twelve years for this."

She scrambled to her feet, facing him. Braydon was covered with blood, the wound oozing. She could still taste him. *Don't think about it. Don't throw up now.*

In Braydon's hand was a knife. He held it up. "Time to die, beautiful."

And he was on her.

PHILIP LEFEVRE OPENED the door himself which surprised Massimo. He was still dressed as if he were about to address a roomful of political lackeys. At four a.m.?

"Gentlemen, this is an unexpected pleasure."

Massimo pushed past the man and strode into the house yelling, "India?"

"Why on Earth would India be *here* of all places?"

"Because it's the last place anyone would look for her?"

"By all means, search the house then. I think you'll find no evidence she was here."

Massimo was already halfway up the stairs. He went into each room, thinking it was odd there was no one else in the large house. LeFevre, a public figure, a billionaire, with no staff, no protection?

No way.

When he went into the guest room India had occupied, he stopped, closing his eyes. The window was open, blowing a soft breeze in, but the scent was unmistakable. India might have changed clothes, maybe put on a disguise, but she hadn't changed the deodorant she always wore, the fresh, comforting smell he loved—fresh laundry and cotton sheets.

India...

Anywhere. LeFevre had removed every trace, but he could not erase her presence entirely.

Massimo went back downstairs. "She was here." He grabbed LeFevre slamming him against the wall. LeFevre had no chance against Massimo's strength and the force of his anger. "You've *given* her to him, motherfucker. Where are they?"

LeFevre laughed arrogantly in his face. "What the fuck are you talking about? Who the hell is Braydon Carter?"

Massimo, his eyes burning with fury, punched him hard in the head. "Did we say his name? Where is she?" He was screaming now, on the edge of losing all self-control, and Lazlo put a warning hand on his arm.

Massimo let go of Philip who slumped to the floor. Massimo and Lazlo waited, glancing at each other, registering the panic in each other's eyes. "LeFevre, this is your only chance. If you know where India is, tell us. Now."

Philip lazily wiped his bloody lip. "She's gone. That's all I can tell you. India's gone." He looked up at them both and started to laugh. "And good riddance."

This time, Lazlo didn't even try to stop Massimo.

IT WAS A FAMILIAR PAIN, the knife sinking deep into her body, but this time it fueled her survival instinct. India jerked away, trying to ignore the agony of the blade slicing through her belly, and she head-butted Carter hard. That he didn't expect. He staggered backward and then with pure animal bloodlust, came at her once more. India twisted, trying to make it hard for him to jam the knife into her, but he stabbed her twice, quickly, once hard in the side, the other in the soft flesh of her abdomen. India felt a wave of dizziness.

No. No, don't lose it now or you're dead. As Carter prepared to stab her again, she suddenly dropped.

Play dead. Play dead.

She made her breathing hitched and ragged, her eyes wide and staring as if she was dying—which she supposed she was—and saw the smile on Carter's face. He crouched down beside her and stroked her face with a bloody hand. "It was always going to end like this, Indy. Always."

She braced herself for the final blow. He stabbed her, driving the knife deep into her belly—and left it there as she arched her back, gasping, then went still.

CARTER GAZED down at her body. His lovely girl, dead at last. Her eyes were open, but he could see she wasn't breathing. Tension seeped out of him. It was done. India was dead.

He moved his hand to close her eyes...and that's when he saw the movement. He couldn't react in time. India yanked the knife from her stomach and plunged it deep between his legs.

The pain was excruciating. Carter screamed, in shock, in agony, rocking back. India scrambled to her feet, her beauty terrifying as she launched herself at him. The knife in his chest felt like a million bullets as she attacked him.

The tables had been turned, and now Carter realized this, too, had been inevitable. India held the knife to his throat, and as his blood gushed from him, she leaned down, her beautiful face contorted with rage. "This is for Mom, for Sun, for me, and for everyone you have hurt because of me, asshole. You lose."

She plunged the knife into his throat and everything went black.

INDIA YANKED the blade from Carter's throat and watched him bleed out. She checked his pulse: non-existent. She cut her bindings and then threw the knife away as far as she could. Her wounds were bleeding profusely, and she felt nausea overwhelm her. She threw up—mostly blood—and knew she was dying.

But Braydon Carter was dead. And Massimo, Lazlo, Gabe, Sun, and Tae were safe now.

Dawn was beginning to creep up over the horizon, and India could see they were not far from the road. She staggered towards it over the soft, sandy ground, but before she could reach it, dark spots appeared at the corners of her eyes. She sank to the ground and struggled for oxygen. "Massimo... I love you," she whispered just once, and closed her eyes.

CHAPTER THIRTY-FIVE – BREATHE

New York State

THE FBI ASSURED Massimo and Lazlo that they had everyone out looking for India and Carter, but that they could not arrest LeFevre without evidence. "Lazlo, Massimo, I know this is frustrating, but the scent of someone's deodorant won't count in court. Our only hope of convicting LeFevre is when we find India."

But finding her alive was becoming ever more unlikely. At dawn, they sent out helicopters and within two hours, Massimo and Lazlo heard their FBI agent shout for them.

"They've found her." His facial expression sent chills down Massimo's spine. *No, no, please....*

"She's alive but in critical condition. Come on, we're flying you to her. Massi, Lazlo... it's bad."

"Was she with Carter?"

The agent nodded. "He's dead. We think there was a fight—quite a doozy. Carter was stabbed to death. India was stabbed, too. Badly. We think she killed Carter." He waited until they were inside the helicopter to continue. "Self-defense, obviously. She had binding marks on her legs and arms when we found her, but Carter had toothmarks in his neck, a bad wound, enough to suggest a pretty comprehensive struggle."

"Was she r—" Massimo couldn't get the words out.

The agent shook his head. "Not that we know of. We think he was driving, and she managed to make the car wreck. We'll know more later."

"Agent?" Lazlo felt like he was in hell. "Her wounds?"

"She was stabbed multiple times. Abdominal wounds. When they found her, she was unconscious. But she has a pulse and she's breathing. That's a good start."

"But it's bad?"

He nodded. "I'm sorry. We'll be at the hospital very soon."

It felt like an eternity before they were ushered into a private room at the hospital. The press mobbed the entrance to the hospital. The FBI, the local police, and Lazlo and Massimo's own security teams were handling them. As Massimo was shown into the waiting room, the surgeon came to see them. "We've stabilized India but she's very sick. She lost a lot of blood."

Lazlo, looking haunted, spoke up. "Doc? Can we see her?"

"She's in recovery at the moment and still unconscious. Maybe later. In the meantime we'll make you comfortable." The doctor gave them a half-smile. "I wish I could give you better news but India's fighting. That's all we can hope for right now."

LEFT ALONE FINALLY, Massimo and Lazlo looked at each other. "She's alive," Lazlo said finally. "We have to believe she'll make it."

"Was this what it was like last time? This... absolute terror of her dying?"

Lazlo nodded. "Yes. And I'll warn you now, there's no respite. Even if she wakes up... what has this done to her psychologically? She killed a man." He sighed. "Last time, she woke up and we thought it was a miracle. But she didn't speak for six months. *Six months.* I'm just saying, things won't be normal for a long time even if she makes it."

Massimo winced but gave a hollow laugh. "What's normal? I don't think one thing about Indy and mine's relationship has been normal."

"True." Lazlo's cell phone rang and he picked it up. "Tae. You heard? Yeah, God. She's stable but it's bad. How's Sun?"

Massimo listened to Lazlo's side of the conversation for a while, then Lazlo handed him the phone.

"Massi?"

"Hi, Tae."

"God, I'm so sorry, Massi. She'll make it, I know she will."

Massimo felt gratitude towards his new friend. "Thank you. How's Sun?"

"He woke up." Tae's voice softened. "He's awake and making jokes, at least he was until we heard about Indy. What happened?"

Massi told him the entire story,, and when he told Tae that India's biological father was involved, Tae became angry. "That son of a bitch."

"He'll get his, Tae, you mark my words."

There was a small silence, then Tae said, "They say Indy killed Carter. She killed the man who shot Sun?"

"Yes, that's what it looks like. And I know, Tae, I know that right at that moment, she wasn't thinking about herself. She would have done it for her mother and for Sun. She was dying and she still wanted justice for them."

"I don't doubt it." Tae sighed. "Listen, keep me updated, would you? And when you see her, tell her we love her so much. Tell her thank you for killing the man who shot my Sun."

"I will. Love to you and Sun, We'll talk later."

THE SURGEON MADE them wait another five hours before they were allowed to see India, and Massimo and Lazlo had been joined by a devastated Gabe and a worried-looking Jess.

India was pale, her usually honey-skin wan, and dark violet shadows under her eyes. A blood bag dripped the precious fluid into her system.

All they could do was wait now.

Twenty-four hours later, one of the security team informed Massimo that a woman identifying herself as his mother was here to see him.

Massimo blinked. "What?"

And yet when he followed the bodyguard back to India's floor, there was Giovanna Verdi, her green eyes large and wary. "Massimo?"

"Mamma... what are you doing here?"

"We got the news in Italy," she said reproachfully, but then her face softened. She touched his cheek. "How is India? *Mio Dio*, Massimo, I cannot believe it, such an appalling tragedy."

Massimo sighed, feeling comforted by his mother's presence. "There's so much more to it than you know, Mamma. If you knew what India had gone through in her life... what she has sacrificed..."

"Tell me, son. Tell me and we'll go see your love together."

When Massimo introduced her to Lazlo, Giovanna kissed Lazlo's cheek. "I'm so sorry, my dear."

She moved to India's side, and Massimo watched as she took India's hand and bent to kiss her forehead. She murmured a prayer in Italian. Massimo felt a profound gratitude to her for coming to be with them when they needed her. And he was grateful his mother had finally acknowledged that India was the love of his life.

The waiting, however, was terrible. Outside of waiting for his love to open her eyes, nothing else seemed to exist.

One week later, Lazlo entered the room and switched on the television. His expression was set and angry. "Look at this asshole."

On the screen, Philip LeFevre, dressed in a black suit with a black tie, was making a speech. His make-up artist had concealed the bruises from Massimo's beating, and he wore an expression of sorrow, talking about his 'daughter.'

"This tragedy only serves to remind us that violence against women is at an all-time high. We will, because we *must,* work together to stem this tide of misogyny and toxic masculinity."

"He gave me to Carter."

Both Massimo and Lazlo whirled around to see India, her eyes open, fixed on her father's image on the television. "He gave me to Carter willingly—he planned it. He planned my murder. He told Carter to butcher me."

Massimo could hardly breathe. Her voice, although scratchy from lack of use and the tubes that had helped her breath, was strong, determined. Her eyes met his then, and all the anger drained from them, and to his joy, his love, his India smiled. "I love you, Massimo Verdi," she said.

Lazlo gave a delighted laugh as Massimo beamed and went to her, kissing her mouth gently. "As I love you, India Blue. God damn, you little *fighter.*"

"You know it." India grinned at him, then at her brother. "Hey, Laz. How's it hanging?"

Lazlo bent to kiss her cheek. "Damn glad to see you, little sis." He smiled at her, stroking her hair back. "Gabe's here, too, and Jess. I'll go get them."

"Please."

When they were alone, India held Massimo's hand as he cupped her cheek with his free hand. "Sun?"

"He's doing good, baby," Massimo told her. "He's awake and making bad jokes, apparently. But he and Tae are desperate to hear good news about you. They love you so much."

India laughed then winced as the movement pulled at the stitches in her abdomen. Her smile faded a little. "Carter?"

"He's dead, baby. Gone." He nodded at the television. "And now that you're awake, that asshole is going down, too. I'm so proud of you, baby."

"There's nothing to be proud of," India said in a small voice. "I was stupid to leave Seoul, to run away. I just didn't want anyone else to get hurt because of me."

Massimo stroked her hair. "Indy... were you... I mean... were you hoping he would come for you?"

India swallowed. "I just wanted it over, one way or another. I'm sorry, but I had reached the end of my tether. Really. When Sun was... God, I can barely say the words. When he was hurt because of me, something switched in my head, and I knew that I could not live with it if Carter hurt you as well. You see, Massimo Verdi, I cannot live without you." There were tears in her eyes now, and Massimo kissed them away as they dripped down her cheeks.

"Don't cry, beautiful. We have forever together now."

"Promise?"

Massimo smiled. "I promise, Indy, my darling love, my *Bella*. I promise you forever.

CHAPTER THIRTY-SIX – SECRET LOVE SONG

Eighteen months later...

INDIA WASN'T in the courtroom when Philip LeFevre, her biological father, was sentenced to life imprisonment for abduction and conspiracy to murder. She had testified against him, of course, telling the court everything and skipping nothing. The horror of it was she also discovered that he had been behind her mother's murder and her own rape and stabbing twelve years previously—or at least, he had hired Carter back then, too. Carter had been tasked with just their murder; he'd added some extra horror himself because of his obsession for India.

But Carter was gone and Philip LeFevre had gone down in flames. India's recovery had been long and arduous, and quite public, thanks to the interest in the case, and eventually, she and Massimo decided to go hide out once again.

They were in Apulia enjoying a summer's day out in the garden when Jess called with the verdict. Massimo's siblings were playing volleyball with Sun and Tae, the youngsters laughing and rowdy. Sun had made a quick and complete recovery from being shot, his natural joyfulness still shone through. He and Tae were so completely head-over-heels for each other that India felt moved to tears whenever she saw them together.

Giovanna sat next to her now, knitting, asking India to help her out with untangling wool. She and India had become incredibly close over the past months; Giovanna was making up for her initial frostiness. Valentina still visited and was noticeably less manipulative and more accepting of the fact that Massimo had moved on. India still didn't completely trust her man's ex, but she had certainly warmed to her. Losing Massimo wasn't something India could comprehend.

And Massimo ... God, she loved him. They had decided to reset their whole relationship once when she recovered: going on dates, travelling together—openly, now—and even doing joint interviews and red carpets. He had brought out a side to her she never knew existed—outgoing, extrovert, almost flamboyant. Most importantly, the darkness was gone. They had *fun*. They teased and joked around in front of the camera together, and India was even persuaded to open an Instagram account which quickly gained millions of followers because of the amusing and hilarious photos she posted.

And she finally told Massimo about her daughter. He had been understanding, sorry for her and asked her if she wanted to get back in contact with her. But India declined. "It would be selfish of me. She's happy. She's loved and cared for. In truth, I was just the carrier. She's someone else's daughter now."

India had used her recovery time to write a new album and work with people she had always wanted to. She had even written a song with Sun and Tae and collaborated on a single which brought their band huge success in the United States and in Europe.

Now, though, before the new album's release, she was taking a break. Giovanna had asked them to come visit, as well as Tae and Sun, to celebrate her seventieth birthday. India and Massimo had flown to Italy a few days before.

Massimo came out from the house carrying a tray of drinks, and the youngsters grabbed at them, thirsty from running around. India grinned at Sun. "Seriously, where do you get your energy from?"

Sun smiled, cutting his eyes to Tae, who chuckled. India beamed at them both. She had thought it impossible that she could be any closer to them, but it was true. They were as close as family now.

Massimo slipped his arms around India's waist and kissed her neck. "Hey, beautiful," he murmured, his lips against her skin. She turned in his arms and pressed her lips to his.

"Hello, my darling." Their gazes locked, and both smiled as if reading the other's thoughts.

EARLIER, they had all agreed to go shopping in the city, but India and Massimo told the others they had changed their minds and decided to stay home. With grins and smirks, the others departed, knowing exactly why the two of them were staying behind.

As soon as they had waved the others off, Massimo lifted India into a fireman's lift, making her laugh and carrying her into the house.

In the bedroom, he set her down on her feet and began stripping her with an urgency she returned. Her lips were fierce against his, her fingers impatiently unbuttoning his shirt. They tumbled naked onto the bed together.

Massimo kissed her lips, her throat, taking each nipple into his mouth in turn, then trailing his lips down her stomach, kissing every scar, old and new, then moving down to take her clit into his mouth. India gave a soft moan as his tongue began to tease and torment her, Massimo's fingers holding her thighs apart, digging into the soft flesh there.

"Oh, God, Massimo... *Massimo...*"

The ecstasy built and built as he worked on her relentlessly, until she could hardly bear it a moment longer. "I want to taste you, my love."

She expected him to move away, but instead, he turned

his whole body around so that they could pleasure each other. India took his long, thick cock into her mouth, sliding her tongue up and down the hot length of it, flicking her tongue across the sensitive tip. God, she loved the taste of him, so familiar now, but always exhilarating.

She wanted him to come in her mouth, and when he did, she swallowed him down as he made her come, her body vibrating with pleasure and release.

As quickly as he withdrew from her mouth, Massimo turned to take her in his arms. As she wrapped her legs around him, he plunged his cock deep inside her, thrusting hard, his gaze intense on hers. His hands pinned hers to the bed, her hard nipples pressed into his chest as they fucked, the bed rocking with the force of their movements. India urged him harder, deeper until they were both crying out and panting for air, coming again and again.

Finally, sated and exhausted, they fell back on the bed, but Massimo couldn't keep his hands off of her for long. He smoothed his hand down her body, over her full breasts, the soft curve of her belly, and he leaned over to kiss her again, her sweet lips irresistible to him.

"*Ti amo*, India Blue," he murmured, a smile on his face.

"*Ti amo*, Massi." She was still trying to catch her breath, but she rolled over, sat up and straddled him, stroking his cock against her belly.

Massimo gazed up at her, wonder in his eyes. "There's no more beautiful a sight that what I see right now," he happily announced, stroking a finger between her breasts and down her belly, resting it gently in her navel before sliding into the crease between her legs.

India smiled at him, her eyes full of lust, desire, and satisfaction. "Yes, there is. What *I'm* looking at."

"Ha."

He stroked her still-hard clit again, watching her head falling back, her eyes closing, her long dark hair falling in soft waves like a waterfall down her back. The sun through the window made her golden skin glow. She looked like an angel.

Massimo smiled. "India?"

"Yes, my love?"

"*Sposami?* Marry me?"

India grinned back at him, and Massimo knew, without a shadow of doubt, what her answer would be...

THE END.

Did you like this book? Then you'll LOVE Fire In The Blood: A Billionaire Single Daddy Romance Their Secret Desire Book two

**Nothing mattered to me more in the last year than putting the man who tried to kill my best friend in jail.
Nothing.**
So, when Hollywood star Teddy Hood asked me to represent him in his child custody battle, I had to turn him down.

Now, a year later, I've never regretted anything more.
Teddy Hood is angry, hurt… and sexy as all hell.
The trouble is he hates me.
The trouble is I can't stop thinking about him.
I have to get him to forgive me and I'll do anything to make that happen.
Because I need him in my life… and in my bed.
I want to feel his skin next to mine, his mouth on my body, his kiss on my lips…
I just have to get him to talk to me first and that…
That's going to be the hardest thing in the world…

Start Reading Fire In The Blood

SNEAK PEEK - CHAPTER 1 PRAYING

Start Reading Fire In The Blood

M*anhattan*

JESS OLDEN IGNORED her phone and waited for Margot to arrive at the restaurant. She hated this, hated it every time she broke up with a boyfriend or girlfriend, but this one was a particularly painful split. For a while there, she had thought Margot was the one: smart, funny, successful.

They had planned a future together without ever discussing whether they actually wanted the same things, and when Margot had tearfully confessed to Jess that she wanted the whole white picket fence and two-point-five kids thing, Jess knew it was over.

Not that she had any problem with that dream—it just wasn't for her. She hated the idea of marriage, and she'd never wanted kids. Something to do with her own upbringing...

"Hey, gorgeous." Margot was standing by her elbow when Jess looked around.

Margot's eyes were soft and sad, and as Jess stood to kiss her hello, they hugged for a beat too long. Finally, both silent with emotion, they sat and ordered, sitting quietly until the waiter brought them their wine.

Margot reached across the table and interlaced her fingers with Jess's. "I keep waking up in the night thinking this is a mistake. Maybe I was wrong; maybe it was just panic that made me say those things."

Jess smiled, but gently removed her hand. "We both know it wasn't, baby. It wasn't. It hurts like to hell to admit it, but..."

"God, Jess..."

"I know."

Neither of them ate much; they lightly talked around the fact that they were in pain, but towards the end of the meal, Margot's shoulders slumped, and she nodded. "You're right. We want different things."

"We do." Jess wasn't someone who cried, especially not in public, but she felt her eyes fill. "But I do love you, Margie. Never forget that."

"I love you, too." Margot's voice cracked, and she looked down as Jess's phone began to ring incessantly. "Answer that. It's driving me crazy."

Jess touched her hand as she answered the call. "Yes?"

"Jessie?"

"Lazlo?" She was immediately alert. Lazlo never called this late unless it was something serious. At first, she couldn't understand him, he was sobbing so hard, then when she caught the words 'Carter' and 'India' and worse still, 'stabbed,' her entire body went cold. "Lazlo, breathe. Tell me."

"She went to LeFevre; that's where she was hiding out. We think he was in league with Carter. Carter took her, Jess. We just found her. He stabbed her, again, Jess! Again!"

The breath froze in her lungs. "Is she..." *Please God, no, please don't let her be dead...*

"No. They're flying her to Lennox Hill now, but she's in bad shape. We're in another chopper on the way."

"I'll meet you there."

Margot looked up as Jess stood. "What is it, babe?"

"It's India. Carter caught up with her. She's hurt." Jess felt her throat close as the shock of what had happened hit her. Margot caught her as her knees gave way. "Come on. I'll drive you."

THEY ARRIVED at the hospital before the helicopter carrying India, and they had to wait around while the place was being locked down by the FBI and Lazlo's security team. Jess overheard the doctor saying the helicopter had arrived, and before anyone could stop her, she took the elevator to the roof.

They were rolling the gurney over to the lift just as she arrived, and Jess couldn't help her cry of distress when she saw her friend. India was covered in blood, deathly pale and unconscious. "Indy!" Jess darted to her friend's side as the paramedics shot her an annoyed look.

"She's my friend," she stuttered, resisting them from trying to push her aside. She grasped India's cold hand as they hurried into the elevator.

"We're taking her straight to surgery." One of the nurses took pity on the distraught woman. "We can't stop the bleeding."

The sheet covering India's abdomen was soaked with blood, and Jess clutched her hand tighter. "You have to fight, Indy, fight! Live! Don't let him win, please."

"Ma'am, please step aside now. We need to get her to surgery."

IN A DAZE, Jess let go of India's hand as they arrived on the surgical floor, and she slowly followed the gurney out until she could no longer move. Margot found her standing stock-still, staring into space, and steered her into the relatives' waiting room.

Jess had pulled herself together by the time Lazlo and

India's lover, Massimo, arrived at the hospital. She quickly told them what she had discovered, leaving out the most gruesome parts.

"He did it," Massimo kept repeating, a man in total shock.

Lazlo was pale and Jess hugged him. "We have to be positive." She took a deep breath in. "What happened to Carter?"

"She killed him."

"Oh, thank God." Jess felt her body relax. Braydon Carter had relentlessly stalked India after she survived his rape and stabbing and the murder of her mother in front of her twelve years prior. A few days previous to today's horror, he had shot one of India's closest friends, a sweet young kid called Sun, who was still recovering in a hospital in Seoul.

Jess rubbed her eyes. "Listen, I hate to be the practical one at a time like this, but we need to get ahead of this in the press. From what you told me, LeFevre is going to try and obfuscate responsibility as long as India is unconscious. I need to get a press statement ready."

"Jesus, Jess…"

"I know, but this is what we do, Laz, and you're in no fit state. Let me just check that they haven't got it already."

She flicked on the television in the waiting room and flicked to the news channels. To her relief, none had picked up the story yet; most of them were concerned with the newly announced divorce of movie stars Teddy Hood and Dorcas Prettyman, the Hollywood power couple for the last ten years. The divorce had come out of nowhere and mud was already being slung, mostly by Prettyman's team. Jess rolled her eyes. She'd had previous run-ins with Dorcas Prettyman and found her to be a vile attention seeker with little regard for anyone else.

Hood she didn't know, but she already had no sympathy for anyone voluntarily involved themselves with Dorcas. Jess flicked off the television and went to work.

AN HOUR LATER, she saw the press gathering at the hospital entrance. She and Lazlo wrote a short statement, and Jess went down to read it, glaring at the surrounding journalists.

"Earlier this evening, India Blue was abducted by Braydon Carter, the man who twelve years ago attacked and seriously injured India and murdered her mother. During the ensuing struggle, Braydon Carter was killed, and India suffered serious abdominal injuries. She is currently in emergency surgery. We'll give you an update later, but in the meantime, we ask you respect both India's and her family's privacy and remember there are many other sick people and their families here who deserve their privacy as well. Thank you."

Jess ignored the flood of questions that exploded as soon as she finished speaking and went back into the hospital. *God.* She felt sick at this whole thing, mainly because of the inevitability of it all. Carter was always going to get to India, wasn't he? Obsession like that was unstoppable. Jess shivered. After her break-up with Margot, she could do with some serious alone-time, away from other people's shit. Not that Margot was ever toxic. She saw her approaching now and hugged her. "Thank you for being here, Margie. I don't know what I would have done."

Margot smiled at her. "You would have done just fine, my little tigress." She raised her hand to stroke Jess's face, then let it drop, realizing it was no longer appropriate to do. Jess felt a pang of sadness. Never again would she wake up to Margot's soft, gentle kiss.

"I should go now," Margot said, "give you all some privacy, but listen. Keep me up to date, right? And you need anything, anything, I'm here for you."

JESS WENT BACK UPSTAIRS after saying goodbye to Margot and found Massimo alone in the waiting room. He looked wrecked. "Lazlo has gone to make some phone calls. He got a message from Tae. The news has broken in Seoul. They're making the link between India and Sun's shooting, so this thing's gone international now."

"Any news from the surgeon?"

Massimo shook his head. "Not yet."

The television was flickering on the wall, the sound muted, and Jess watched as the news shifted from the Hood/Prettyman divorce to outside of Lennox Hill. She and Massimo watched her statement to the press, then it cut to a package of India performing and doing interviews. They also managed to rehash the Rome scandal, the nude photographs taken by a snoop paparazzi of India and Massimo making love. *So much for respecting India,* Jess thought grimly.

Massimo gave a choked laugh. "God, how beautiful does she look? Why would anyone want to destroy it?"

Jess put her hand on his shoulder. "Sick fucks will always be sick fucks, Massi. He's gone. He can't hurt her anymore."

Massimo nodded. "If she lives. Otherwise... he won."

"She *will* live," Jess said fiercely, hurt and anger in her voice. "There's no way India would give up now. Did you hear what she did to him? She wanted to live, Massi. For you, for Sun, for her Mom. For herself. She wanted to live. She's not going to give up now."

For the first time there was a faint smile on Massimo's handsome face. "Thank you. I needed to hear that."

"Look, why don't I go get us some coffee and maybe something to eat? We're no good to India if we collapse from hunger and thirst."

Jess patted his shoulder and went out of the room. She walked down the stairs to the cafeteria, hoping it was open this late, but as she came to the bottom of the stairwell, she stopped and bent double, trying to quell her sudden urge to scream, to cry, to indulge in everything her broken heart wanted to do. She sank to the floor, pulling her knees up to her chest and took several deep breaths. *Don't. Don't lose it now. This isn't about you.*

She took a deep lungful. India will live. Believe what you told Massimo.

"Yes," she said quietly to herself, "yes. She'll be fine. She'll be okay."

As she pulled herself to her feet, Jess told herself the same thing again and again, ignoring the simmering fear inside her that her friend might be too far gone this time.

Chapter Two – Waiting Game

Los Angeles

TEDDY HOOD STOOD in the empty house on Mulholland Drive and shook his head. Dorcas had finally agreed to selling their home, and now that she had finally moved her stuff out, the house was ready to be handed over to the new owner, an excited young actor who'd made his first million and wanted the now-legendary Hood/Prettyman mansion for himself.

Good. Let him have it. Teddy Hood was tired. Tired of the fighting, of the divorce, of Hollywood. Of Dorcas's spite.

He checked his watch. He would have to leave now to get to his supervised visit time with his daughter, DJ. His mood lightened at the thought of seeing his darling tomboy daughter, only six and yet so headstrong. The only downside was…

Supervised visits. He swallowed the anger that the restriction riled in him. Damn you, Dorcas, and your lies. She'd made a big deal of his 'temper' to the press, and then to the custody judge who had been starstruck by her and had taken against Teddy. Unfairly, too, but Dorcas had the upper hand in the divorce and she knew it.

She knew way too much about Teddy's past. All of it: the early days of his acting career and what he had been put through. The stuff of nightmares and nothing he wanted out in the world. Nothing. And Dorcas had been gleeful when she told him that she would think nothing of revealing everything if she didn't come out as the 'winner' in their divorce.

He was just grateful she finally agreed to it. The face that the caring 'humanitarian' Dorcas Prettyman showed to the world was in sharp contrast to the destructive narcissist she actually was.

It had fooled him for a few years, too.

Teddy got into his car and drove across the city, glancing in the mirror to check he didn't look too grungy. He'd been growing his dark brown beard out, not to hipster lengths, but so it covered his handsome face enough that he felt as if he had a mask on. Of course, his brilliant cornflower blue eyes would always give him away, but that wasn't the point. He didn't want to be 'Teddy Hood,' pretty-boy movie star anymore… he wanted out of the game entirely.

No more Hollywood. God, what an appealing idea.

When he arrived at Dorcas's new 'rental,' a behemoth that was costing *him* nearly a quarter of a million a month, the supervisor greeted him and led him in. "We've had a bit of an upset," she whispered to him. The supervisor, Fliss, unlike the judge, had seen through Dorcas immediately and adored Teddy—not for his reputation, but for the way he was with DJ.

"What happened?"

"*Mommy* wanted DJ to wear a dress for some press photos. DJ had other ideas." Fliss, a non-nonsense middle-aged Englishwoman, tried to hide a grin. "Oh, DJ put on a dress but halfway through the photos, ripped it off. Underneath she had a *Never Mind the Bollocks* shirt on. Mommy wasn't pleased."

Teddy grinned widely. "How the hell did she get her hands on that?"

Fliss opened her eyes wide in innocence. "Can I help it if I leave my laptop open on Amazon.com?"

"You are a bad, bad influence. But thank you," he patted her back, laughing. "So, I take it Dorcas went into one of her screaming jags?"

"Yup. She's now in bed with one of her *heads*."

Teddy rolled his eyes in unison with Fliss. "Good."

In the living room, DJ looked up with pure joy as her father entered the room and flew into his arms. She looked cheerful enough. "Did Fliss tell you?"

"She did. You are a bad, bad child, Dinah-Jane."

"Then why are you smiling, Daddy?" DJ grinned widely at him and threw her arms around his neck. "How long can you stay tonight?"

Teddy shot a look at Fliss who made a face. "Just the usual hour, Monkey."

DJ's face fell. "Oh."

Teddy hugged his daughter tightly. "It'll get better soon, I swear it will. In the meantime, let's not waste any time moping, hey?"

DJ rallied, smiled, and they played together for an hour, laughing and joking around.

Teddy hated saying goodbye; it was the only time DJ got teary, but tonight, she clung on even more. "Can't I come live with you, Daddy? I promise I'll be good."

Teddy's heart shattered. "Monkey, you don't know how much I wish you could. I wish, I wish, I wish you could."

He hated to leave her crying, but Dorcas was fierce about him leaving exactly on the hour. As he walked out of the mansion, he heard his ex-wife calling to him. Bunching his hands into fists to stop himself breaking down in front of her, he turned.

Dorcas Prettyman had always relied on her good looks for everything in life. The daughter of a screen legend herself, her path to stardom was also eased by her spectacular looks, silky dark hair, and silver eyes. When she had been younger, her body was the stuff of legend, Jessica-Rabbit curves, but once she had built a reputation not just as an actress but as a charity maven, she had simply stopped eating. Teddy also suspected she was using but could never find proof. Dorcas could run classes on how to hide a person's vices.

A title which, of all people, Dorcas Prettyman was least entitled. She would host benefits but would ask an extortionate fee to do it and insist on NDAs for everyone. Anyone that crossed her was met with a tsunami of spite so vicious it could leave someone speechless for days. She was, quite simply, terrifying.

And now in her mid-forties, her looks were starting to fade, her dark hair was now dyed an unflattering straw-blonde, and younger, prettier, easier to work with actresses were taking the roles she had always expected to be offered. Rather than move into character roles like her contemporaries, she began to write her own roles... which were *not* well-received. Dorcas had become a laughingstock behind the scenes in Hollywood, and Teddy had borne the brunt of her rage.

She hadn't started to beat him until DJ was three years old. It was on the night of the Oscars and nominee Dorcas had been passed over for an actress she hated. The actress in question, Tiger Rose, had won Best Actress for a film starring opposite Teddy and their onscreen chemistry had been the talk of Hollywood.

Dorcas, of course, immediately suspected they had been fucking, despite Teddy's denials. Unlike most Hollywood husbands, he had remained faithful, even through the last few years when any love between him and Dorcas had been minimal.

Teddy was dead on his feet, having taken a red-eye flight back from a film set in the Ukraine the previous day. He'd supported Dorcas on the red carpet, of course, and commiserated when she had lost. Of course, he had to applaud his costar for her own win, and that had set Dorcas off. In the limousine on the way home, she had practically screamed at him, blaming him for her loss.

He had gone to sleep in the guest room, eager to fend off any further argument, but in the early hours, he had been rocked awake by searing pain as Dorcas beat him with an empty vodka bottle. It smashed across his brow eventually, and Teddy had been left with a scar above his right eye.

It was all hushed up, of course, and Teddy declined to press charges for DJ's sake. Dorcas had been repentant... *that* time. She never made the mistake of hitting him where it showed again. Teddy, his male pride more than dented, made a show of putting up with her moods, never telling anyone how miserable he was, but inevitably, rumors started. A former nanny to DJ, whom Dorcas had verbally abused, broke her NDA and sold a story to the press of Dorcas's moods and how whipped Teddy was. Teddy was humiliated.

But it wasn't until his beloved younger brother Billy had been diagnosed with a terminal brain tumor did Teddy see the light. As Billy wasted away in hospital, he begged his older brother, Teddy, not to waste any more time. "She's poison," Billy had said, his honesty forthright because he had nothing to lose. "She always has been. Teddy, please, take DJ and go. You'll both be happier."

Teddy told Dorcas he was leaving her the evening of Billy's funeral. She reacted as expected, laughing in his face, not taking him seriously.

She soon found out he was deadly serious and went into damage control mode. Nannies, bodyguards were all paid off to say he was a bad father and neglectful. Dorcas was clever—she never outright said he was abusive—that would be very hard to prove, because he was the farthest thing from it, but she started a whisper campaign. Going into one of her saintly martyr modes, she gave interviews where she would espouse how hard it was for a single mother out there, how she barely had time to shower because of it, that she cared little for the trappings of fame—all while renting a beautiful mansion and making Teddy pay for it.

TEDDY DROVE HOME NOW, his heart heavy at leaving DJ, and when he got to the small apartment he had rented—private, out of the way, and nowhere a movie star was expected to live—he took his jacket off and slumped onto the sofa. He flicked the news on, expecting to hear more about himself and Dorcas, but instead saw a beautiful woman speaking outside a hospital building, surrounded by press. He turned the television up.

"During the ensuing struggle, Braydon Carter was killed, and India suffered serious abdominal injuries. She is currently in emergency surgery. We'll give you an update later, but in the meantime, we ask you respect both India's and her family's privacy and remember there are many other sick people and their families here who deserve their privacy as well. Thank you."

Jesus. India Blue was hurt? Teddy felt a pang of sadness. He didn't know the singer well, had only met her a couple of times, but she was a sweetheart, a rare talent. Teddy watched as the spokeswoman walked back into the hospital. She looked tired and distressed, but still walked with purpose and with confidence. The reporter at the scene identified her as India's lawyer, Jess Olden.

Jess Olden... Teddy had definitely heard of her; in fact, she was legendary in Hollywood circles for winning the best possible outcomes for her clients in savage, bitter battles regarding alimony, property, and more importantly, custody.

An idea formed in his mind, but he put it aside for now. Jess Olden was clearly devastated by her friend's attempted murder, and now wouldn't be the ideal time to ask if she could take him on.

But when—and if—India Blue made it, and Teddy hoped she would, he would approach Jess Olden. Ask for her help.

Because he wanted his daughter back for more than a supervised hour every two days, and he had the strangest idea that Jess Olden was the right person to help him.

And it had nothing, nothing at all to do with the fact that she was the most beautiful woman he had ever seen.

Nothing.

Chapter Three – Dreaming with a Broken Heart

New York

JESS DIDN'T CRY until Lazlo told her that India was awake, that her beloved friend was going to make it. Then, glad to be alone in her apartment, she was able to bawl, to sob out her utter relief. She let all her emotions out, finally hiccupping to a halt and cranking on the shower. She let the water run down her body for longer than usual, hoping to ease some of the muscle ache.

After drying her hair and dressing, she grimaced as she glanced into the mirror. Her dark hazel eyes were puffy, thick violet circles underneath them, and her usually glowing skin was wan.

"Nope, not a good look." She decided she would work from home today before going to the hospital. Lazlo had told her that although India was awake, she was exhausted, unsurprisingly, and that the doctor had advised no more than two visitors at a time. Jess knew India would want her brother and her lover with her, so she agreed to provide relief later. She couldn't wait to hold her friend though.

Lazlo also told her that India had positively identified her politician father as the one who had instigated her attempted murder, and Jess went into work mode, contacting the police and finding out what charges were being brought against Philip LeFevre. She also wanted to make absolutely sure that India would not face any charges for killing Braydon Carter, the man who had been so obsessed with her that he had almost killed her twice.

The District Attorney reassured her. "It was self-defense, pure and simple. There will be no charges filed against India, I can assure you. As for LeFevre, at least one count of murder for India's mother, three counts of attempted murder, but really, Jess, I could be here for hours reciting what we're going to charge that son-of-a-bitch with. He's going away forever."

"To think he almost ran for president."

The DA had laughed humorlessly. "I'd say he would have never gotten in, but apparently, right now, anything goes."

"Right? What a world."

Jess called her Los Angeles office to update them on India's condition, smiling when she heard their relief. "There's a long way to go yet, but it's good news." She heard her assistant, Bee, relay the news to the others in the office and heard their cries of delight. There was a reason India was so popular both with her fans and those she worked with.

Jess smiled. "Listen, I'm going to be here in New York for the foreseeable future. I'm going to help the DA send Philip LeFevre down, so as of now, no new clients whoever they might be. We will, of course, keep working with our existing client list, and I'll fly back and forth, but as I say, no newbies."

"Sure thing, boss. Give our love to India when you see her, won't you?"

Jess smiled. "Of course. Thanks, Bee."

She snagged her laptop from the bedroom and sat down to work, keeping half an eye on the television news in case anything leaked about India that they didn't want out there.

Since the news that India was awake was made public, the ardor outside the hospital had died down a little, but it didn't stop some of the more gutter-like press from trying to get in to see her. Jess smirked when she remembered Massimo, half-crazed with grief, discovering a *pap* hovering outside the door of India's room. The whole floor knew of Massimo's anger that day. Jess wondered how he was coping.

She picked up the phone and made a call. In Seoul, Tae

picked up and greeted her, sounding more cheerful than for a while. "Hi, Jessie."

"Hey, Tae. How's Sun?"

"Comparing scars with another patient at the moment—it's the cutest thing. Well, if seeing your lover with a hole in his chest can be described as cute." His breath hitched a little, and Jess could tell he was trying to keep from screaming at that thought. He rallied and chuckled softly. "Honestly, nothing can keep this little angel down. How's Indy?"

"I think if she were with Sun right now, they would be comparing scars. Tae, I think it's just their way of being happy to be alive. I know it must be hard to hear the morgue humor."

"A little, but I'm just glad he's here to make bad jokes. Listen, I'd like to call Indy, but I don't want to intrude. How're Massi and Lazlo holding up?"

"Exhausted but relieved."

"And you?"

"Same."

Tae sighed. "When they're well... we have to all get together."

"I agree, honey. Listen, Tae... it's over. They're hurt, yes, but they made it. Carter is dead. It's over."

THE CONVERSATION WAS on her mind later, when she'd replied to every important email she had, deleted the rest, and gone to the kitchen to make herself a snack. *Family.* That's what they were, despite the distance in geography, despite the cultural differences, despite everything. In this industry, Jess thought, there are so many fake relationships, lavender marriages, PR romances, false friends. But not them. *Not us*, she thought, *not us*. The love between all of them was real, palpable... forever.

But Jess also felt lonely, seeing the love between India and Massimo, and Sun and Tae. Oh, to have that perfect love. Not that she believed in it, most of the time, but her four friends were the most convincing evidence she had ever seen. To find that one person who fit you exactly.

It would be nice, Jess thought, taking her cup of tea back to the couch as she waited for her pasta to cook. *Nice, but not necessary. Right?*

She pushed the thought away. Too much was happening for her to lose focus now. She glanced at the television and grimaced. Dorcas Prettyman was simpering as she was being awarded a star on the Hollywood Boulevard. *Yeah, we know you paid for that, bitch.* Jess's lip curled as she watched the overly-exaggerated mannerisms of the other woman.

"Stupid woman thinks she's Grace Kelly," Jess muttered to herself. The screen cut to a shot of Prettyman with Teddy Hood, who looked miserable. Dude's gorgeous, Jess thought, but what the hell was he doing with her? *Good move divorcing the spider, man.*

She didn't listen to the rest of the segment, but Teddy Hood's blue eyes haunted her. That was misery right there. Poor guy. Distracted, she looked him up. He was five years younger than his soon-to-be-ex-wife, forty to her forty-five. A successful actor in his own right and had quietly built his own resume with small, independent parts before marrying Dorcas and being propelled into the big time. He didn't seem the type to do Oscar-bait-ey films, happy to play character parts and take second or third billing, but he constantly garnered good reviews and had been nominated for some minor awards, even winning a few.

What on earth did you get out of this marriage? Jess's interest was piqued then, and instead of concentrating on her own work, she did some research into the Hood/Prettyman marriage until Lazlo called her and asked her to come back to the hospital.

Los Angeles

Teddy arrived at Dorcas's home a little early but didn't wait for the appointed time to be buzzed in. Expecting to see Fliss, he was taken aback to see a new woman coming toward him. She didn't smile. "Mr. Hood. You're early."

He pointedly checked his watch. "By about two minutes. Where's Fliss?"

"Ms. Chambers has been replaced at the request of Ms. Prettyman. She felt the young lady was not a good influence on Dinah-Jane."

Teddy clenched his jaw in irritation. "And why was I not informed or consulted?"

Was he imagining it or was there a slight smirk on the

woman's face? "You would have to ask Ms. Prettyman." She mimicked him checking his watch. "You can see your daughter now."

DJ WAS QUIET, subdued and Teddy could tell she was upset about Fliss. "Why did Fliss have to go away, Daddy?"

"I don't know, sweetie, but I'll be asking Mommy."

DJ's eyes slid away from his at the mention of her mother, and suddenly Teddy's heart clenched. He shot a look at the supervisor. "Monkey... is anything wrong?"

DJ shook her head, cutting her eyes at the stranger, and Teddy knew she didn't want to say anything in front of her lest it get back to Dorcas. He was haunted by the same thought again. God, please... not that...

Was Dorcas abusing DJ? Was she taking her anger out on her child? Teddy held her tightly. He couldn't ask her in front of the supervisor, nor could he examine his daughter for bruises. "Sweetie..." He made her look at him. "You know you can tell me anything, right? Anything?"

"I know." The way her voice quivered made his heart shatter. DJ hugged him tightly.

It was a somber hour together, and Teddy had to fight back tears leaving her behind. Dorcas hadn't made an appearance, wisely avoiding the anger he felt like unleashing on her. Strange. Usually she would use that to smear his character further, especially if she had witnesses.

It was only after he'd gotten home that he found it. He pulled the screwed-up piece of paper from his pocket and opened it. His already fractured heart gave another crack as he read the childish scrawl.

"Daddy, please help me. Mommy is angry all the time."

"Oh, God..." Without thinking, he snagged his cellphone and called his agent, asking for the phone number he needed now.

When she'd given it to him, he didn't wait, dialing the cellphone number. When the call was picked up, he didn't bother with hellos. "God, please... this is Teddy Hood... you have to help me..."

Chapter Four – Hello

Los Angeles

ONE YEAR LATER...

JESS STRETCHED out her limbs and glanced out of the window. Christmas Eve and it was still eighty degrees in Southern California. She laughed to herself and got out of bed, hearing voices in the kitchen of her condo.

"You fiends had better not be eating all my food," she called out as she tugged her robe around her and padded down the hallway. In her kitchen, four very guilty faces grinned back at her, and she laughed, rolling her eyes.

"We didn't eat much," India said with a smirk. She was perched on Massimo's knees, her arm around his neck. She was still recovering and was thinner than her usual curvy weight, but the color had started to come back into her skin now, and the relief of knowing she was finally safe also played a part. Massimo looked like a man wiped out by love as he cradled her in his arms.

Their friends, Alex and Coco, best friends but not lovers—Alex was gay—were busy flipping pancakes onto plates. Coco was pregnant... with Alex's baby. They had both wanted kids for so long, but when Coco found out she had very little chance of conceiving and that the chance was rapidly decreasing as she entered her late thirties, Alex had offered to father a child with her through IVF. After the second try, they'd gotten pregnant and were both so excited about the baby, they could hardly wait.

Jess had dated a few people since Margot, but nothing had stuck. She'd been concentrating so much on putting Philip LeFevre behind bars for what he had done to India that nothing else had mattered.

Now that he was in prison for the rest of his life, she felt like a weight had been lifted. Time to get some space—to enjoy life. Hence, inviting her friends for Christmas. Tonight, they would all attend a party thrown by one of Jess's clients, Cole Henning, an actor hoping for his first Oscar nomination the following January.

Until then, the friends sat around playing games, eating, being with each other, and talking about the future. India and Massimo were planning their wedding for the following

May, a double wedding with Sun and Tae, and Jess listened as they excitedly told them the plans for their special day.

Coco and Alex talked about their child due in the summer, and how it would work between them. "We're going to live together for as long as it both woks for us," Alex explained, his hand resting on Coco's back. "If either of us feel we need space... we'll work something else out, but this kid is going to be the most loved ever."

"I don't doubt it," Jess said, smiling at them both. She looked over at India, catching her and Massimo sharing a long look, a brief kiss. "Don't tell me you're broody, too?"

India laughed, but Jess noticed the slight catch in her voice. "Not yet. I'm selfish enough that I don't want to share Massi for a while." India smiled a little. "And to be honest..." She shared another loaded glance with Massi. "We don't know yet if I'll be able to carry a child. The knife... it damaged my uterus. They were able to repair it, and the docs tell me a pregnancy could go ahead, but no one really knows until we try. So..."

"...so, we're waiting. Until India has fully healed. Until we're ready to try." Massi stroked his love's face tenderly. "And we're going to explore every option, right? So, there's no pressure."

India smiled at him gratefully, and Jess felt again the pang of longing she always felt around them. *Nope. You're a strong, independent woman. You don't need anyone.*

Start Reading Fire In The Blood

If you want to read the entire Their Secret Desire Series at a discount, you can get the complete box set by clicking here.

Their Secret Desire: Billionaire Romance

https://books2read.com/u/3RKkQn

www.ingramcontent.com/pod-product-compliance
Lightning Source LLC
LaVergne TN
LVHW021652060526
838200LV00050B/2311